"I *like* you, Jerro[d] [...] like me."

Dawn shook her head. "What I mean is, are we ever going to acknowledge this thing between us?"

His head jerked back. In an instant, the air around her changed. The sound of the waves lapping the shore grew louder.

"Say something, will you?" Was he going to leave her standing there feeling like a fool?

"I don't know what to say, except that I'm sorry." He took a couple of steps away from her. "You don't want to *like* me in any way other than as a client and casual friend."

In for a penny, in for a pound. In an instant that old saw had popped into her head. Why? Maybe because she was trembling and wasn't thinking straight. But the adage fit. She'd taken a chance and might as well commit to it all the way. "Is that so? Well, then tell me, why is that?"

"Because the good things about you don't make up for what's missing in me."

Dear Reader,

Welcome back to Two Moon Bay, Wisconsin, a small town on Lake Michigan. In *Something to Treasure*, the town is a place where both a newcomer and a longtime resident hope to find the changes and challenges they've been seeking. I'm delighted to offer a new look at the town so many readers were drawn to in my debut Harlequin Heartwarming book, *Girl in the Spotlight*.

Something to Treasure is about valuing the past and learning from the tragedies and losses it sometimes leaves us with. Two single parents, Jerrod and Dawn, meet when each is at a crossroads. Will they stay stuck in the past, or will they find the courage to take a chance on the future? Dawn and Jerrod's story is about the fragility and strength of family bonds, the value of friendships and community, and a belief in possibilities.

Enjoy *Something to Treasure*, a story of hope, healing and second chances. I hope you'll visit my website and sign up for my mailing list at www.virginiamccullough.com, or find me on Twitter, @vemccullough, and Facebook, www.Facebook.com/virginia.mccullough.7.

To Happy Endings,

Virginia McCullough

HEARTWARMING

Something to Treasure

———

Virginia McCullough

Recycling programs
for this product may
not exist in your area.

ISBN-13: 978-1-335-63347-7

Something to Treasure

Printed in U.S.A.

After a childhood spent on Chicago's sandy beaches, **Virginia McCullough** moved to a rocky island in Maine, where she began writing magazine articles. She soon turned to coauthoring and ghostwriting nonfiction books, and eventually began listening to the fictional characters whispering in her ear. Today, when not writing stories, Virginia likes to wander the world.

To contact the author, please visit www.virginiamccullough.com, or find her on Twitter, @vemccullough, and Facebook, www.Facebook.com/virginia.mccullough.7.

Books by Virginia McCullough

Harlequin Heartwarming

Girl in the Spotlight

For my two grandsons, CJ and Kyle,
adventurers in training.

CHAPTER ONE

CLUTCHING THE WOODEN PLAQUE to her chest, Dawn Larsen laughed with joy at the sound of applause, along with the loud chant, "Speech, speech, speech." Tingling with excitement, and almost reeling from a jolt of nervous energy, Dawn stepped up to the microphone to give her colleagues what they demanded.

"And to think I almost didn't come to the conference this weekend." She grinned at Barb, the conference chair and her good friend, who stood to the side of the podium. "But thanks to Barb, I'm here. She's encouraged me every step of the way."

Dawn held up the plaque and turned it so the audience could see the engraving: Outstanding Public Relations Campaign of the Year. "My clients, the owners of the party planning business, get some credit, too. Party Perfect is a great firm and a joy to promote. And this award is especially gratifying because my peers in public relations have honored me in this way."

"Two firsts for you this weekend, Dawn," Barb said, coming to stand next to her. "Your first conference presentation and your first award."

Once again, the one hundred or so attendees broke into applause. Dawn took that as a signal to end her speech and called out, "Thanks again, everyone." She gave the audience a quick wave and went to her seat at the panelists' table, still in shock over receiving the award.

Barb quickly gave the group a rundown of the afternoon programs and then directed everyone to tables in the hall set up for their afternoon coffee break. "I'll check out the snacks for us," Barb said before heading out of the meeting room.

Her face still warm with excitement, Dawn stayed put. She wasn't finished coming down to earth. Gradually, though, her heartbeat slowed and she began to feel like herself again.

She even tried to wiggle her toes inside her black high heels. If her feet could speak, though, they'd beg to be set free from the prison of the shoes. But then she ran her fingers down her opposite arm, enjoying the feel of the silky fabric of her new spring green suit. She chose the perfect color for her fair skin, and for this very occasion, her debut as a speaker at this professional conference. A milestone for Dawn. The award was the icing on the cake.

Finally, her attention back in the present, Dawn noticed a woman lingering in the room. She was occupying herself with looking out the meeting room window. Not much to see from the twenty-third floor, since the glass was being pelted with sleet that blocked the view of Lake Michigan. This April storm had started about the time Dawn had backed out of the driveway of her house in Two Moon Bay, Wisconsin, almost two days ago.

"Hi," Dawn called out to the tiny older woman with a halo of salt-and-pepper curls. And who was wearing sensible flats, too.

"Hi, yourself," she said, turning away from the window and approaching the table. "I'm Kym Nation. An old friend of Barb's. Congratulations on your award, and that terrific talk. And I hung back in the room because

I wanted to ask you about that town you're from."

Dawn shook the woman's outstretched hand, amused at the teasing sparkle in Kym's eyes. She pointed to a chair at the now empty panelists' table. "Have a seat and tell me what you'd like to know about my corner of the world."

Kym plunked a thick portfolio on the table. She folded one leg under her as she settled in the chair. "So, you really *are* from that place with the outrageously cute name, Two Moon Bay?"

Dawn chuckled at Kym's mock skepticism. "I am, indeed. But people usually call the town's name charming—or romantic and alluring. Not *cute*."

Swatting the air, Kym said, "I know, I'm just joshing you a little. Couldn't resist." Her expression becoming serious, she added, "You see, not long ago, I talked to an old acquaintance of mine. He was telling me about his plan to relocate to Two Moon Bay—I had to get my road atlas out and find out where it was." She paused. "That was a couple of months ago. He might even be there as we speak."

"Really? Does he happen to have a business?" Dawn asked, more as a joke from one businesswoman to another than a serious question.

"As a matter of fact, he has a tourist business...diving and water tours," Kym said. "I knew him a few years back when I was based in Key West. We've stayed in touch— the occasional phone calls and emails, that sort of thing. He contacted me because he needs some promo help. Brochures, ads, feature stories. And that's just a start."

"Tell me more," Dawn said, curious about the newcomer to her hometown. "It's true, the party planners are terrific clients, but I'm looking for some fresh challenges."

"Well, okay, then," Kym said, her features animated. "He runs scuba diving excursions and much tamer water tours for kids and older folks—anyone of any age who doesn't want to dive but would like to spend a little time out on a boat. He told me he leased dock space up in Two Moon Bay. He plans to take divers out to some legendary shipwrecks off the coast. That's his specialty, shipwrecks." Kym's eyes sparkled. "I didn't know there *were* any wrecks up your way?"

Playfully taking the bait, Dawn held up her left hand and ran her opposite index finger along the outside of her thumb. "People describe Wisconsin like a mitten, and this is the peninsula that forms the thumb. Two Moon Bay is along the lower edge of the peninsula. And there are shipwrecks up and down the whole coast—in *all* the Great Lakes, as a matter of fact." She made big circles in the air with her index finger.

Kym threw up her hands in surrender. "Okay, okay, I get it. Seems he was raised on one of those lakes and had relatives who worked on boats way back when. Must have sparked something in him, because he's been exploring shipwrecks all over the world for years now."

"Was he a client of yours?" Dawn asked.

Kim paused, frowning. "Not exactly. He had a couple of dive boats in Key West back when my husband and I ran a tourist information kiosk near the docks." She rubbed at what seemed like an imaginary spot on the back of her hand. Without looking up, she said, "We got to know all the folks doing tours and such."

Why the hesitation, and why so serious all of a sudden?

"My ex-husband and I got our scuba diving certifications at home and then did some diving in the Caribbean on a vacation once." Dawn left her discussion of diving at that. Otherwise, she might have meandered into unpleasant memories. She'd only mentioned it to reassure Kym she had what it took to promote a marine business. She trembled a bit inside, but brushed the negative memories out of her mind.

Scuba aside, promoting an outdoor venture appealed, especially now that the cold Midwest winter would soon give way to spring. It wouldn't be long before the orchards transformed the landscape into clouds of pink and white blossoms and tourists flocked to town.

"We have kayaking and diving businesses operating on the shore in Wisconsin all summer." In a deliberately amused tone, she added, "By the way, Kym, you wouldn't *believe* the number of books written about shipwrecks—just in Lake Michigan alone."

"So, is it okay if I pass on your information?" Kym patted her portfolio. "I already picked up your press kit off the display table."

"By all means," she said. "I'd be happy to talk to your friend. What's his name?"

Kym stared out into the empty room. "Jerrod Walters."

Dawn waited, sensing Kym was gathering her thoughts.

"Uh, I don't want to overstate this, but he's not…" Kym paused. "He's not an *exuberant* kind of guy."

Hmm…what did that mean? "Could you elaborate on that a little?"

Keeping her gaze lowered, Kym fidgeted with a corner of her portfolio. "Let's just say he's known some trouble."

Dawn released the breath she'd been holding and folded her arms across her chest. "It's a good thing that's not a disqualifier. I've had a spot of trouble now and again myself." She expected to see Kym smile at that, but she didn't.

Despite the woman's somber expression, Dawn wouldn't second-guess a referral just yet. Even one new client could mean a solid return on the investment she'd made to come to this conference. Besides, much as she'd enjoyed working with Party Perfect, the thought of a guy with an adventure business whetted her appetite. Hadn't she come to the conference because she wanted to stretch professionally? This might be the opportunity she'd been looking for.

JERROD WALTERS PROPPED UP the picture of a wooden steamship, the *Franklin Stone*, against the wall at the end of the table. He'd had the poster-size print of the 280-foot ship framed and it would soon hang in his office in Two Moon Bay. The original oil painting had never been considered a masterpiece. Far from it. An art critic would laugh at the amateurish rendering of the people and the landscape. But Jerrod didn't care about any of that. The painting showed the steamship burning like a giant torch out in the lake. Men in two lifeboats were rowing to shore and a smaller boat was headed out to meet them. Jerrod could put himself in that painting and play any of the roles, from the captain who'd ordered the ship abandoned to the fisherman on the shore who spotted the distant flames and rowed out to see if he could lend a hand.

Jerrod knew many facts about the *Franklin Stone* but hadn't seen her yet. Few people had, since what was left of her sat on the bottom of the lake sixty feet below the surface. This legendary wreck would soon be the primary site of his diving excursions in his new location. What better way to introduce the site than to have a poster showing what destroyed the ship mounted on the office wall?

A pile of old books about shipping on the Great Lakes sat next to his open laptop, but he picked them up and moved them to a box on the floor. If he kept them in his sight he'd be tempted to lose the day to marine history. Lose *another* day was more like it. Much as he wanted to keep reading about grain and iron ore tonnage transported on the Great Lakes in the early 1900s, he had a more pressing task.

He rolled his office chair a few feet to his right and spread out the dive site map and navigation chart. He needed to double-check the accuracy of the distances and location of the site map against the course he laid out on the chart showing a section of Lake Michigan surrounding the Door Peninsula. He'd chosen the *Franklin Stone* because it had all the elements he needed. First, it was well-known by historians and shipwreck divers alike. Resting in only sixty feet of water, newly certified divers could gain a little experience without committing a lot of time. Finally, it was the right distance from the shore of the popular tourist town, Two Moon Bay, to take divers for short day trips. Later, if this new arm of his adventure business panned out, he could add sites at greater depths and distances from shore. Even weekend trips could be part of his future in Wisconsin, but he didn't want to get too far ahead of himself.

Jerrod had also settled on a second shipwreck, the eighty-foot schooner *Alice Swann*, not as exciting, but closer to shore in about eighteen feet of water. Some divers bypassed the boat trip and visited the site from the shore, walking in fins until they were able to swim and snorkel the rest of the way. That was certainly possible, but not how he chose to lead his diving excursions.

He eyed the reference book he'd been using to write the script for the day tours he'd run on a converted ferry. If he were a guy prone to easy laughter, he'd certainly laugh at himself. The outside world thought of the physical demands of diving, never the quiet preparation. Looking at him, they'd see an adventurer who'd traveled the world and had trained others to explore reefs and wrecks. But Jerrod liked to think of himself as an amateur archeologist. The site map grids were almost like those used to explore ruins of lost cities. The ships that fascinated him most were indeed like lost cities in miniature.

For sure, his academic interest in the history and lore of commercial shipping on the Great Lakes wasn't what had built his reputation or his business. He was known for big-sea diving in Key West and the Virgin Islands—and for a time, Thailand. Now, in a matter of weeks, he'd begin taking people down to visit these bones of ships at the bottom of Lake Michigan.

New location, new start. That was the plan.

Although difficult to admit, neglect had led to a shrinking business. At one point, he'd faced the crossroads. He either had to reverse the downward trend of his business or give it up altogether. He'd chosen to stick with what he knew and loved and had launched an aggressive plan to breathe new life into his Key West location. Then he'd added his Two Moon Bay plan to satisfy his own need for a new direction.

As he studied the site map, Jerrod's

thoughts drifted back to the days when diving had dominated everything, including his family life. Adventure Dives & Water Tours had offered both diving trips and sightseeing tours and was more successful than he'd ever imagined. But in a flash, that had all changed, and for a couple of years, he'd let much of the business he'd built crumble around him. It was kept alive only because he had such an able crew. But with renewed resolve, he was approaching his scattered life as if it were a jigsaw puzzle, and it was time to make the pieces fit together again.

Pushing away from the table, Jerrod stood and grabbed a thick envelope off the nightstand. It contained the handful of listing sheets for rental houses. The cramped hotel suite in Chicago he currently called home motivated him to find two summer rental houses in Two Moon Bay. He needed one house for himself, his little girl, Carrie, and her nanny, Melody, and a second for his crew, Wyatt and Rob.

Maybe being settled in a real home would do the trick and wipe out the lingering anxiety over his new direction. In his rational mind he was certain he'd made the right decisions, but on some days, he had trouble making his heart understand.

His buzzing phone signaled a text from Melody. He read it quickly, to be sure it was just a routine check-in and nothing urgent. Melody and Carrie had left the zoo and would stop for lunch at their new favorite hole-in-the-wall to get a couple of Chicago's famous hot dogs before coming back to the hotel.

Jerrod smiled to himself. When the rain had stopped, Carrie, who'd celebrated her fifth birthday only last month with a trip to the Lincoln Park Zoo, had wanted to go visit her animal friends. She couldn't get enough of the zoo families—giraffes, chimpanzees, even lions—that lived in the zoo less than a mile away from the hotel.

Fortunately, the rain and bluster had left them with a cloudy but dry late Saturday afternoon that made it possible for the zoo trip. Jerrod shook his head sadly. In order to give Carrie a real home again, rather than this residential hotel, he'd need to uproot her once more. He hoped she wouldn't mind, not as long as she still had Melody, who, lucky for him, was willing to make the move with him and Carrie.

In spite of losses and changes no child should have to endure, Carrie was a lively little girl, about as well-adjusted as Jerrod could imagine. That was great, but he was still finding his way to healing from the past. Carrie was the most important part of his present. More than anything he had left in the world, she was his heart.

His phone alerted him to a new email. Nice surprise, he thought when he saw the name, Kym Nation, his old friend. In his mind's eye, he could see Kym's welcoming face as she greeted tourists and encouraged them to explore Key West. She and her husband had worked side by side in a kiosk and promoted every Hemingway tour and shrimp shack the iconic little city offered. But they'd eventually gone home to landlocked Kansas City.

Kym's message delivered exactly what he wanted to hear:

Ran into a PR consultant today—lives in that 2 moon town you told me about. How 'bout that? Heard her speak on a panel this morning. Impressive, experienced, familiar with diving. She won an award for her work, too. A dazzler. Call her.

Kym had included this award-winning dazzler's name, Dawn Larsen, her email address and a phone number.

The message immediately lifted his mood. She no doubt had her reasons for throwing in that bit about Dawn Larsen being a dazzler. She'd known Augusta, Jerrod's wife, and Dabny, his older daughter, long before Jerrod had lost them both. He'd stayed in touch with Kym and Guy, who regularly expressed their concerns about how he was recovering—or not—from the tragedy that left him to raise Carrie alone.

Jerrod could read between the lines. Kym believed this dazzler was a woman he just might like. No matter how hard they tried, his friends couldn't perform the miracle it would take for him to open his heart to another woman. *Ever.* On the other hand, he was a man of action, and he needed public relations help…now. He called the number Kym provided. Irrationally, his energy dropped a notch when he reached Dawn Larsen's voice mail, but he followed through and left a message asking her to return his call.

What had he expected, anyway? That she'd pick up on the first ring? Kym had only met this woman that day at the conference. Kym didn't know he was still in Chicago. Even he'd expected to be settled into Two Moon Bay by now. But finding the right tour and dive boats had taken longer than he'd planned. Meanwhile, the search for housing went on. Too bad he couldn't hire Kym herself. She'd made a successful transition from being a Key West booster to an independent PR consultant in Kansas.

Grabbing his jacket, he headed out of the hotel and down Clark Street toward the hot dog place a block away where he'd find Carrie and Melody. His little girl spotted him as he entered the restaurant, but not before he'd had a chance to take in the vision of his child with her dark hair in two long braids. She was swinging her sneakered feet from the molded plastic bench of the booth. A basket of fries sat in front of her, along with a squeeze bottle of ketchup.

"Hi, Daddy." She raised her hand and waved. "We're having hot dogs. Want one?" She scooted over to make room for him and patted the seat the way he did when he wanted her to sit next to him.

He gave her a one-arm shoulder hug and

kissed the top of her head, but moved his upper body just in time to avoid the smear of ketchup getting ready to transfer from her mouth to his jacket. "As a matter of fact, baby, that's why I'm here. Melody sent me a text saying you were stopping for lunch." He made a show of studying the counter. "Do you think they have any hot dogs left?"

She craned her neck to look behind him. "I think so—better hurry."

His phone chimed the familiar melody of the old Jimmy Buffet song about a lovely cruise. He kept it on his phone because Carrie knew all the words. Her favorite line was about the sailors having water in their shoes.

Sure enough, Dawn Larsen's name appeared on the screen. Holding up one finger to Melody to indicate he needed to take the call, Jerrod stepped outside.

"Hello, Ms. Larsen. Thanks for returning my call."

"*Dawn*, please."

A light, pleasant, voice—he was grateful. "Well, by any name you come highly recommended. My pal Kym Nation is your newest fan."

"I feel the same way about her, and she

thinks the world of you." She paused. "I understand your plans for shipwreck diving excursions are well underway. So, you've already moved into your dock space in Two Moon Bay?"

He pressed his finger over his other ear to block out the street noise. "Not quite. Only one of my two boats is up in Two Moon Bay. I'm still in Chicago, where I've been outfitting the tour boat. My crew is bringing her up in a few days. Admittedly, my time line is short." No sense trying to make excuses for it, either, he thought. "You see, I made the decision to open a Great Lakes location only a couple of months ago. That means I'm still a stranger in the area. But I got in under the wire and bought some ad space in some of your local tourist papers. It's a start, but obviously, I need a lot more."

"I'd be happy to listen to your plans and see how I might be able to help you. I'm curious about your business, of course."

Businesslike, professional, Jerrod thought, and he had a hunch Dawn meant what she said. "If you have time, I could come to your hotel and meet you for a cup of coffee. I realize you're busy at the conference, so I'll understand if that's not possible. Kym had high praise for the talk you gave about one of your successful campaigns."

"It was great fun," Dawn said, "but between you and me, Kym inspired everyone, too. She just finished a speech about the need for professional reinvention when life intervenes. I think we learn more from each other's stories than we do from flowcharts and ten-point strategies."

True, Jerrod agreed. He was up for hearing someone else's stories. He'd become sick and tired of his own.

"I'm going on and on a bit here," Dawn said with a lilt in her voice, "so I'll get to the point. The conference ends tomorrow at one, and I'll have a little time before I need to catch my train. Any chance you can come around that time? We could talk before I grab a cab and head to Union Station."

"Sounds doable," he said, trying to hold back his sudden and inexplicable eagerness to sit down and talk to her. "Why don't I meet you in the lobby by the registration desk around one fifteen or so? I'll check your website, so I'll know what you look like."

"That's good...uh, I was going to say I'll be

the woman with the rolling suitcase, but since this is a hotel, that's not particularly helpful," she said, her tone breezy. "I'll be the one with the short strawberry blonde hair. And I *won't* be wearing high heels."

"I will check the shoes of everyone in the lobby until I find you, Dawn." Where had that little one-liner come from? He didn't know, but he instantly felt lighter, almost buoyant. But then he winced against the screech of a bus braking up at the stoplight on the corner not far away. "The traffic noise is bad. I better go. See you tomorrow."

"Looking forward to it, Jerrod."

The call ended, and he went back inside, conscious of his better mood. First, because of Carrie. There she was, cheerful and happy in a beat-up old plastic booth dipping fries in ketchup and still swinging her legs. And Dawn had amused him, too, with her melodic laugh and lack of pretention.

When he slid into the booth, Melody pushed his basket of food in front of him. "Here, we ordered for you. Better eat while it's still hot."

"Hey, cutie," he said to Carrie. "Could be I found someone who can help me get some passengers for the trips to shipwrecks I was telling you about."

"I saw the pictures of those boats," Carrie told Melody. "They're really old, just like in Key West, and they broke into lots of pieces."

"They don't get too many visitors, either, or so I hear." Melody turned down the corners of her mouth. "They must be lonely out there in the cold lake all by themselves."

Carrie shrugged and dipped another fry in the ketchup. "Could be."

Apparently, lonely shipwrecks weren't as alluring as lunch.

"So, you found a PR person?" Melody asked.

"A possibility. We'll see. She was referred by someone I knew years ago. I'm meeting her at her hotel tomorrow. Best of all, she lives in Two Moon Bay."

Melody's eyes opened in surprise. "*Cool.* I hope it works out."

"Me, too." He didn't want to be dramatic, but the success of his new direction and the safe and secure life he wanted to create for Carrie could depend on getting this venture off the ground.

CHAPTER TWO

ONCE SHE AND JERROD had settled into a couple of chairs in a quiet corner of the lobby, Dawn pulled out her notebook and pen. "I'm ready to work," she said.

"Is that really a pen? And actual paper, too?" Jerrod asked. "How old school of you."

She tapped the end of the pen against her temple. "Maybe so, but this is where it all begins. The computer folders and files and spreadsheets are launched in phase two." She grinned. "I just made that up."

Suddenly, she wished she'd accepted Jerrod's offer of coffee. She could have used something to distract her from the man himself. She'd found him online, of course, and Jerrod had looked very good in his website photo. But it didn't do him justice. Not even close. She guessed him to be around her age, maybe closer to forty, as opposed to her thirty-six. His almost-black hair showed no hint of gray to match his penetrating, but solemn gray eyes. Because of the nature of his business, she expected a guy with weathered, rugged looks. His open, unlined face had immediately thrown her at first. The tall, lean man in a fisherman's knit sweater and jeans would have looked at home in a courtroom or maybe a classroom.

She'd come into the meeting wary, because a few red flags already waved and grabbed her attention. The oddly outdated website. Articles posted there were at least three years old. He had no active social media. Despite his up-to-date appearance, his promotion plan, such as it was, came out of the last decade. She hadn't done a complete search. That could wait, but still, it was a little strange.

Jerrod leaned forward and rested his forearms on his knees. "Why don't I fill you in on the background of the business?"

She nodded, eager to stop thinking about how appealing he was and get down to the nitty-gritty of the meeting. For the next few minutes, she took notes about his fifteen-year-old business, headquartered in Key West, but sometimes working from outposts in St. Thomas and even as far away as Thailand.

"And you want to expand into the fairly small shipwreck diving market in the Great Lakes?" Dawn asked. Somehow, Two Moon Bay seemed an odd place to branch out, especially for someone with his extensive experience in tropical waters.

"I'll be honest with you, Dawn, it's an experiment. I…uh…lost my wife a couple of years ago, which led to cutting back my role in the business. My diving guides and the crew carried on at our home base in Florida. They kept us going. But I've recommitted to the business and I'm responsible for launching the changes it needs."

That sounded reasonable enough, except… what? Why Wisconsin, why the Lakes? "Moving your company to the chilly Great Lakes is a big change. Especially for shipwreck diving," she said. "It certainly exists up my way, but the summers are pretty short."

"True, but my hometown is Erie, Pennsylvania. I grew up on the water."

Dawn spent the next several minutes scribbling background information about the stories Jerrod grew up on, including his great-grandfather's life on barges and ore boats on the lakes.

"Even as a kid I was caught up in the image of shipping in the area. My dad always said it was part of settling the whole country and making us rich." Jerrod raised his hands in the air for emphasis.

"Well, when you put it like *that*," Dawn said in a wry tone, noting the change in his expression. Finally, she'd managed to bring a smile to his face.

"I was fascinated with shipwrecks, too, which is why they've figured into the kind of diving business my wife and I created."

My wife and I created. A partnership based on adventure? He'd piqued her curiosity. The more Jerrod talked, the more Dawn's vision of a PR program for him expanded to include interviews and speaking engagements. Only a few of her clients were good media guests and public speakers. Jerrod might be one of them. His deep voice was matched with an easy manner of bantering back and forth. She was certain he could handle interviews and speeches. He already was a walking encyclopedia of the shipwrecks in Lake Michigan. But he'd be even better if more enjoyment or happiness came through. Hmm…she couldn't coach that.

"So, do you think you can help me?" Jerrod asked. "I know I still have loose ends, but I'll do what it takes to kick-start the season."

And it would take a major push. Dawn liked the sense of bubbling excitement inside her. She'd asked for a challenge. Jerrod's business was certainly that.

"Fortunately, I've got experienced diving guides and crew. You'll get to know them, but they handle a lot of the desk work, the customer service end. Also, Wyatt is one of my instructors and guides, but she's willing to help me create a new website."

Wyatt, a woman, Dawn wrote in the margin on her page, along with notes about Jerrod's short-term plans. It was only a matter of days before he and his crew would arrive in Two Moon Bay.

"Until I nail down the summer housing situation," Jerrod said, "we'll be staying in a place called, if you can believe it, The Sleepy Moon Inn."

Amused, Dawn said, "Of course I believe it. The Sleepy Moon Inn is the town's newest hotel." She cocked her head. "You see, we have a law that you have to refer to the moon in any business name in town."

"Kind of like Hemingway and Key West."

She nodded. "Exactly. As it happens, though, the Half Moon Café is one of the best restaurants in town. Don't write it off as a tourist trap." Dawn gathered her thoughts. She had a hunch Jerrod might misunderstand Two Moon Bay. "Visitors give the place a chance because of its obvious theme, but as you'll see, they stay or come back because they like the kind of town it is. It was once a fishing haven, but now it's a tourist hub that local people enjoy." She could have listed a few points, but she'd wait until he was in town and let him see for himself. Or not.

"I'll remember that," Jerrod said, his expression warm and thoughtful.

Dawn shifted in her chair and went back to her notes, a feeble attempt to quell her rising excitement about the prospects of working with Jerrod. He was a mystery, though. Details were sketchy about the last couple of years since he'd lost his wife. His business had continued. Barely, even by his own admission.

"If Wyatt has any trouble nailing down the housing you need, let me know," she said. "I have a couple of friends who might be able to offer suggestions."

He nodded his thanks. "Speaking of that, what do you think I need to get my venture off the ground, even this late? Give me the bare bones."

A dizzying number of ideas raced through her head. Since anything she said could be altered later, she tapped her pen on the notepad and began reading from her hastily scribbled list, starting with brochures right up to an attempt to start up a social media campaign.

"You're a natural for a blog. There's the basic allure of shipwrecks." She looked up from her notes. "You know what I mean. Barnacled ships and colorful fish."

He rolled his eyes. "You're a poet, huh? I'm going to steal that last line and use it somewhere."

"I guess it came out that way, didn't it?" *Barnacled ships and colorful fish indeed!*

"One of the best things we do on our day tours is take guests back in time, give them a sense of history," Jerrod said. "We've done well with both the diving and the day trips because they satisfy natural curiosity about the past."

It struck Dawn that other than laughing at her poetic line and the occasional faint smile, his expression didn't change much. Still, despite the serious—cerebral—way he'd approached their meeting, Dawn had no trouble envisioning Jerrod running a group dive or narrating a tour. Thinking of Two Moon Bay, she easily pictured him in the reception hall at the yacht club after a talk. She wrote a reminder to touch base with her contacts at yacht clubs and libraries throughout the peninsula. They were always looking for people who could do programs about local history or lore or things going on in the area.

When Kym first mentioned Jerrod, Dawn knew she was capable of promoting a diving excursion business without being drawn to scuba diving herself. She had no intention of sampling the diving excursions. Not on her life. But so far, nothing Jerrod had said about his business made her doubt her ability to do a good job for him.

Jerrod pointed to her notebook. "So, you got enough out of my rambling to organize a PR program?"

"Absolutely. Especially since you realize you're off to a late start. Typically, I'd have started planning to establish a business like yours last fall, January at the latest. Oh, I can pull a few strings with editors and advertising departments and call in a favor or two." She shrugged. "I bring local publications a fair amount of business."

"I get it," Jerrod said, staring out into the lobby. "It's good to be so well connected."

Dawn followed his gaze, but she saw he wasn't staring at anything in particular. He had lost himself in his own world of thought. But when she caught a glimpse of his watch, she jolted into high alert. She stuffed her notebook in her bag and scooted to the edge of the chair. If his watch was right, she barely had enough time to get to Union Station.

"I'm sorry to cut this short." She stood and grabbed her coat. "I should have checked the time, but I got caught up in all the ideas popping in my brain. We'll need to finish this on the phone. Right now, I need to hustle to catch my train—it leaves in about twenty-five minutes."

"So sorry, Dawn," he said, getting to his feet. "My questions kept coming up nonstop, and I never thought about the time."

As they hurried through the lobby to the

revolving doors, Dawn saw Jerrod pull cash from his pocket and assumed it was to tip the doorman. She started to protest that she could handle the tip herself, but she didn't bother. She was impressed that he'd thought of it.

"I'll call you tomorrow to discuss details," Jerrod said after he told the doorman they needed two cabs. "We never got to your fee, but we can settle that in the morning. We're planning to move into The Sleepy Moon Inn by the end of the week." He held out his hand. "So, can we shake on a deal, and tomorrow we'll finalize our terms?"

Running late or not, Dawn stifled a strong urge to dance a jig right there on the sidewalk in front of the hotel. Instead, she took his outstretched hand. It was reassuring and he held it firmly for just the right amount of time. She was thrilled to have a new project. No, not any project, *this* one. With him. Her conference fee and the hefty hotel bill had paid off. But it wasn't only about the money. Jerrod himself had an intriguing air about him. Not the warm-and-fuzzy type, maybe, but worldly and serious.

When a taxi pulled up, the doorman opened the back seat door for her while Jerrod rolled her suitcase to the car so the driver could put it in the trunk. When he reappeared, he put his hand to his ear as if holding a phone and again said, "I'll call you." He backed away and waved.

As the cab pulled away from the curb, she checked the dashboard clock. Only twenty minutes until her train pulled out of Union Station. Why hadn't she paid attention? Because she'd been stimulated and focused, her brain occupied with ticking off ideas. The ability to block out distractions was one of her strengths. It served her well, except when it backfired. Like now.

Why was the cab creeping along, coming to a full stop, then swerving out from behind one bus and then another? It was Sunday, after all, not rush hour on a Monday morning. Suddenly anxious, she repeated familiar clichés in her mind about worrying being useless, a waste of time. But her self-talk was a bigger waste of time. She went right back to willing the cab to speed up. The driver threaded through streets at normal speed when possible, but slammed on the brakes when he couldn't run a yellow light or was forced to a sudden stop because a pair of red rear lights appeared perilously close.

It wasn't the driver's or Jerrod's fault. It was hers alone. When the cab pulled up to the curb in front of Union Station, she reached into her pocket and brought out cash, but the driver waved his index finger back and forth. "No, no, no." In his lilting accent, he told her the gentleman at the hotel had paid the fare.

When had he done that? Must have been when he rolled her suitcase to the trunk. With theatrical flourish, the driver lifted her suitcase from the trunk like it was a bag of feathers and wheeled it to the revolving door. He touched his fingertips to his cap and hurried back to his cab before she could tip him. Jerrod must have taken care of that, too.

She rushed into the station and onto the escalator. On the lower level, she checked for the track number on the departure board and broke into a jog. She picked up even more speed as she passed the deserted glassed-off waiting area. When she got to a set of double doors, she saw the track, as empty as the waiting room. And what could she expect? She was nearly ten minutes late. Stopping in place, she let out a loud sigh.

"Was that your train?" a man in an Amtrak uniform called out from a few tracks away.

"It sure was. I just missed it."

He walked toward her, his expression sympathetic. "The next one leaves in two hours."

Offering a weak smile in return, she muttered, "Thanks. I'll be sure to be on it."

She dreaded having to call her ex-husband, but she had no choice. He and his wife, Carla, were expecting her, but she'd be delayed now. Gordon, at thirteen, wouldn't care. He was happy enough with spending time with Dad. Bill wouldn't mind, either. But Carla? That could be another story.

It took only a minute to get Bill on the phone to deliver the bad news. "Long story short, I missed my train. Traffic downtown was heavier than usual. Anyway, it doesn't matter. I'll be a couple of hours late picking up Gordon."

"Okay, no problem," Bill said, his voice friendly as usual. "We'll see you when you get here."

Easy enough. She exhaled and the anxiety dissipated in an instant. She nearly laughed out loud. "Thanks. I really am sorry."

"Oh, wait…hang on a minute," he said.

She heard two voices, but Bill was obviously trying to muffle the sound, so she couldn't understand what was being said.

"Uh, Carla wanted me to ask if you're certain you'll get here tonight," Bill said when he came back on the line.

She wouldn't let her irritation bleed through. "I'll be there, Bill. I had planned everything pretty much down to the minute. But the plan went awry. I can explain when I get there."

"It's just that Zinnie has been fussy the last few days. Carla thinks she's teething. Gordon's spent most of his time making faces to try to distract her."

"Sounds nice, Bill," she whispered. Unwittingly, he'd painted a simple picture of what was going on in his house, and she envied it all out of proportion. "Like I said, I'm sorry."

Why was she eating humble pie? Their arrangements almost always revolved around Carla, especially with the new baby. Not *so* new. She was already ten months old. And probably crawling into everything, Dawn thought, trying to be fair. But when it came to Bill and Carla, nothing seemed fair.

When she ended the call, Dawn walked to

the waiting room and tried to recapture the excitement of the conference, especially winning an award. It was the first time she'd been recognized for work by her colleagues in the public relations industry. To top it off, she'd landed a new client, who also happened to be an interesting, attractive man. Well, more than that. Bringing his face to mind, movie star handsome seemed to fit. She gave her head a little chastising shake. *Stop, stop it right now.*

She opened her tablet and began transferring her handwritten notes and sprinkling in the new ideas springing into her head. She started a separate file for her estimates of Jerrod's initial expenses, mainly the cost of the ads and his brochures. She sent an email to Ian Shepherd, the photographer she'd used for her fitness center client. She was crossing her fingers that he had some free hours in his schedule. He had a great eye for design and he'd done brochures for sleek sailboats, too.

The email to Ian sent, Dawn indulged in a grumpy sigh. She'd been "on" all weekend, but she'd run out of steam. Missing the train and the obligatory apology to Bill left her deflated. But then her thoughts flipped back to her meeting with Jerrod in the hotel lobby. He had such serious gray eyes, but they occasionally surprised her with flashes of warmth. Sure, he'd been all business in demeanor, but she'd enjoyed the easy way he answered her questions. And he'd showed hints of passion about his life on the water. Like it was a calling, not only a business. But what had happened to his wife, she wondered, and would he tell her?

When her thoughts circled back to the present, the letdown returned, particularly when it came to Bill and his cozy new life. He'd left her four years ago, announcing it one cold January night after what Dawn had naively believed were their best holidays ever, starting with the huge Thanksgiving open house for a few dozen family and friends and ending with a quiet New Year's Eve spent with their next-door neighbors and their three kids.

No wonder she was surprised that night when Bill said he needed to talk. She'd only been mildly concerned when they sat down together at the kitchen table, because she'd assumed his mood had something to do with office politics. But, not wasting a second, Bill opened their conversation by saying, "I want a divorce."

She froze in place, stunned and silent. When she at last found her voice the first words she uttered were, "But we've been talking about having a baby. A couple of weeks ago. In the car. It was Christmas Eve."

Bill had run his fingers through his prematurely gray hair and did her the courtesy of confirming their conversation about a second child wasn't a figment of her imagination. In fact, her desire to have another baby was why he considered it imperative to own up to what had happened. He'd fallen in love with Carla, a colleague at the insurance company where he worked as an actuary. He was sorry, he'd said. *So sorry.*

Right.

Dawn had descended into crushing grief, but ultimately worked through it and moved on with a vengeance, starting with her business. In the first twelve months of living as a single mom, she'd doubled her business income. In the second twelve months, she'd begun dating. Mixed results for sure, including with Chip, the man she'd hoped could be her second chance. At first, he'd claimed to be enthusiastic about having a child if their relationship blossomed, but he showed zero interest in Gordon. Not exactly stepdad material. She'd collected all the warning signs she needed, but it still hurt to give up on what at the beginning seemed like a promising relationship.

Sitting alone in the waiting room at the train station, she tried mightily to ignore those thoughts. For all her so-called adjustment to life after her difficult divorce, Dawn hadn't allowed herself to think that Bill and Carla would have a baby of their own. Why had that been so difficult to accept?

As if she didn't know.

Carla was living the life she'd wanted—expected—for herself. That was the heartbreaking truth. It was as if an imposter had stepped in and taken over Dawn's life.

Tired of sitting, she stood and slung the attaché over her shoulder and left the waiting room. Still an hour to go. She needed to move, walk, observe, absorb. She wouldn't lift her mood sitting alone, thinking about little teething Zinnie.

CHAPTER THREE

HOLDING CARRIE'S HAND, Jerrod pointed to the boat tied up at the dock on the blustery April day. "See? Rob and Wyatt got here safe and sound."

The two waved at Carrie from the stern of the *Lucy Bee*. Jerrod greeted Nelson White, the owner of the boatyard-marina, who he'd dealt with on the phone over a period of several weeks. Nelson stood at the end of the dock dressed for winter in a knit hat and heavy gloves. So far, Dawn's weather prediction for the week had played out exactly as she'd described: cold and mostly rainy. Count on miserable, she'd warned Jerrod the day before he drove up and checked into the hotel. In his texted reply he'd teased her about being a meteorologist on the side. He enjoyed teasing her, maybe because she laughed so easily at even his lame remarks.

Nelson pointed to the *Lucy Bee*, a seventy-foot passenger ferry designed to take guests out on day tours along the coast and to the sites of wrecks. "Nice-looking," he said. "We don't have nearly enough of these excursion boats down our way. Most of them cluster up a little north of us in Sturgeon Bay. I'm glad to see you set up shop here in Two Moon Bay."

Jerrod nodded, pleased at Nelson's response. *Lucy Bee* had started her life as a ferry and later was converted to a tour boat on the Mississippi, but Jerrod liked to think he was giving the vessel a third incarnation on Lake Michigan. Rob suggested changing the boat's name to something more distinguished, maybe, but Jerrod had nixed that idea. He didn't consider himself a superstitious man, but as far back as he could remember he'd been warned that changing the name of a boat was asking for trouble. He couldn't shake the notion that boats of any kind were alive in their way. That meant the *Lucy Bee* started her life with a name of her own, and that's how it should stay.

"I'm eager to get the business moving," Jerrod said, pulling the hood of his jacket up over his head to ward off the rising wind. At least the rain had stopped for the moment.

Nelson motioned with his chin at the water. "All well and good, but you still have a few weeks before it's fit to take people out there. It's only April, man. It can be raw up here even in May. Most folks won't put their boats in the water 'til close to Memorial Day."

"I know. Dawn Larsen, who's doing some promotion for me, warned me that the weather can be iffy all the way to Memorial Day and into June." At Dawn's suggestion, Jerrod was adding an all-caps line to his brochure about bringing along jackets and hats. Dawn suggested taking one more step and keeping a backup supply of sweatshirts and caps in a storage bin.

Nelson gestured to the empty space behind the tour boat. "When we get your dive boat in the water this afternoon, we'll dock her right there. You'll have easy-on, easy-off for both boats. You need anything, you know where to find me."

Jerrod had the feeling Nelson would be as good as his word. Something about the down-to-earth guy reminded him of people he'd grown up with.

"Rob, Wyatt!" Carrie shouted. "I'm going to a new school."

"So I heard," Rob called back in a loud voice. "Very exciting, Miss Carrie."

Her giggles instantly turned Jerrod's heart to butter. Rob and Wyatt called her Miss Carrie precisely because it brought on her little-girl laughter. But then, he'd been able to count on his two younger crew, both not much over thirty. They'd been with him through these last years, the darkest time of his life. Wyatt, in particular, had used her business savvy to patch together a viable, if scaled-down version of Adventure Dives & Water Tours when Jerrod barely cared anymore. Rob made sure their equipment stayed top-of-the-line and their boats in good repair. The two had been the glue that held the operation together. Even more important, they acted like older siblings or aunt and uncle to Carrie, who had lost her big sister when she was too young to understand why.

Jerrod was suddenly conscious of Rob looking past him and down the dock. Pivoting on his heel, he saw Dawn coming toward him, dressed in practical jeans, a jacket and sneakers. But she had that large hand-

VIRGINIA McCULLOUGH
51

bag slung over her shoulder, looking like a woman on a mission—an organized mission at that. They'd been in touch by email and text throughout the week, sending a letter of agreement and priority lists back and forth. Watching her shade her eyes as she approached, looking beyond him to the boat, he once again had the strong feeling he'd found exactly who he needed to help him launch this phase of his business. He'd had a specialty food basket sent to Kym as his way to say thanks.

Although Dawn hadn't yet been formally introduced to his crew, she waved at Rob and Wyatt. Jerrod would handle the social rituals later, but he couldn't help but notice the way Rob stared at her. Even from a distance he was certain her distinctive reddish blonde curly hair had caught Rob's eye. And his crew member didn't even know Dawn had the clearest light brown eyes he'd ever seen. Or maybe her eyes were green. He couldn't be sure, but they were unusual—and, he'd learned, unforgettable.

Throughout their initial meeting, Jerrod had tried not to focus too much on Dawn's natural beauty, but even her teal blue reading glasses added to her unique look. All week he'd made a studied effort not to be too eager for their next meeting. Knowing she was single wasn't helping that effort, but even hinting that he found her attractive was out of the question. To a *T*, he fit the description of what many women feared: *unavailable*. In every way. It hadn't been that long since he'd become a fully present dad again to his little girl.

"Hey, Nelson," Dawn said, playfully elbowing the boatyard owner. "How are you doing? I haven't run into you in a long time."

"Good, good. So, you're part of the welcome wagon," Nelson observed.

"I am, and you'll be seeing a lot of me down here at the docks."

"Oh, yeah?" Nelson smacked his hands together. "How did I get so lucky?"

Jerrod snorted a laugh. As if this pretty woman would ever date an old-timer like Nelson.

"Hey, Nelson and I go way back," she explained, casting Jerrod a distinct look that said "cool off." "His grandson goes to school with my son. They hang out with the brainy kids who started a chess club."

Embarrassed by his own ridiculous assumption, Jerrod decided his best bet was to say nothing.

Dawn crouched down in front of his daughter. "Let me guess. Is your name Carrie?"

His little girl nodded, not a bit shy. She tugged on Melody's hand. "This is Melody. She takes care of me. She took me to my new school."

"I'm sorry," Jerrod said, "I didn't get to all the introductions."

As if wanting to be in the know, Carrie said, "Daddy, is this the lady who's going to help you get customers on your boats?"

"Yes, she is. This is Ms. Dawn Larsen. Like I told you, she's what people call a public relations consultant." Carrie had no idea how much he needed Ms. Dawn Larsen, the pro.

"It's fine if she calls me Dawn." She peered down at Carrie and said. "I bet you're about five years old. Am I right?"

Carrie nodded.

Jerrod looked on as his daughter told her new friend about the other kids at her morning preschool. Carrie didn't know Dawn helped him find it. Thanks to her, two houses would also be available the next week, so his stay at The Sleepy Moon Inn would be short. Nice as it was in his spacious room, he was looking forward to feeling at least a little like he actually lived somewhere.

Waving goodbye, Nelson said, "Well, Jerrod, I leave you in good hands. Dawn can show you every inch of this town."

After Nelson left, Wyatt and Rob joined them on the deck and Jerrod made the introductions. For him, it was like bringing Dawn into his family. Besides Carrie, Melody, Wyatt and Rob were the most important people in his life.

"Let me give you a quick overview of the immediate area," she said to the assembled group. She started by explaining that the town's waterfront was divided into two main parts. "We're in the heart of the working waterfront now." She waved toward a multifloor storefront building set in a cluster of trees farther down the shore. "That's Donovan's Marine, the closest marine supply store. They either stock everything you'll need or they'll special order it." She grinned at Jerrod. "The other day, I stopped in to see Art and Zeke Donovan, the father and son who own the business. I told them all about you."

Dawn pointed to an area beyond the boat-yard. "The yacht club is down that way, and you'll also find a food market, a couple of restaurants and the Silver Moon Winery over there. There's a playground in the big lake-shore park that connects to our downtown. People gather in the center of town all summer for various things. Most important of all, it's where you'll find the Bean Grinder, the busiest coffeehouse for miles. You can't miss it—it's in an old but refurbished octagonal building painted red."

"I don't think we'll get lost," Wyatt said with a grin. "I like that we can walk to most everything we need."

"A trolley comes around, too, and stops at all the major landmarks and will let riders off in front of stores on Bay Street."

Speaking directly to Carrie, she said, "I have to be going now, but I'm sure I'll see you again soon. It was so nice to meet you—all of you." She nodded at Melody and then at his crew. "Let me know if you need anything. If I can't answer the question, I can find some-one who can."

Whoosh…that's what he thought of when he realized she was hurrying off in the same energetic manner in which she'd come down the dock. Before she had a chance to rush off, Jerrod moved to her side and walked with her to the marina parking lot. "Uh, I need to talk with you about the diving excursions and what I'd like highlighted in the brochures to add to their appeal. Make them sound exciting. I'm wondering if we can meet soon. Maybe grab some coffee?"

He was about to suggest getting together later that day, but she pointed out that Ian was due the next morning to take preliminary photos of the boats. "That's fine. I wanted to go over brochure ideas with both of you and direct some shots, anyway," she said. "So, maybe we can find time after Ian has finished." She knit her brows in thought. "I don't have other appointments scheduled for tomorrow afternoon."

Her expression communicated that she'd already jumped ahead to her next stop of the day, probably another client meeting.

"That would be fine," he said, resigned to wait.

"So, until tomorrow morning," she said. "It's sure to be a big day for your business."

"Yes, thanks to you."

"We're a team," she said, patting his upper

arm, her face reddening a little. Her eyes softened when she added, "Before I forget to say this, Carrie is adorable—breathtaking, really."

Thrown by her wistful tone, he muttered a quick thank you. But he doubted she'd heard him. She'd fixed her gaze on her car and was fidgeting with her keys. He stepped aside to give her space to get behind the wheel and start the engine. She quickly drove out of the spot without so much as a backward glance.

"See you tomorrow," he murmured. He walked toward the office he'd rented in the square frame addition behind the marina. Her words about Carrie circled through his mind. Dawn wasn't the first person to comment on his daughter's charm, but usually the remarks were just part of casual social banter. Instead, real emotion had seeped into Dawn's words about Carrie. In an instant, this woman he'd just met had touched his heart. Again. There was something wonderfully sunny about her. Even her hair, which brought to mind sunrises he'd seen all over the world, matched her personality.

Shaking his head, he whispered, "Not good, not good."

DAWN TURNED DOWN Night Beach Road and pulled into Lark's driveway. Not so long ago, Lark had lived in this compact cottage on the shore with her son, Evan. Not anymore. After marrying Miles last fall, what had been a small home for two was transformed into a large office—and a guest house when needed. Lark and Miles had bought a large waterfront home down the block, which led Lark to joke about her short commute. So many changes in her best friend's life, Dawn thought, and she'd been right there with Lark personally and professionally.

She knocked on the cottage door before pushing it open and calling out, "Hey, Lark, I'm here."

"Come on in," Lark said. "Give me a second. I'm finishing up one last paragraph."

Dawn spent much of her work life on the road seeing clients in their offices or shops or meeting with graphic artists, media professionals and visitors' center staff throughout the region. On the other hand, Lark spent most of her days sitting at her computer writing articles on health care and parenting—and enjoying herself every bit as much as Dawn thrived on being on the go.

Dawn dropped her shoulder bag on the couch and shrugged out of her coat. Instantly at home in Lark's cottage, she sniffed the air and immediately recognized the scent. Hazelnut. Lark knew it was one of her favorite coffee flavors. The pot and mugs were already on the coffee table.

"There," Lark said, "the end… Well, not quite. It's the end of the first draft, anyway."

"The wordsmith is done for the day?"

"Not exactly. One interview to go. How about you?"

Dawn frowned, needing a minute to think. "Two strategy sessions on the phone." She glanced at her watch. "I almost forgot."

"Hmm… Is that because you're preoccupied with your new client?" Lark asked in a light tone. "How did you describe him again? Good-looking, super fit, interesting, an adventurer. What more could a woman want?"

"Let's put *available* at the top of that wish list." Dawn made an effort to keep her voice light. "I met Melody today, who could be his much younger partner, as well as the little girl's nanny. Hard to tell. And then there's Wyatt."

"Wyatt?"

"She's one of his crew, but maybe she's his girlfriend." She threw up her hands. "I know next to nothing about the man's private life. Matter of fact, I don't know all that much about his business yet, either. We're meeting tomorrow, so I expect to pick up more of the flavor of what he does."

Lark came out from behind her desk, tablet in hand, and sat in one of the reading chairs in what had once been the living room.

"There's something closed off about him, though," Dawn said, thinking about his somber expressions. "He mentioned losing his wife, and that's as far as it went."

There was more to it than that, but she didn't want to talk about it. Seeing Jerrod's daughter only reminded Dawn of a recent painful memory. On Sunday, when she'd stopped to pick up Gordon, Bill had opened the front door and stepped back so she could come inside the entryway. Snug in his arms, Zinnie was happily gnawing a teething ring. Bill had shared a light laugh with Dawn when the baby shyly hid her face in Bill's shoulder in the presence of a stranger. Then Carla came to the foyer. She nodded tersely and lifted the baby out of Bill's arms and walked away. Fortunately, Gordon had been ready to leave, so she could escape Carla's icy way of ignoring her.

Gordon had been unusually talkative on the drive home, telling her stories about bowling with his dad on Saturday. Just the two of them.

"Earth to Dawn." Lark waved her hand. "Where did you go?"

"Sorry. I was thinking about the conference," she lied. She quickly changed the subject to the appointment with Ian and the need for graphic design. All business, all the time. Much as she loved running her firm, she hadn't planned to spend her thirties living quite like this.

"I'm looking forward to meeting Jerrod and his crew," Lark said. "Aren't you glad you and Bill did some diving years ago? You start off with a good understanding of what he does."

Dawn nodded and fidgeted with the pages of her planner. "That was tropical diving."

"I suppose you'll go on a dive with him, so you can see the *Franklin Stone* and the other one. What is it again? The *Alice Swann*?"

"Listen to you," Dawn teased. "Already up on the shipwrecks."

"Just doing my job. I got the names from the notes you sent and I came up with a few ideas for the copy. How early do you think he'll go for a trial run—trial dive, I should call it? In May?"

Dawn glanced down and consciously stopped her fingers from continuing to nervously ruffle the page of the planner. She looked up only to see Lark peering into her face. "What?"

"What, indeed," Lark said. "What's bothering you? I can see you're not yourself."

She couldn't deny she was troubled. "I guess I'll tell you my secret. I have to tell someone."

Lark leaned forward in the chair. "You can trust me. You know that."

In the past few years Dawn had almost no occasion to think about her bad experience. Even hearing about Jerrod's business hadn't brought it back, other than in an abstract way. Now that a diving business was not only in town, but the owner was her client, her fears had returned in a bigger way than she'd expected.

"Bill and I went to a diving class at the YMCA down in Bratton so we could have our certification when we visited St. Croix. Gordon was only three years old, and he stayed with Bill's parents while we went away for a few days over Christmas break. Bill was still teaching math at the middle school then." Was it really necessary to go into all that? Probably not, but she hadn't known Lark then. "Anyway, we did some snorkeling and then we did two dives, which were okay."

"Just okay?"

Dawn nodded. "Bill loved it, but I was a little afraid all along." She pressed her fingertips to her temples as if she could massage away the memory of the rising fear. "On the third dive I panicked. I thought I didn't have any air and couldn't breathe. I lost sight of the guide, had no sense of where I was. We were well within the water depth that matched our certification, but I did everything wrong. I flailed around and held my breath. Bill saw what was happening and alerted the guide and the two of them surfaced with me."

"Oh, that sounds awful. And you didn't dive again?"

"Absolutely not, and I have *no* desire to.

Zero. But I don't like being afraid of any-thing. That's what bothers me." Even the aftermath hadn't been pleasant. The panic hadn't easily subsided once she knew she was safe. For weeks she'd had dreams of being suffocated. Irrational, crazy stuff. Bill would shake her awake, quick to reassure her she wasn't drowning. It was all a bad dream, start to finish.

Lark frowned. "But Dawn, we had that weekend trip in Florida with the boys just three years ago. We took them snorkeling. You were fine. At least you seemed okay."

"Oh, I was. Believe me, snorkeling is *not* diving. Big difference. With snorkeling you easily break the surface and tread water. But in my panic deep underwater, it felt like I had no control over anything, not even my breath."

Lark's expression seemed thoughtful. "Nothing says you have to see those ship-wrecks or experience an excursion with Jer-rod. You simply say it's not your thing. Or you could tell him what happened. Maybe he'd have ideas about getting past your fears."

Or, better yet, maybe she could sidestep the whole issue. "I'm a consultant, not his employee. I have nothing to do with the nuts and bolts." She sat a little straighter in the chair. "Yeah, that's right. Why am I even worrying about it?"

"Good. That's the spirit," Lark agreed, matching Dawn's tone.

"Now that I've tabled that little problem, I suppose I should be on my way." Dawn yawned and let her head fall back. "But it's so comfortable here. I wish I didn't have those phone meetings. I'd stretch out on this couch and take a nap." She gave her thighs a light slap as she rose from the couch, feeling the shot of energy needed to keep her moving. "By the way," she said, "I'm putting out some feelers for speaking gigs for Jerrod."

"You seem to be supplying the whole of Northeast Wisconsin with all the speakers we can handle," Lark said.

"I take him seriously. He's so many things. Archeologist, environmentalist, historian and, of course, the big draw, international adventurer. I have a feeling he could make his mark here in Two Moon Bay—and the entire region—in any number of ways."

Lark cocked her head. "You've got my attention. Knowing you as I do, I'm eager to see what kind of a campaign you put together for him." She opened her front door. "Do you want me to bring Gordon home after practice?"

Dawn let her shoulders drop in relief. "That would be great."

"Better yet, he can go to Lou's for pizza with Evan and me. Miles is in Boston for a couple of days, so Evan and I are on our own. You can meet us for dinner there when you're done with your calls."

"Thanks so much. Now I don't have to worry about fixing dinner." She gave Lark a quick hug and hurried to her car.

As she drove through town, Dawn's thoughts turned to Lark and the enormous changes in her friend's life. It made Dawn's head spin to think Lark was reunited with Miles, the father of a baby girl they'd given up for adoption when they were college students. Eighteen years later, they'd discovered their daughter was the rising figure skating star Perrie Lynn Olson. Dawn still found it remarkable that in working together to learn about their daughter, Lark and Miles had fallen deeply in love. Perrie Lynn had even come to their wedding. It was a matter of addition, not subtraction, Lark had said about how their family formed. She had become stepmom to Miles's nine-year-old daughter, Brooke, and Lark's son, Evan, gained a stepdad.

A miracle, Dawn thought, feeling the same surge of pleasure she always did when recalling Lark and Miles's small but joyful wedding.

Maybe it will happen for me one day, Dawn thought, pulling into her driveway. Maybe. Baby Zinnie had been on her mind, ever since she'd seen her happily snuggled in her daddy's arms. Bill was a good dad, too. Dawn had never denied that fact, no matter how she'd claimed to hate him for what he'd done to their family. Did Jerrod know how lucky he was to have Carrie, a little sprite full of curiosity?

What was she doing? She had no business asking questions like that.

CHAPTER FOUR

JERROD PREFERRED TO wait for Dawn to arrive, but Ian Shepherd showed up right on time at 10:00 a.m. Nothing laid-back about the photographer.

Jerrod stood silent as he observed Ian examining the exterior of the two boats as they moved gently at the dock. He took a few shots that seemed random to Jerrod, but based on what he'd seen of Ian's work on his website, he trusted the photographer had a sharp eye—and a plan. It was a good day for a photo shoot, starting with the calm waters. The scattered clouds in an otherwise blue sky provided a background more dramatic than a clear day.

Ian wore an expression that went way beyond curious. Jerrod knew that look. He'd seen it plenty of times before when the sight of his dive boats sparked someone's imagination. He'd bet Ian was hungry to experience at least a day trip, maybe some diving. No problem. The trial runs would begin soon.

"From what Dawn told me," Ian said, "we'll get some shots today with the boats at the dock. Later, we'll take more when you're underway on the water. But she needs some visuals now to send to newspapers and feature writers."

Ian fixed his gaze on the *Lucy Bee*. Nodding toward her, he said, "I need a feel for what you're selling. A sense of what the business is all about."

Jerrod shrugged. "That's easy. I sell adventure. And while that tour boat looks tame to me, and maybe to you, everyone defines that a little differently." That was his philosophy, anyway. For some, adventure was nothing more than a new experience—a short, safe jaunt on a tour boat. For others, his small company offered a chance to explore the mysteries of diving. "Divers are our most satisfied customers. Some people take to scuba like fish to water, and that's not even a pun."

"I've always known there's shipwreck diving going on up here," Ian said pensively, "but I personally don't know anyone who's done it. It's almost like a well-kept secret."

"Maybe I can change that," Jerrod said. "As long as people are willing to suit up for cold water, there's no reason not to enjoy it." Jerrod was aware of several companies, but they offered less than he did. Fewer diving days and not as much structured training.

Jerrod stared at the dock and kicked away stray clusters of gravel with the toe of his shoe. He was conscious of Ian waiting, not jumping in with a comment just to fill the silence. "My late wife liked to arrange dinner reservations as part of a two- or four-person package. She liked the idea of enhancing visitors' vacations—she'd even make some calls to get a golf outing add-on and make it a two-day deal. Over the years, quite a few couples or groups took her up on it." He stared at the ground again. "She was one of a kind, my wife."

Why had he said all that? He looked up into Ian's questioning eyes. He'd wandered right up to the door of the danger zone, but he wouldn't let himself cross the threshold. He changed his tone when he continued. "Sorry, didn't mean to take that detour. Now that I'm up here for the season, we might try the same kind of packaging ideas. We won't invest a lot of time on it for our first season, but we'll see if some extra customer service works."

Ian pointed to the *Lucy Bee*. "But I expect your day trips will be the bread and butter, huh?"

"I think so, especially for this first summer." He spoke with determination, but he was desperate not to get lost in nostalgia, reliving the best years of his life. He thought he was mostly over those jaunts into the past. He hadn't expected that filling in the history of his business would stir up so much emotion.

Refocusing on providing Ian with facts, Jerrod cleared his throat and pointed to the open water.

"Hold it right there, skipper," Ian said with a laugh. "I want to catch you in the act of gesturing toward the water—it communicates partly what you feel about the lake itself."

For some reason, Ian's words didn't lift Jerrod's spirits much, but it wasn't the photographer's fault. Faking it, Jerrod grinned. "Follow me."

"At last," Ian said, following Jerrod aboard the *Lucy Bee*.

"This is a classic passenger ferry, redone, refitted, repurposed," Jerrod quipped. "Since

Dawn tells me anything considered classic sells, we'll use those exact words in the brochure."

"Hmm…she's right. 'Repurposed' is big these days, too." Ian stepped down to the passenger well and aimed his camera at the wooden benches and the planked deck.

"What made you choose our neck of the woods?" Ian asked, as he kept at it, aiming his camera, angling it over the stern, up the companionway to the wheelhouse. He climbed on a side bench and from that perch, shot the bow of the dive boat, *Wind Spray.*

Good question. It wasn't just the story of the ships, with colorful names like *Fountain City* or *Empire Lake.* Nor was it the venerable shipbuilders, whose stories fascinated him and he found himself retelling to Wyatt and Rob. "This is a beautiful stretch of coast on both sides of the lake, right down to Chicago and up to Mackinac Island. People are drawn here. *I* was drawn here."

Jerrod struggled to quiet the new bittersweet feelings his surroundings triggered. Augusta had grown up in Milwaukee, but he wasn't so foolish to think he'd keep her alive for Carrie in some mystical way by coming all the way to the thumb of Wisconsin. He was clear about that.

"I don't know if this will make sense to you, but I like places that don't take themselves too seriously. There was nothing pretentious about the Lake Erie shore where I grew up, or the Milwaukee lakeshore where my wife spent her childhood and I did some commercial diving. And it's the same here."

Ian laughed as if Jerrod had made a really funny joke. He waved at the plain wooden marina and boatyard building. "No curlicue silver lettering on that sign—or even a fresh coat of paint."

Amused, Jerrod could see the two-story building and what looked like its makeshift additions. It was neither cute and quaint nor upscale and elegant. It desperately needed a makeover. "Watch it, Ian. My office is in one of those square sections stuck on the back."

"If lack of pretention attracted you," Ian said, still chuckling, "you won't be disappointed. But Two Moon Bay has many strong points. Nelson's building may not be fancy, but all summer long, sailboats and motor yachts stay at his docks and visitors and locals wander around town and always end up down here."

Jerrod agreed with Ian's take about the feel of this small town. It didn't surprise him the waterfront attracted lots of marine and foot traffic. It spoke of safety, too. After the horror of what had happened, Jerrod sought as much safety for Carrie as possible. He also craved a lack of drama, even in the landscape. Two Moon Bay provided the comfort and a degree of anonymity he wanted. That's why he hadn't told Dawn about what happened to his wife, just that he'd lost her. He hadn't even mentioned Dabny.

"I wonder what's keeping Dawn," Ian said, lowering his camera. "I usually arrive early to appointments she arranges. Most of the time, she's already there."

"I haven't heard anything from her," Jerrod said. In the back of his mind, he'd also been wondering where she was. "I just started working with her, but she sure seems reliable. Always does exactly what she says she's going to do." He pointed to Ian. "She said she'd arrange today's photo shoot, and here you are."

"Why don't we keep going, as long as I'm

here? Dawn and the writer she works with, Lark McGee, will do the copy later, anyway."

Jerrod was reluctant, but then they'd already started, more or less. Before leaving the *Lucy Bee*, he pointed out all the basics, from the safety to the snack bar. He described the video and slideshow that went with his tour scripts, including the graphics of old newspaper headlines and accounts that always appealed to audiences in Florida and the Virgin Islands. Just because they weren't diving didn't mean they weren't interested in hearing folklore about storms and sunken treasure.

"I guess you'd say I'm an amateur cultural historian of the unpretentious Great Lakes."

"I've got terrific shots of you as you're talking." Ian patted the camera. "Your passion comes through, exactly as Dawn described. And the camera doesn't ignore it nor lie about what it picks up."

At another mention of Dawn, Jerrod finally admitted he was annoyed. Until he got information to contradict it, it appeared Dawn had stood him up. In fact, the longer he thought about it, Dawn's absence went from annoying to really maddening. She'd let him down in a major way. But he kept his professional demeanor long enough to give Ian some space to shoot photos of *Wind Spray*, a white fiberglass boat gleaming in the sun. Every piece of equipment and even the way it was arranged communicated care and safety. He was proud of that.

"We don't settle for anything less than the best equipment kept in top shape." He patted the tank racks and pointed to the storage bins. "We provide everything, although some people bring their own gear. Masks, gloves, hats, dive boots, and wet and dry suits suitable for the climate."

Ian's quick camera work kept Jerrod animated. "I like working with new divers, and kids, too. Teenagers can dive safely, as long as they're taught well. Besides, they aren't jaded. They think spotting old bottles on the bottom is cool."

Ian began talking about his own desire to dive and Jerrod tried to listen, but he couldn't stop himself from staring off the stern of the boat and craning his neck to look for Dawn's blue car.

Jerrod led the way off the boat and onto the dock.

"I'll be in touch," Ian said tentatively. "I'm

sure Dawn has a good explanation for not showing up."

Jerrod nodded, but wasn't so confident. Ian stayed put, as if waiting for something. Jerrod jumped when his phone signaled a new text. "Maybe this is something from her." He pulled his phone out of his pocket and glanced at the screen. "Sure enough, here it is, Ian. She says she was in a car accident, rear-ended. She's at the *emergency room*. Her car was towed away. But she's okay. If that's the case, then why…" He stopped talking when Ian's phone pinged.

Ian read his text and nodded. "It's Dawn. She's at Northeast Memorial Hospital. Not far from here. A mile or so down the road."

"That car of hers, it's so small," Jerrod said, giving voicc to his visions of a bashed-in trunk and back seat. Irrationally, he was angry that she didn't drive a sturdier minivan or even a truck.

"It's a standard compact car," Ian said, frowning at him. "It's not especially small."

Jerrod caught Ian's puzzled expression, but was too distracted by his heart beating wildly in his chest to say anything. *Calm down. She said she's fine.* "Uh, she's going to need a ride home, assuming she'll be released."

Ian waved him off. "No problem, man, I can go. I know where the hospital is."

No, that wasn't right. He should go. He should make sure she was okay. She'd been hurt on her way to see him. Swallowing hard, he forced himself to sound casual when he said, "No, I insist. I'll go. I'll get directions on my phone."

Ian stared at him as if searching for something in his face. "Are you sure? It's no trouble. Besides, she might have called someone by now. Probably Lark. You might want to check with her before taking off."

Maybe so, but she'd only probably protest that she was fine. It wouldn't do any harm to show up there. "I'll check it out. My little girl is at school and her nanny is picking her up later." Swatting the air dismissively, he said, "You go on, Ian. I've got this."

Jerrod started down the dock to his van, with Ian following right behind. Of course, Jerrod knew he should call Dawn. But he chose to ignore logic. It made no sense, but the closing fist in his gut told him he had to see for himself that she was okay.

THE NURSE HANDED Dawn the envelope with the six pain pills. "Take as needed. You can talk to your doctor if you need more."

"Thanks, Adele, but I'll be fine," she said. Why had she been so quick to say that? Her wrist was badly sprained and secured in a removable splint. An immobilizer, Adele called it. She'd twisted her knee and banged her head in her rapid escape from her mangled car. But no, she told Adele, a nurse who, as it happened, used to work for Gordon's pediatrician, she was fine. What a joke.

"Don't be a martyr, Dawn. You've had one pill, and you can have another in six hours. I recommend taking it to stop a pain cycle in its tracks." The nurse tapped the straps holding the splint in place around her hand and wrist. "In a day or two you'll still be sore, but probably not in unbearable pain."

"But if I took the med, I can't drive today. Is that true?"

"Well, you don't have a car. Remember?" Adele picked up Dawn's good hand and held it between both of hers. "I know you, so I can imagine your mind is jumping ahead to whatever was in that appointment book you lug around in your attaché. It makes me think of the carry-on bag I take on flights."

Dawn laughed in spite of herself. "I get it. I'll slow down. Tomorrow is soon enough to get a loaner or a rental." She gently walked her fingers over the lump on her head starting at her hairline and ending at the outer edge of her eyebrow. Even without seeing it she knew it was turning into a spreading purple bruise she'd walk around with for a couple weeks.

"Fortunately, I only missed one actual appointment today. I planned the afternoon for phone calls and writing press releases."

"All that can wait." Adele waved the paper she held in her hand. "I have your aftercare instructions right here. Point number three," she said, poking at a number on the page, "is rest."

Dawn managed a grin and nodded to her phone on the chair. "Now it's time to call a cab." Knowing she'd come through the three-car accident without being badly hurt, her thoughts turned to the others involved. "By the way, Dr. Adams said no one was seriously injured. Is that true?"

"Yes—even the guy who plowed into the

car behind you is okay. Apparently, his brakes failed and that's why he couldn't stop."

Dawn winced against the memory of the shock when the car behind her inexplicably hit the back of her car at the stop sign. She tried to get away by flooring the accelerator, but the car came faster than she could move forward. The sharp turn she made to avoid—unsuccessfully, as it turned out—hitting another car caused her to careen into a mailbox. Ironically, she'd sprained her wrist, twisted her knee and banged her head during her effort to escape from the car as quickly as possible. Fear of an explosion had pushed her to act so quickly. Fortunately, the fiery demise of her car never came, although it was badly damaged. Still, as upset as she'd been, in her heart she was aware how close she'd come to a real catastrophe.

"They can call a taxi for you at the desk," Adele said, taking hold of her elbow so she could help her off the exam table. Dawn moved gingerly to avoid landing too hard and fast on her wrapped knee, the least of her injuries. A little light-headed, Dawn was grateful for Adele's firm grasp as she draped her coat around her shoulders. The curtain sud-

denly pulled back, startling her. She rocked
to one side, but was righted again by Adele's
firm hold on her. Dawn recognized the
woman as the front desk clerk she'd spoken
to when the police had brought her in.

"Uh, there's a man at the desk asking about
Ms. Larsen. He's not family, but he said he
was here to see how she was. He can drive
her home."

"Ah, Ian," Dawn said. "I had an appointment with him and a new client. I texted
him to let him know what happened." She
looked at the desk clerk. "Tall guy, unruly
blond hair?"

"Tall, but dark-haired. He said his name
was Waters...no, Walters."

"Jerrod?" She let her aching head drop
back. "Oh, no."

"What?" Adele studied her face as if looking for clues. "Who is Jerrod? And why is it
a bad thing he's here?"

"He's my new client. I texted him to let him
know why I didn't show up this morning for
a photo shoot." She looked down at herself
and moaned. She had a rip in the knee of her
best jeans. The sleeve of her coat had an ugly
tear, as well. All that to go with her bruised

face. "I didn't want anyone seeing me like this, but especially a client. Here I am, not only disheveled, but wobbly, too."

"So you'll let him grip your elbow and keep you on your feet." Adele spoke in a firm tone. "Get real, Dawn. You've been hurt and someone stepped up to offer his help. Accept it."

What choice did she have? Besides, Jerrod was only being kind. She'd already seen his kindness—and loyalty—on display interacting with Wyatt and Rob, and his little girl.

"Please, tell him I'll be right out." When the clerk disappeared, she turned to Adele. "Thanks for bringing me back to reality. I had the idea I'd walk out of here and restart my day like nothing happened."

"I know the type," Adele said with a laugh. "Takes one to know one. Now, hang on to my arm so I can walk you to the waiting room and deliver you into capable hands."

"Yes, ma'am."

With Adele setting the slow shuffling pace, it took a couple of minutes to reach the exit doors leading to the intake area. She spotted Jerrod immediately.

"There he is," Dawn said, raising her

wrapped hand to indicate Jerrod. He turned when they were a few feet behind him.

"You're walking." The muscles in Jerrod's face visibly relaxed. "That's a good sign."

"I came in sitting in a wheelchair, but I'm determined to leave on my own two feet."

She caught Jerrod's quick glance at Adele. Was that a not-so-subtle eye roll?

"She's supposed to rest," Adele said to Jerrod.

"I see." Jerrod looked at Adele in the serious way Dawn already had come to recognize. "I think I can handle it from here."

"Quit talking about me like I'm not here," Dawn said.

Looking amused and a little smug, Adele said goodbye and disappeared through the doors to the treatment cubicles. Dawn sat in the nearest chair while Jerrod left to move his van to the entrance. Then, after shuffling to the van, she had no choice but to accept help to lift her hip and slide onto the seat. That brought her a little too close to Jerrod for comfort. For a few seconds she could feel his warm breath on her cheek and neck. It would have been so easy to drop her head against his chest and just rest there. Even in her hazy mind, she was aware that what seemed such a pleasant fantasy was a really terrible idea.

On the drive home, Jerrod filled her in on his meeting with Ian. Satisfied that it had gone well, she perked up a little. So, the day wasn't a total loss. When they pulled into her driveway, she invited Jerrod inside because it seemed like the polite thing to do, and then was surprised when he accepted. She'd imagined him eager to get on with his day. Once in the house, he shed his jacket and tossed it in a chair. Then he steered her to the couch and offered to make tea.

"That sounds good." She sighed as she surrendered to the puffy cushions that enveloped her. "I'll even share the bag of sugar cookies I picked up at the bakery. They're in the cabinet with the tea." Her living room and dining room-kitchen were open, so she could see into the kitchen and watch Jerrod fill the kettle and find the mugs. What a relief her house was pretty neat. On another day, it could have been a whole different story.

With thoughts of moving to the table, she tried to scoot to the edge of the couch seat.

"You stay where you are," he said. "I can handle this."

Losing steam by the second, Dawn offered no protest. She kicked off her sneakers and lifted her injured leg up to rest on the coffee table and thought about all the lost time in her day. The hours had passed quickly and now it wouldn't be long before Gordon's bus pulled up to the curb. Since he couldn't come pick her up or do anything else to help her, she hadn't sent her son a text. No sense interrupting the normal course of his day.

Jerrod brought the tea and cookies in two trips and then settled in the chair closest to the couch. Dawn picked up the hot mug and blew across the top of the strong black tea. "I didn't know how much I needed this until now."

"I know what you mean," Jerrod said, his voice low. He opened his mouth as if to speak, closed it.

She flashed back to his serious demeanor as he walked her to her car. Was that only yesterday? She kept quiet, but she was pretty sure she knew what was on his mind. "We were due to talk after the photo shoot. I was going to suggest coffee at the Bean Grinder." She lifted her injured arm. "Best-laid plans and all that."

Seeing his expression darken, she held back the probing question on the tip of her tongue. "Okay, I'm listening."

With nothing else to say, she reached for a cookie, surprised by the beads of sweat forming at the back of her neck. She wrote it off to the hot tea, the pain pill, even the stress of the accident, but it was hard to ignore the tension in the air.

"To put it bluntly, I've only told you part of my story," Jerrod began.

Putting the mug on the coffee table, he said, "I told you I lost my wife, which is true. But what I left out was that I also lost my older daughter. At the same time. In the same way."

She drew in a breath. "I'm so sorry." Hearing him say the words out loud, especially after reading about his tragedy on the internet, she understood why his expressions and moods shifted moment to moment, almost like a sudden change of wind direction. With Gordon's face immediately flashing through her mind, Dawn could barely bring herself to imagine such a loss.

"It was my fault, you see."

She swallowed back her impulse to break in, spare him from going into self-blame mode. But what did she know about him, anyway? Not much. What if it was true, that it was his fault?

A grimace distorted his features, and as if reading her mind he said, "Thanks for not immediately jumping in to negate what I just said."

"Is that what most people do when you blame yourself for what happened?"

He lowered his head in a solemn nod. "Exactly. But denying it would make it even harder to describe what killed my wife and daughter."

Sensing he needed to tell her in his own words, she made a quick decision to keep up the ruse that she knew none of this. "Can you start at the beginning?" Her mind on alert, she sat up a little straighter.

"I can, but the short version is easier, and then I can backtrack. Augusta, my wife, and Dabny, our daughter, were killed in a terrorist attack overseas. In Bali. Carrie and I, along with Wyatt and Rob, weren't with them, and nothing happened to us."

Dawn rubbed her fingers across her breast-bone as if she was soothing the ache that had settled there.

"The day it happened, Carrie pleaded to go with me on what she assumed were wonderful adventures off the boat. Augusta and I relented and let her come along. This was a few weeks before her third birthday and for her, most everything was fun. Earlier, she'd wanted to go off with Rob and Wyatt, who were exploring some of the local tourist attractions."

Jerrod stared off into space again, his gray eyes filled with pain. He shook his head. "It's hard to explain, but I can't think about the day without including all the good things going on. In fact, every one of us was having a great day. When Carrie and I left the boat, Augusta and Dabny were doing her social studies lesson. Like a magician, Augusta had made homeschooling exciting for Dabny."

"Were you diving, I assume?" Dawn tried not to focus on him too intently. She wanted to temper her own electric response to hearing him reveal such personal information. When she'd read the articles on the internet about this attack, it had seemed unreal. But hearing him say the word *terrorism*, her mind took flight and formed horrible images of explosions and fire. The chaos inherent in disasters, natural or otherwise. Her heart picked up speed. She couldn't entirely bring herself back to the safety of her living room. Even the peaceful atmosphere of the town she called home suddenly seemed fragile.

Jerrod nodded again. "We were location scouting. Augusta and I were preparing to branch out. We chartered a boat in Bali so we could get some experience in the area and plan new excursions. We checked out marinas and met with officials at the tourism bureau. Typical information gathering."

"Were you planning to relocate the whole business?"

"No, no, nothing that drastic." A wistful smile crossed his face. "After we had the girls, Augusta and I thought in terms of two or three year chunks of time. We used those chunks to guide our plans."

Over the next few minutes, the facts Dawn already had gathered about Augusta's and Dabny's deaths receded as pictures of their lives emerged. Dawn listened to Jerrod describe the off-beat, adventurous way he and Augusta and their kids had lived.

"Of course, we knew we'd settle down one day," Jerrod said, rubbing his hand up and down his cheek as he spoke, "but while the girls were young, we tried to pack in as much novelty as we could."

Jerrod stopped talking and turned his attention to draining the mug. Dawn took advantage of his silence and said, "I don't want to make assumptions, so I need to ask *why* you blame yourself."

His expression unchanged, Jerrod said, "Extremist groups had been tracked to other parts of Indonesia, but Bali was considered relatively safe—at that time." He shook his head, regret dominating his face. "But I can't claim we were kept in the dark about potential dangers. Threats existed everywhere and we always weighed them. Most of our clientele would have come from Australia and New Zealand." His shoulders stiffened when he stopped talking. "It's hard to believe now, but we were assured these tourist divers accepted a certain level of risk, just like we Americans do when we travel. It all seemed so doable."

He still hadn't answered the question, Dawn thought, deciding to let him work his way to his full answer.

"A dozen people were killed that day by a bomb planted under the dock and detonated in the middle of a typically busy day. Many more were wounded. A lot of tourists. And *I* wasn't there. Looking back, I blame myself for being cavalier—much too willing to brush off risk." He glanced up and met her gaze. "Before that day, when I was challenged about the life Augusta and I chose, I argued that life is filled with hazards, and we can't protect ourselves or even our families from every bad thing."

She stretched her arm toward him. "You weren't wrong about that." Wasn't that obvious?

Cocking his head, he said, "Let's just say I pushed the logical limit. Yes, diving itself poses risks, but I was always a super-safety kind of guy. Even Rob and Wyatt used to tease me about it. They don't tease anymore." He jabbed his index finger into his chest. "But, the fact is, I tempted fate. I put my family at risk and my wife and daughter paid the price."

That statement took on an air of finality. Dawn sensed he'd disclosed all he cared to. For the time being, anyway.

"I'm glad you told me about…your situation." That was the only word that came to mind. "I know that word is inadequate."

The faint smile Jerrod gave her relieved some of the tension in the air.

"I'll fill you in another time about what's gone on the last couple of years." His voice returned to his typical businesslike tone. "But establishing myself up here is part of my company's comeback."

A comeback for the business, or for him? Maybe both. "New location, new website, new home. You have a full plate." She wanted to acknowledge Carrie, and how happy she seemed, but was afraid of going to places she didn't belong. She was saved from making a decision when the school bus pulled up in front of the house.

"That'll be Gordon," she said.

"Sorry, I should go." Jerrod stood and retrieved his jacket off the chair.

Dawn raised her hand to stop him. "You don't need to rush off. In fact, I'm glad you're here to meet him. I've told him about your business. Naturally, he thinks it's very cool— or rather, *you're* cool in his eyes."

The wider smile in response wasn't lost on Dawn. He also watched the front door, as if eager for Gordon to come in. But why? Especially now, knowing more about his past, the new client in her lineup was in some ways even more of an enigma.

Gordon registered his surprise when he pushed the front door open. First, he rarely saw her sitting on the couch on a weekday, or more to the point, a work day. His eyes opened wide when he got a better look at her. And saw Jerrod standing by the chair.

"I was in an accident," she said, "but I'm not badly hurt. Just bumps and bruises."

"Is your wrist broken?" Gordon asked, nodding at her hand.

She dismissed that concern with a flick of her good wrist. "No, no, just a sprain. I wanted you to meet Jerrod, the new client I was telling you about."

"And I've heard a lot about you, Gordon." Jerrod approached and held out his hand.

Dawn almost laughed out loud to see how eagerly Gordon shook Jerrod's hand. And not in a little boy way. Her son looked like a grown-up making a connection with another person…another man.

"I was able to make sure your mom got home okay," Jerrod said.

"Uh, that's good. Thanks." He paused. "What happened to the car?"

"Bad body damage. It was towed over to Vandenburg's garage. I'll get the estimate tomorrow. Or, they'll tell me it's totaled." A moment of silence passed. "Why don't you sit with us a minute?" she suggested. Gordon didn't need to be coaxed or asked twice, but immediately sat in the chair across from her.

Without a hint of shyness, Gordon said, "I've been asking Mom about your business. As soon as school is out, I'm going up north to be with my dad at my grandparents' cottage on Redwing Lake. I'll be learning scuba up there."

"By the way, Jerrod, 'up north' is a generic term for anyplace north of here," Dawn said, a laugh in her voice. "Could be sixty miles where Redwing is or a long trek of a couple of hundred miles to the Lake Superior shore. Bill's family has had a cottage up on Redwing Lake since the 1920s."

"My dad can go back and forth to work, or just come up on the weekends," Gordon explained.

How different her son's family life was from Jerrod's daughters before the tragedy altered everything, Dawn thought. They didn't have a typical lifestyle, but what did that matter? They were a real family. Two parents who loved each other and their kids all lived together in the same place. Would she ever get used to the idea that her son had to leave one house and go to another to see his own father? Yeah, yeah, it was common and all that, but she'd never become accustomed to it. *Never.*

"If it's okay with your mom, I'd be happy to take you diving when you get back," Jerrod said.

"Sure it's okay," she said, getting to her feet to get an ice pack from the freezer for her head, but mostly just to move around and energize her body. She weaved forward, though, and Jerrod and Gordon both got to their feet, their arms outstretched to catch her. Before they got to her, though, she flopped back down. Suddenly, her knee was a ball of fire. Her head didn't feel so good, either. "I better stay off my feet. I'm feeling kinda woozy."

"What do you need?" Jerrod asked, glancing at Gordon. "We can get it for you."

"Just an ice pack from the freezer. Adele told me to put ice on my temple to keep the bruising down. She said to do it right away, but I forgot. I can put one of those packs on my knee, too."

"I'll get them." Gordon dashed to the kitchen.

"I should have known you'd need to ice that bump," Jerrod said. "I'm sorry I didn't think of it."

"Oh, please, it's not your job to look after me. Besides, you have your hands full with Carrie—and your crew. Right down to the housing."

Jerrod started to respond, but Gordon came back and handed her the packs.

"I've been down to Key West," Gordon said. "We went snorkeling with my friend Evan and his mom, Lark."

"Dawn mentioned that," Jerrod said. "So you liked it, huh? Snorkeling?"

"Oh, yeah." He hesitated before adding, "I'm thinking maybe I want to be a marine biologist…you know, it's something I'm considering."

"Now that's a great ambition." An expression of pleasant surprise spread across Jerrod's face and stayed there. "There's so much left to learn about this planet's oceans, and even the lakes and rivers."

"Our trip was four years ago when the boys were nine," Dawn said. "At the conference, Kym and I compared notes and it turns out that she and her husband had just left. It seems we missed crossing paths by a matter of weeks."

"I think we'd gone to St. Thomas in March and April that year to check in on our charters there. We only ran two boats then, but it was a busy season."

Gordon's eyes lit up. "Do you still have those boats?"

"Not that he's eager or anything." Dawn deliberately kept her tone dry. She could almost see the wheels turning in Gordon's head thinking about diving in the Virgin Islands.

"My company technically owns them," he said, going on to explain that he leased the boats to some former crew, with the idea they could keep the company operating out of both St. Croix and St. Thomas.

As she listened to more of Gordon's questions and Jerrod's answers, she was impressed by the respectful way her new client treated her son's interest. He responded to his curiosity with the same seriousness that Gordon displayed. She relaxed deeper into the couch, the muscles in her body loosening.

"Are you hungry?" Jerrod asked, breaking the silence.

She shook her head. "No doubt my growing kid is, but he can—"

"I have an idea," Jerrod blurted. "You two need to eat, and Carrie and I do, too. Why don't I fix us all something?" He glanced at Dawn. "If you don't mind me using your kitchen."

Seeing Gordon's face light up, she laughed and said, "No, I don't mind. Gordon can help. He knows his way around the pots and pans. Melody is welcome, too."

Getting up to retrieve his phone from his jacket, Jerrod said, "I'll text her now. Believe me, Melody will be happy to have a night off. We more or less split the cooking…well, that's an exaggeration. We're doing mostly takeout now that we're all in hotel rooms. But I like to be there with Carrie, mostly to make her life as routine as possible."

His fingers moved rapidly as he texted. "How about tacos?" He glanced to Gordon, who nodded enthusiastically.

"Do I have a say?" Dawn asked.

Gordon chuckled, but Jerrod's neck turned red. So, it was possible to embarrass this serious man.

"Just teasing. Tacos happen to be one of my favorites. Gordon and I feast on them a lot," she said, although her mind was focused elsewhere. It seemed Melody was only the nanny, after all, Dawn thought. Lark had been right about her jumping to conclusions.

"She makes me stir the ground beef on the stove and chop up stuff, so I know what I'm doing." Gordon spoke as if bragging about a big accomplishment.

Dawn saw Jerrod sucking in his cheeks in his attempt not to grin—or maybe laugh. Then he was on his feet and getting into his jacket. "Let's get this dinner underway," he said, hastily adding, "if you're sure you're up to having us."

Dawn rested her head on the back of the couch. "As long as I'm not expected to help in the kitchen, I'm good."

"You stay right where you are. We'll handle the rest." He nodded to Gordon and then disappeared out the door.

Gordon picked up his backpack and headed

to his room, but not before calling over his shoulder, "He's cool."

What just happened? Whatever it was, Gordon was right. Her new client was definitely cool.

DAWN SAT AT the table with her arm companionably resting on the back of Carrie's chair. Jerrod watched his little girl's shy side show itself since they'd come into the house, although Dawn welcomed her like she was the special guest she'd been waiting for. Dawn even took care to explain that her temple, swollen and still bruised close to her eye, didn't hurt too much.

Carrie had rewarded Gordon with a bright smile when he admired the big polar bear stuffed animal she'd carried in by its ear. Lately, that bear she'd named Candy was her new security blanket. The only place she didn't bring it with her was to preschool.

Earlier, in the grocery store with Carrie, he'd had a few shaky moments while he let her help him pile food into the cart. Hard and soft shells, refried beans, guacamole and seasoning plus all the fresh ingredients needed for a perfect taco. He added soft drinks and ice cream, just because. Carrie was happy having a new adventure, but he had to honestly ask himself what he thought he was doing. A dinner between friends? Helping Dawn out after a bad day? Getting to know this newest member of his team? Maybe all of that was true, but was that as far as it went? It had to be.

He and Gordon put the platters of the vegetables and beans on the table. "Time to put it all together," he said to Carrie as he assembled a taco for her and cut it into pieces.

"Looks like I have to cut up a taco for my mom." Gordon directed his comment to Carrie.

Finding that notion very amusing, Carrie took special interest in Dawn's plate of food being turned into manageable bites. With her right hand unencumbered, Jerrod knew perfectly well that Dawn could have used her fork to break up the shell. But they'd have missed a moment of playfulness with Carrie.

Jerrod shook off the hint of sadness and turned his attention to the food. He hadn't realized how hungry he was until he inhaled the aroma of browning meat and taco spices. It had been so long since he'd experienced the

sense of normalcy to be found in simply sharing a meal around a table with new friends.
But danger loomed like an invisible line just
beyond him. A couple of steps more and he'd
be in trouble. Dawn's pretty face and open
heart. Gordon's poise for his early teenage
years. It was all just a little too much.

"Did your daddy die?" Carrie asked out of
the blue. She was looking at Gordon.

An uncomfortable silence followed.

"No, Carrie, he didn't die," Gordon said
after a second or two had passed. "He lives
in Bellwood, not too far away."

"Oh, okay," Carrie said, apparently satisfied with the answer. "My mommy died. But
I don't remember her much. I don't remember
my big sister, either."

Jerrod put his fork on the plate and stared
down. It wasn't the first time Carrie had said
that, but it never stopped feeling like a hot
poker searing his heart. "But we look at pictures sometimes, don't we? Of Mommy and
Dabny." Jerrod swallowed hard.

"I bet your mom was very special. Dabny,
too." Dawn leaned closer to Carrie, almost as
if protecting her.

"Uh-huh," Carrie said. "Her name was Augusta. She was pretty." Hunching her shoulders, she looked a little embarrassed when she added, "Like you."

Reality hit hard. No one knew what to say, not even him. Yes, Augusta was pretty. And so was Dawn. Talk about confusing. It was only natural that Carrie would form an attachment to a woman like Dawn, and even to Gordon. They were on the edges of Carrie's life. Far edges, but still.

"Thanks, sweetie," Dawn said. "What a nice thing to say."

Gordon left the table and walked to the freezer. "Does anyone else want ice cream… let's see, we have vanilla, and the chocolate chip and peppermint stick you brought. What'll it be?"

Trust a kid to save the day.

"I want chocolate chip *and* peppermint stick." Carrie cut her eyes at Jerrod, as if waiting for him to object.

On another night he might have, but he said, "Okay, a little of each. And I'll make decaf coffee."

"My daddy drinks a lot of coffee," Carrie said as if making an announcement.

Gordon put the bowl of ice cream in front of

Carrie. "So does my mom. She and her friend Lark meet for coffee at the Bean Grinder and if Lark comes here they drink more coffee. And my dad is just as bad."

"Enough," Dawn said, laughing. "We get it."

"I go to the Bean Grinder, too." Carrie held a huge spoonful of peppermint stick ice cream over the dish bowl and claimed the floor while she had the chance. "Melody lets me get an oatmeal cookie. The cookies crunch when I chew 'em."

Dawn patted Carrie's shoulder. "Ooh, there's nothing quite like a Bean Grinder oatmeal cookie. They're my favorite, too."

The warmth that defined the mood of the evening had settled in Jerrod's heart. He'd been 100 percent unprepared for the range of emotions the day had brought on. These feelings were like strangers to him now, and he wasn't sure he wanted them hanging around.

Glancing at Dawn, seeing through the pleasant expression on her beautiful face, he saw she was fading fast. It was a signal he could use to make his exit. He stood and began gathering empty plates. Gordon did the same and said he'd take care of the pile of dirty dishes on the counter.

"It's time we said good night and let you get some rest," Jerrod said.

Dawn didn't argue. "I'll be in touch as soon as I hear back from the newspaper and the tourist weekly I was telling you about."

"Great. Meanwhile, focus on taking care of yourself."

"Thanks for this evening," Dawn said. "It lifted my spirits after such a crummy day."

"We should be thanking you," Jerrod said, leading Carrie through the living room to the front door. He didn't add anything to what Dawn said. If he did, he'd reveal too much about what he missed about his old life. That wasn't Dawn's problem.

CHAPTER FIVE

WITH WYATT NEXT to him, Jerrod moved slowly through the water, adjusting the video camera and getting the shots he wanted. Small fish he didn't recognize and a school of white-fish darted around the propeller and in and out of a piece of the intact bow. Not many other complete structures were evident in the wreck of the *Franklin Stone*. Freshwater diving would take some getting used to, Jerrod thought.

He'd done a lot of it earlier in his life, even a short stint as a contract diver for police departments in counties on Lake Erie and for the public works department in Milwaukee. But it had been a while since he adjusted to the difference in buoyancy in freshwater.

Wyatt directed his attention to a dense cluster of zebra mussels, a reality he and his guests would see. He first knew about them when they appeared in Lake Erie and for a time some seemed to be part of Mother Nature's grand cleanup crew, even making freshwater clearer. A deceptive view, for sure, because these mussels drove out other species, including birds. In truth, their presence was a threat to all the Great Lakes. Part of a diving company's job involved talking about these problems.

He and Wyatt moved around the propeller as he kept filming. He'd never planned to talk about the ecology of the lake as part of his dives or tours, any more than he and Augusta intended to make their tropical dives a lesson on the fragility of reefs. But realities changed and the presence of the zebra mussels made it impossible to avoid the subject, if for no other reason than their presence had made the shipwrecks themselves harder to view. Some random wooden sections of the ship that hadn't burned were hidden under mounds of mussels.

Jerrod had any number of wrecks to choose from, but there was something spectacular about the 280-foot *Franklin Stone* as a ship to visit. In some ways it had an ordinary life. When it sank off the shore of Two Moon Bay in 1913, it was carrying 2,500 tons of coal to

Sheboygan. The fact it was just one more ship doing its work was exactly what he wanted to convey to the divers. Even being lost in a fire wasn't unusual. A crew of nineteen managed to climb into lifeboats and row away toward the shore unharmed. Not unheard of, maybe, but it was a stroke of luck, the likes of which sailors pray for.

The bottom was flat where the remains of the ship rested, which was an advantage when taking divers out to it. It was one of the reasons *Franklin Stone* had made the final cut of his options. For one thing, the relatively concentrated space made it easier to keep track of his divers, who would use their fins to move through relatively clear water to see the steam engine and still-attached ten-foot propeller sitting on the bottom where it landed over one hundred years ago. Every hard surface was covered with mussels—zebras and quaggas. They loved hard surfaces like flies loved honey.

The conversation he'd had with Gordon came back to him. The boy had said he might want to be a marine biologist, so he most likely knew all about these invaders. He made a mental note to mention them to Dawn and ask her about bringing up in interviews the mounds of data about the rapid spread of these unwelcome guests. Her answer would likely be no. He could almost hear her reminding him that there were plenty of local experts to book for speeches or panels about the ecological threats to Lake Michigan. But he still wanted to run his idea by her. In such a short time she'd become a voice inside his head. Amazing.

He went back to focusing on the site, studying the bottom for items, like anchors and even the giant bolts that held the vessel together. The wreck was a doorway to the past. For as long as he could remember, diving deep into the water and using all the modern equipment to adapt to the foreign environment was like going to live in another world. In some ways it might as well be Mars. The diving gear was like a spacesuit, the underwater world fragile, always changing. He and Wyatt were just tourists that day.

Dawn had used the word *ambassador* to characterize the kind of guide he'd always wanted to be—and that had led to his success in the past. Sometimes Jerrod believed he was speaking for the lake itself in the way he described the treasures silently waiting to be discovered in the sometimes harsh conditions underwater. Most people will never know what it's like to be submerged in even twenty or thirty feet in any body of water. Yes, he was lucky. As Dawn suggested, he'd write about it in his new blog.

Signaling Wyatt, he drew her attention to how the engine sat straight as if it had been purposely dropped into place. Responding with a yes sign, he was satisfied she'd noted the position of the wreck. The fire had made the wooden sides of the ship collapse. So the intact engine sat among the scattered pieces of the hull. Two anchors had drifted to the edges of the site.

When they explained the wreck to the guests, they'd point out that the ship burned so fast it sank at that straight angle, not like the bow or stern first like the dramatic depiction of a sinking most people saw in the movies. And the surviving engine and boilers would likely be unmoved for a century or two more. Pieces of coal were spread on the bottom of the site, thinning out as they moved farther away from the center.

On his day tour, he could tell the stories of attempts to salvage the coal even years after the fact. Jerrod's granddad had told him many tales about the guys who'd take a chance and claim ownership of whatever they could bring to the surface.

He raised his thumb, signaling it was time to end the dive. Together, he and Wyatt began their slow ascent. No rushing to reach the surface. They climbed onto *Wind Spray*'s stern, and took off their tanks and weight belts, the fins and hoods and other equipment as Rob steered the boat back to the marina. Once the lines were secured and their dry suits and gear taken care of, he and Wyatt went into the office. Jerrod ordered a large everything pizza for their lunch.

"It should be here in forty-five minutes," Jerrod said.

"Let's see how the video turned out," Rob suggested. "I want to know what to expect when we go out again. Anything new we need to add to what we tell people on the day tour?"

Wyatt pointed at the poster hanging behind Jerrod. "It's one thing to know the *Franklin Stone* was in flames when it went down. The painting tells that story. It's another thing to see the wooden hull in pieces but the engine sitting on the bottom upright. There's also something about those nineteen men getting to shore safely."

"True," Jerrod said, "and it's an important part of the story to tell our divers. Then we can elaborate and add a couple of colorful stories on our day tours. We have plenty of photos of the ship—and of this painting."

He made a note on his tablet to work on the *Franklin Stone* section of his script. Mussels, coal scattered on the bottom, and the nineteen survivors. Those men occupied his mind, too.

Rob started the video on the computer and Wyatt filled in detail as the images changed. He smiled to himself. The two got along so well, anticipating each other's thoughts, finishing each other's sentences. As well suited as they were, hc sometimes wondered why they hadn't drifted together, become a couple. Or if they had, they were good at keeping it private. That was fine with him. No need for complications, he thought, suddenly aware of how dispassionate, even cold, he sounded about the prospects of staff romance. He could almost hear Augusta chastising him. "Heave a heart," she'd have said.

"Aren't you doing some interviews tomorrow?" Wyatt asked.

"Four, to be exact. Dawn will introduce me to these editors and people running tourist information centers."

"That was fast," Rob observed. "We've only been here a few weeks."

"Seems my PR consultant is very well connected. She was honest about being able to call in some favors and nail down some space in a couple of papers."

"Will you talk about the *Franklin Stone*?" Rob asked. "Give the flavor of what divers can see in their own backyard."

"It's the primary site for this season. So, yes, I'll mention it." He leaned back in the desk chair and laced his hands behind his head. The dive was responsible for his pensive mood. "All these shipwrecks provide a historical trail. You could almost write a history of the coasts of all five great lakes simply by taking a trip through the known marine accidents and boats in their graves at the bottom. Treasures everywhere—not for the taking, but for the viewing."

"I'd use those words in an interview," Wyatt said. "You have a way of bringing the

meaning of what's underwater to the surface."
She raised her hands defensively as if to stop
the inevitable teasing. "I know, I know. Bad
pun. But it works."

Jerrod laughed. "I do intend to mention the
history. But Dawn is trying to book some presentations for that. She's afraid I'll veer off
topic, as people in her business say. For these
interviews, I'll mostly describe our dives and
the wreck. It's all about rustling up enough
business to make our summer worthwhile."

Dawn had read him like a book. It hadn't
taken her long to pick up on his tendency to
get lost in the lore and the history and lose
sight that he was selling his products, dives
and tours. A familiar heaviness settled in his
chest. It was impossible to ignore it, because
Augusta used to chide him about taking side
trips into history.

The arrival of lunch pulled him out of his
thoughts. "Let's run that video again while
we eat," he said. "There might be things we
see we can highlight."

Watching the video lifted his spirits in an
odd sort of way. Once lunch was over, Rob
went to the *Lucy Bee* to work on the engine
and Wyatt headed to the house to answer

emails and check in with the Key West crew. That left him alone in the office for the afternoon. Or, he could go home and spend time with Carrie or find out if Melody planned to take her to the park after lunch. But he didn't trust himself to be able to be more than half present with his daughter.

His mind was kind of jumbled lately, or maybe it was his heart that needed to settle down. Ever since telling Dawn about the past, she'd been on his mind. But he'd finally reached the point that thoughts of Augusta and Dabny made him smile and not reel from the pain. At first the horror of what happened had left him physically weak—unable to trust his legs to bear his weight. Then numbness had set in, like paralysis that robbed him of what he had to give to other people, even his little girl. But now, even when he was talking with Dawn, describing what happened, he felt different, more at ease with himself. For sure, it was all as real as ever. Maybe, though, he'd turned a corner and the vision of that part of his life was changing. The memory wasn't fading so much as getting smaller and losing some of its power as he moved forward with Carrie and embraced a new, if limited, life.

Jerrod grabbed his jacket and took off for home—and Carrie.

"YOU'LL GET A top-of-the-line tour of the area today. I can show you lots of off-the-beaten path spots." Dawn pulled the seat belt across her body and managed to move her hip just enough that she could click it into place with her good hand. She'd scheduled back-to-back appointments in key places, including two stops in Door County. Jerrod had insisted on doing the driving, so Dawn wouldn't put any strain on her wrist. To make it even easier on her, he'd traded vehicles with Melody, so they could avoid the need to strain her wrist or knee—or both—to get in and out of the van.

"It's odd to be a passenger," Dawn said, watching the gas stations on the edge of town give way to dairy farms, orchards, and a few stables. Not that she could see any of it, but the road was as familiar as an old shoe. Today, though, the heavy fog even obscured the taillights of the car ahead.

"It's like being in a tunnel," Jerrod said,

"but if you live on these lakes, you get used to fog, huh?"

Dawn raised a finger in the air next to her ear. "And foghorns. Listen to that sound."

He smiled at the next faint blast.

After an initial email exchange where they'd each mentioned enjoying their dinner, Dawn had said nothing more about it. Neither had Jerrod. Since the immediate items on her to-do list for Jerrod could be handled online and by phone, including arranging these interviews, she hadn't seen him for several days. In the interim, April had turned to May and Jerrod and his crew were settled into the two houses that would be their summer headquarters.

She directed him to the state road that would take them directly to the headquarters of the company that produced half the free papers and magazines that promoted the Two Moon Bay tourist hub and neighboring towns. Jerrod would be drawing diving guests and tour boat passengers from both areas.

"The most in-depth interview is with Wilson Cone at *Peninsula News*, the weekly events paper. They want lots of background, so you can elaborate on what you've done in the Virgin Islands and Thailand. Wilson is very excited about talking to you."

Trying not to bog him down in detail, she described the other stops she'd scheduled, ending with a shorter interview for a glossy life-on-the-peninsula magazine. The shorter two appointments in the middle were typical tourist ad books with some short pieces. "They don't claim to be journalists, so the interviews tend to be short and not exactly deep."

"Got it. I've done many of those over the years. Augusta called them overview interviews with a teaser."

He didn't look happy as he said that, but Dawn was glad he mentioned his wife. It explained the somber demeanor she'd observed. The pleasant way he interacted with Gordon over dinner—and with her—gave Dawn a sense of the Jerrod as he was before the tragedy. Could he be that way again? She was almost afraid to answer the question.

Making these rounds of publications was a big part of her job, but that morning nothing seemed routine about the day ahead. For one thing, she'd taken more care with her clothes and makeup than usual. Even choosing between the turquoise drop earrings or gold hoops took longer than it normally did. Like getting ready for a date, she reluctantly admitted when she settled on the turquoise pair, not a formal work appointment.

"Thanks for getting this type of exposure off the ground," Jerrod said, glancing sideways to meet her eye. "I know we got in just under the wire."

"I'm glad it happened. And I didn't have to twist too many arms to get appointments for you." She stared out the window knowing the landscape was greening, even if she couldn't see it clearly through the dense fog. "If I waved a wand and cleared the fog up ahead, you'd see the lake appear right around the next corner."

"According to the weather radio the fog is in here to stay," Jerrod said. "So it's not a good day to take the boats out, anyway. Besides, thinking about these interviews helped me pull my thoughts together about diving and shipwrecks and the adventure and beauty involved."

"Hey, keep talking like that and you'll do fine," Dawn said, grinning. "That's what you're selling after all, adventure, beauty, something out of the ordinary."

"And, as you'll hear me say—again and again—each dive is unlike any other. Every trip under the surface of any body of water is unique."

"Every drive around the peninsula is unique, too. With the fog and snow and fall colors and clouds of apple and cherry blossoms and summer flowers, it's never the same twice." Although this day trip was about business, Dawn was glad the legwork was done.

Riding along next to him, Jerrod himself occupied her thoughts, just as he had earlier that morning when she was nervous with anticipation. Sometimes she had to stop herself from jumping too far ahead, but she'd asked for a challenging project and she got it. Dawn wished they were traveling in comfortable silence, feeling no need to talk. That wasn't quite true. The warmth of their previous time together hung between them, almost as a barrier to business as usual.

It had been his idea to bring their families together after her trip to the hospital. She wasn't expecting that evening and what had felt like intimacy between them. Saying goodbye to Carrie that evening had left Dawn needing to come down from surprisingly intense emotions. She'd said good night to Gordon and hurried to her bedroom trying to calm a wave of unexpected attraction—and longing.

Even Gordon felt a shift, as if something important happened. For the last couple of weeks he'd peppered her with questions about Jerrod and diving. She was sure other questions lurked beneath the surface. Like her, Gordon was drawn to Jerrod.

A street sign barely visible in the mist jolted her back to the present. Just in time. "Take the next right and then after the stoplight, you can take another right into the parking lot. I was daydreaming and almost missed seeing the turnoff to Rock Hill."

A few minutes later, she led the way into the two-story glass and stone *Peninsula News* headquarters.

"What a building," Jerrod said, scanning the open space and atrium.

"It's a real showpiece in Rock Hill," Dawn said. "They replaced an old wooden 1950s building that looked like it had been glued together in a day or two. This building sends a signal that tourism is a serious industry, not an afterthought behind fishing and farming."

Jerrod frowned. "I imagine there's an argument whether that's good news or bad news."

"Right you are," she agreed. "So far, co-existence has prevailed, mainly because the orchards and farms bring a lot of visitors. We can't have farm stores without produce, namely the local specialties, cherries and apples. You can buy tarts and tortes and pies, jam and jelly and chocolate-covered everything. And in the fall, the apple products share space with pumpkin desserts and such."

Seeing she'd finally amused him, she added, "Nowadays, these farm stores have added big selections of wine, too, from the many wineries that have sprung up around here. Good wine, too." She grinned. "And that, Mr. Walters, is the end of the local commercial."

The receptionist recognized her and directed them to the cushioned benches on the second level. On a clear day they could look downhill to the waterfront, where a series of walkways and docks led to shops and restaurants. Rock Hill was upscale and touristy, but as beautiful as it was, Dawn liked the atmosphere of Two Moon Bay so much better. Her town sent out a warmer invitation to stay awhile. Even Jerrod had mentioned how quickly he'd learned to navigate around the pedestrian-friendly town. The Bean Grinder staff had quickly adopted him and his crew as regulars and called them by name. She liked that he was beginning to feel at home there.

When they sat side by side on a bench outside Wilson's office, Dawn decided she had to speak up, knowing she wouldn't be doing her job as a PR consultant if she kept quiet. She put her hand on his arm to make sure she had his full attention. "How would you feel if Bali comes up? I understand you wouldn't welcome nosy journalists probing, but we're deliberately doing things that will put you in the public eye."

Jerrod lowered his head. "I need to settle in here with Carrie first, before I'd be ready to talk about that. I've got to feel at home, to the extent any place can feel like home to me now, and maybe then, down the road, if someone asks, I'll answer." He paused. "I used to be paralyzed, almost mute. Couldn't talk about any of it. But things are different.

I don't want people to pity me. That would be too much."

Dawn bit the corner of her bottom lip, a sure sign she was frustrated.

Some part of her wanted to assure Jerrod that in no way did he elicit anyone's pity. Sympathy, yes. What had happened to him was a true tragedy. She'd wondered about his serious demeanor, the reasons he smiled so little.

"I don't get why it would even come up. Really."

"The internet, Jerrod. Easy access to information that just pops up." Dawn lifted her arms in a show of exasperation. What fantasy world was he living in? "You can be looking for one thing and then all of a sudden the search brings up something you weren't expecting."

"Oh, sure, like these writers are going to go snooping around about me." He cast a pointed look her way. "These are tourist guides, Dawn."

Nice put-down. "These are *interviews*, and you don't get chances like this just by snapping your fingers, you know," she said, snapping her own fingers in the space between them. "And, of course, these writers are looking you up. You're being naive to think otherwise."

"Naive?" he said in a loud voice.

"That's what I said." She pointed to herself. "How do you think I learned about what happened to Augusta and Dabny? The internet, of course."

Stunned by her own admission, Dawn glanced around her, relieved no one was around to hear them.

Jerrod stared at her, his eyes icy. The vein in his temple pulsated. Finally, he spoke. "I suppose you saw this information before I sat in your living room and brought it up."

Dawn closed her eyes and drew in a breath. "Yes, but I didn't go looking…" Behind Jerrod, the office door opened and Wilson's face appeared. "Oh, good morning, Wilson."

"Nice to see you, Dawn. How have you been?" Wilson asked.

"Good. Let me do the introductions," she said, willing her voice to a normal tone as she approached Wilson standing in the doorway.

They followed Wilson into his office, but she moved aside to give Jerrod room at the small table in the corner in the paper-cluttered office. "I'll sit over here," she said, pointing to an empty desk chair several feet from the table. She stole a glance at him and saw his face looked no more serious than usual.

"I see you and your clients' names in papers and local guides everywhere," Wilson said, apparently not puzzled by the distance she'd created. "And on the radio. Lots of action."

Dawn smiled. "Can't hurt to have my newest client hear about the success of some other ones."

"I've heard a lot about a fitness center and party planning business," Jerrod said flatly. He quickly added, "And it's all been good."

As if she weren't in the room, Wilson pointed to Dawn. "We call her the publicity maven. You chose well, Jerrod. Dawn's clients become regulars of ours around here. They're always doing something newsworthy."

"Ah, flattery. I love it. And by the way, maven is much better than diva. But he's already hired me, Wilson." To keep her hands still, Dawn reached into her bag and pulled out her planner. "You two go ahead." Looking at Jerrod, she added, "I can step out if you'd like."

"No, that's not necessary." His voice remained flat.

Wilson looked quizzically from Jerrod to Dawn, no doubt wondering if her client was always so stiff, Dawn thought. She smiled at Wilson and took her seat. She kept her hands busy writing a grocery list in her planner. Ridiculous. She never made grocery lists.

"Okay, then, let's get started." Wilson pulled a reporter's spiral-top notebook out from under a stack of what looked to Dawn like regional dailies. Dawn didn't see many of those old-fashioned journalists' tools anymore among the staff writers and freelancers she encountered. Wilson was not only an older man by anyone's definition, he was also old school.

As Wilson flipped the notebook open and grabbed a pencil out of a coffee mug filled with them, Dawn went back to pretending she was working. Jumping ahead, she was relieved knowing Jerrod wouldn't need any coaching to prepare for their next stops.

"I've read the background material, so I see you have extensive experience," Wilson said.

"I've pigeonholed you, more or less. You're in the adventure business."

"Fair enough," Jerrod said.

"Your photographs are fine," Wilson said, lifting a printout of eight-by-ten photos, "but I'd like to see the boats for myself. Before you leave, we can set up a time for me to come down to the docks in Two Moon."

"You're welcome to come on one of our trial runs," Jerrod said. "I've made a couple of dives, but we're doing a few more before we bring the divers or the tour boat passengers."

Wilson shook his head. "Thanks, but I'll pass on that invitation. I'm not exactly water phobic, but I don't spend much time on the lake—or under it."

You and me both, Wilson. She almost blurted those words, but wisely held back. Snorkeling in really warm water aside, Dawn was almost grateful for the immobilizer on her wrist and the bump on her head. It gave her an excuse to avoid the diving issue at least for the time being. She'd not reacted one way or another when Jerrod had mentioned diving with him in the future.

"I get it," Jerrod said, "Lots of people feel

that way, and needless to say, they aren't my customers."

From there, everything went exactly as Dawn had imagined and she listened in and watched as Jerrod loosened up. This phase of her plan was off to a good start.

It didn't hurt that Wilson was a solid sports and outdoor life journalist. He wouldn't take this article lightly. He probed deeply, too, letting Jerrod explain the lure of shipwrecks and how they were a window to the past.

"But what about diving itself?" Wilson asked. "It's so cold up this way, and the water never gets all that warm, not even in August. Is a dive really worth it?"

"Each dive is different, unique." Jerrod rested his forearms on the tabletop. "Each time you venture beneath the surface of a body of water, whether it's the Caribbean or Lake Michigan, you can expect to see—and feel—something new."

"And you believe it's safe?"

Dawn saw Jerrod's quick change of focus as he looked toward the window, which showed nothing but the gray fog. Still, Dawn saw the faraway look in his eyes. For the moment, the only sound in the room was the faint scratch of Wilson's pencil jotting notes.

"It's safe if people are trained and up for a challenge," Jerrod said, shifting in the chair. "My crew has as much expertise as any diving operation you'd find anywhere in any country. They've been with me for several years and have taken others on coral reef and shipwreck dives in locations all over the world. So, does that make it risk free? No. But no adventure is."

"I know you understand that better than most people," Wilson said, his voice low. "I saw a couple of online pieces about the terrorist attack in Bali. Such a terrible tragedy for you and your family."

Jerrod shot Dawn a look. But she lowered her gaze.

"Since I'm not known in the area and am starting fresh," Jerrod said slowly, "I'd rather not have that story follow me around."

Wilson knit his brows. "Look, I wasn't planning to mention it, because it isn't related to your local business. But others might ask you about it, even your passengers…" He shrugged and left it at that, but stood as a signal that the interview was done.

They were awkwardly silent on the way back to the car and the drive to the next two stops. Each time, they went through the similar round of introductions and quick questions for short blurbs in tourist monthlies. If the situation weren't so sad, Dawn would have had a good laugh over the front they put up. They were like a feuding married couple, riding along in grim silence in the car and putting on their professional game face at each venue.

On the way to the last stop, Dawn said, "Jerrod, let's clear the air."

"I need to do one more interview," he said, following her directions to the office of the regional publisher in Sturgeon Bay. At least he wasn't so cold. Still, her impatience with him grew. She might have made a mistake, but she hadn't shared his secrets with anyone. Besides, they weren't secrets in the first place. Hadn't she said as much?

Jerrod was deep into the fourth interview when he seemed fully himself again. Serious, yes, but friendly to the editor, Josie. He acted like he'd decided to make himself at home, Dawn thought. He responded to questions about what Dawn had learned were his favorite topics, the history of the two shipwrecks, the *Franklin Stone* and the *Alice Swann*.

"The history is part of the lure for me. These wrecks are unpretentious, like the area itself. These two ships were solid and hard-working, like their owners and crews. Coral reefs, with their exotic colors and sea creatures, are like the shiny objects that get all the attention. It's time for this area to make the most of its waters and its history."

"I believe I read that your late wife was from Milwaukee," Josie said.

"Uh, yes, that's true. I don't talk about that a lot."

"It's part of your bio," Josie said, her voice matter-of-fact.

"Maybe so, but, it's not something I do interviews about, not specifically, anyway."

Josie pushed a printed sheet toward Jerrod. "Is there anything in this article from the *Miami Herald* that's inaccurate?"

Jerrod's head jerked back in surprise, but he immediately recovered and scanned the page. "Since you're pressing me for an answer, yes, it's accurate."

Josie's eyebrows lifted. "Okay, I think we

have what we need. The piece will run in our Weekender insert."

Dawn stood, and Jerrod followed her lead. He offered his hand to Josie.

"Thanks," Dawn said, shaking Josie's hand. "See you soon."

"I hope so. We need interesting stories…" she nodded to Jerrod "…like this one."

Walking out of the building, she noticed Jerrod's stride was looser and the tension in his face had eased.

"Well, that's over and done with," he said, approaching the car. "Overall it wasn't so bad."

"Good. I'm glad you feel that way." She stood at the passenger-side door. "So, are we going to talk about this?"

"What's to talk about?" he asked, flicking his hand. "You already knew what happened to Augusta and Dabny. You let me go on about it…"

"I didn't see the point of stopping you." They were looking at each other over the top of the car, a barrier literally between them. "I'm sorry, Jerrod. Really."

"It's just that it's so hard for me to talk about

it," he said, his voice rising. "I was opening myself up about these painful things."

Dawn walked around the back of the car to stand with him. When she pressed her hand lightly on his upper arm, his eyes flashed in surprise. "That's exactly why I didn't stop you, why I didn't break in. You seemed to need to tell me this awful story in your own words. So I decided not to interrupt and blurt out that I already knew about it from the internet. Are you kidding me?"

"Okay, okay, but maybe I wouldn't have gone into it so much, I guess."

"I wanted you to." Dawn knew the air would never be clear between them if she left it at that. "I was afraid you'd think I was just snooping around. But I wasn't. The same *Miami Herald* piece Josie just showed you was what the search engine brought up."

Jerrod shook his head. "I was naive. You were right about that. After the attack, when we went back to Florida and Wyatt and Rob helped me save the business, everyone knew what happened. But I thought up here where no one knows me it would be a different story."

"It was two years ago, too, Jerrod. So,

you're right, it is different here, but to be frank, your story is dramatic." She again touched his arm. "It was the kind of tragedy almost everyone fears nowadays. That sounds cold, but it's true. That's why I didn't want you to think you could hide it. I didn't want you caught flat-footed."

Jerrod covered her hand with his, increasing the pressure against his arm. "I get it. I'm sorry I went all cold on you."

She nodded. "That's okay. And if I had to do things over, I'd have told you what I found. But to be honest, I'd still have wanted you to confide in me, you know, let me hear it in your words."

Jerrod let go of her hand and lightly pulled her to him in a quick embrace. Her muscles relaxed as her cheek brushed against the smooth fabric of his jacket. She was surprised, but not in a negative way. For a few seconds she held her breath.

"Wasn't I promised lunch in some special place up this way?" Jerrod asked, lowering his arm.

Reluctantly, she exhaled as she backed away and returned to the passenger side and opened the door. "I seem to recall making that promise. So, let's go."

AS THEY FINISHED their Swedish pancake platters at Al Johnson's restaurant, the sun had defied the forecast and burned off the fog. They'd had a late lunch at this particular place because it was one of her favorite restaurants outside of Two Moon Bay. With the tension gone between them, Jerrod felt lighter than he had in a long time. All four appointments were behind him and he could relax. He'd been wrong about what would happen if Dawn knew Augusta's and Dabny's deaths were his fault. He'd feared she'd shrink from him as if avoiding something toxic. But she hadn't. Maybe that was the real reason he'd needed to be closer to her. It was his way of thanking her without actually saying the words.

"The restaurant was the only stop we made today where you didn't know pretty much everyone," he said, switching his train of thought as they left the restaurant.

"Oh, that's what you think," she shot back, feigning a self-satisfied look. "As a matter of fact, I ran into an old friend in the ladies' room."

"I might have known. But it's good to navigate new places with someone familiar with everything."

As they climbed into the car, she said, "Now that the sun's out, there's something I'd like to show you. It won't take long to get there, maybe twenty minutes. Are you up for a side trip?"

"Lead the way," he said, wondering where she got all her energy. After four appointments, she was as fresh as when they'd started their trip up the peninsula earlier that day. He used to be like that himself, he mused. It came from enjoying his work the same way he could see Dawn enjoyed hers. But her energy also rose from a clear conscience, a lack of burden. That's how he read Dawn. He'd once thought self-blame was a permanent part of him. Now he wondered if could let that piece of himself off the hook. He hadn't even considered it before. Only as he settled into life in Two Moon Bay had he thought it possible.

He followed her directions onto the main highway and then the state road in the next town north. She directed him down an un-paved road full of bumps and ruts that slowed his speed to less than twenty miles an hour. He began to regret saying yes to this extra jaunt. "This place better be good," he teased.

"This is the worst of it," she said, "but the reward is at hand." She pointed ahead to a parking area. "This is actually a county park, but it's the lookout that draws people from ev-erywhere. These bluffs are the highest point in the area, so we get a beautiful panoramic view of the lake and the small islands around the peninsula."

They were alone in the park on that week-day in May and under a now clear blue sky.

"Follow me." She led the way down steep and winding wooden stairs to a platform and fence that offered a view of the lake from a point higher than he'd seen before. The fresh breeze created an even pattern of whitecaps broken up only by the wooded islands. "This is the reward for going down that awful road." She encompassed the view with an exagger-ated sweep of her arm. "It seems a shame to come as far as the famous Al Johnson's and not go this one leg more."

He stood still and took it all in. The fishy

scent carried on the breeze, the sound of the waves slapping the rocky boulders below, the spray flying high into the air. He'd trekked to the panoramic views of oceans and lakes, waterfalls and rivers. They almost always left him awestruck, even overwhelmed. For reasons Jerrod couldn't explain, he found this view both majestic and oddly comforting. "There's nothing *un*pretentious about this view."

"Ha! That's so funny. I've never heard anyone describe it quite like that, but you're right. It's more dramatic than most of our landscape. I think of this part of the state as a showpiece of *gentle* beauty. Two Moon Bay is one of the best of its gems." She tilted her head back and inhaled deeply. "I can't get enough of that lake smell."

Dawn was so much more than to-do lists and that satchel she called a handbag she hauled around. "You really love it here, don't you?"

"I do." She shrugged. "I love to travel, but I always want to come back to this neck of the woods. It's home."

He thought about home, and what that meant for him. He didn't know anymore. But being around Dawn made him ask questions he hadn't allowed himself to think about for the past couple of years.

"I suppose for you, Key West is home?"

She phrased that as a question, so she probably expected an answer. He searched for one, but finally said, "I don't know if that's true anymore. It was always the base, the place we called home. But I'm not attached to it."

He gazed at the grayish blue lake. "I can't even imagine not having water as my, oh, I don't know, point of reference."

"Me, too," she said, turning away from the fence. "I suppose we ought to head back."

He glanced at his watch. "I like to be home for dinner with Carrie. On most days I spend time with her in the evening. It's our special time, and Melody gets her breaks, too."

"Now that you know where this place is, you can tell Wyatt and Rob about it, and you can bring Carrie to see it, too." She stopped and glanced over her shoulder. "I wanted you to know it's here. After all, not all the beauty around here is found under the water."

Not by a long shot. He almost laughed out loud at the direction of his thoughts. "I understand why you wanted to bring me here."

"I had a feeling you would," she said, getting into the car.

When they'd settled into their seats, Dawn said, "One more thing. I propose a toast." She picked up her bottle of water from the cup holder.

Puzzled, he did the same.

"To the success of your new venture for however long you choose to make this little corner of the world your home."

They bumped the water bottles and Dawn laughed. "It's not exactly fine wine and crystal glasses."

Who needed crystal? He drove back down the rutted road thinking about Dawn and mulling over her question about home.

CHAPTER SIX

DAWN PULLED THE hood of her jacket up over her head and hurried from her car to the docks in the light rain. Seeing the lights on in Jerrod's office, she changed her mind and ducked inside. She saw no sign of Jerrod, but Wyatt sat at the desk working on a laptop.

"Hi, Dawn," Wyatt said, glancing away from the screen. "I didn't expect to see you here today."

"I've got some news for Jerrod," Dawn said, pushing her hood back. "Since I was passing by I thought I'd tell him in person."

"You just missed him," Wyatt said, "but he'll be back soon."

The walls of the square room were lined with shelving and bins and a dozen or so folding chairs set up and a few others closed and propped up against the wall. The poster of the *Franklin Stone* added something. Maybe a little character and sense of permanence. Nothing was thrown together haphazardly.

"I've only seen this office when you first moved into it. But it looks like you're in business now." She glanced at the diving gear, from dry suits to buoyancy controllers and weight belts neatly arranged on labeled shelves. "It looks like someone around here is an expert organizer."

Wyatt closed the computer and gestured to the empty chair. "That would be Jerrod. He insists on good order, as he calls it, especially now that Memorial Day is behind us and the tourist season is finally underway. He links our systems to his two primary goals. Naturally, safety tops the list, with success right behind it."

"That could sound stuffy and formal," Dawn said, slipping out of her coat. She sat on the chair next to the desk. "But somehow, it doesn't strike me that way at all."

From where she sat, Dawn could see the shelf of framed photographs behind Wyatt. She wasn't able to see it clearly, but a photo of a woman and a little girl sat between some pictures of dive boats and crew, including Wyatt. "You have a photo gallery, huh? Is that new? I don't recall seeing photos in here before."

"Jerrod brought them over the weekend. We used to have a wall of photos in the Key West office...years ago, I mean," Wyatt said, "Since we did our first tour on *Lucy Bee* last weekend, he wanted to start posting new pictures showing our guests having a good time. These framed photos reinforce the idea that the business has a long history."

Wyatt frowned as she swiveled in the chair and grabbed two of the pictures. "This one was taken in Thailand when Carrie was still a baby." She pointed to Jerrod standing in the well of the dive boat with Carrie in his arms. "This one is from St. Croix the next year."

Speaking softly, Dawn said, "I know what happened in Bali. Jerrod told me about it."

"Good," Wyatt said. "When he came in with the photos I thought he might be taking a step to be more open about the past."

"Is that Dabny?" Dawn asked, pointing to a girl sitting on Wyatt's lap.

Wyatt's features changed as a look of sadness crossed her face. Recovering quickly, she managed a weak smile. "Uh-huh. I used to call her Dabs. She was a great kid. Like

Carrie is now." Wyatt turned back to the shelf and picked up another photo. "Here's one of Augusta and the girls not long before…well, before she and Dabny died." She grunted in frustration. "I don't know why I said that. Augusta and Dabny were killed. Murdered. They didn't just die." Wyatt passed the picture to Dawn.

She hoped Wyatt didn't see her hand shaking ever so slightly as she took the photo. She felt a little like an intruder. Her curiosity was more than a passing thing. Like Wyatt said, though, these pictures were now out in the open. She glanced down and saw a woman with long blond hair gathered over one shoulder offering a bright smile to the photographer, whoever it was. Carrie stood on a cockpit seat next to her mom, and Dabny, whose hair was blond like Augusta's, stared away from the camera, a dreamy look on her little face.

"Did Jerrod take this picture?" Dawn asked.

Wyatt shook her head. "I took it. Jerrod was off with Rob and a local guy he'd hired to help maintain the two dive boats. Augusta called it our 'girls only' afternoon." She flashed a wistful smile. "She liked having those special days, and she always included me."

Dawn tapped Dabny's image. "Her expression makes me wonder what she was thinking about."

Glancing down, Wyatt wrinkled her forehead in thought. "If I had to guess, she was making up a story. She had a great imagination and sometimes fancied herself a mermaid—she claimed she lived her mermaid life at night for real, not just in her dreams." Wyatt's smile was soft, full of affection. "Dabs used to say her tail was blue and glowed in the dark underwater."

The air around Dawn's head buzzed and her hands tingled. Every cell in her body responded to the image of the little mermaid girl. But she fought back the tears threatening to spill down her cheeks. "On some level I'm grateful to know that one thing about Dabny, but another part of me wishes I'd never asked." Or seen the photos. The happy mom and dreamy little girl would haunt her. "It breaks my heart."

"I understand," Wyatt said. Then she quickly took the two photos and placed them back on the shelf, finishing up about the same time Jerrod and Rob came through the door, each carrying a box with the Donovan's Marine Supply logo on it.

Jerrod's face showed pleasant surprise. "I didn't expect to see you today."

"From the logo on the boxes, it looks like you've become well acquainted with Art and Zeke Donovan."

"Yep, and we like dealing with them," Jerrod said.

"I came here with a purpose." She explained that the head librarian at the Two Moon Bay Library had some time that afternoon to meet Jerrod and set up his first talk. "She wants to fill a spot left open because another speaker is in the midst of a health crisis and had to cancel. I told her I couldn't commit without asking you. She'd like to meet you."

Jerrod shrugged. "I can free up time this afternoon."

"Good. She said two o'clock works for her."

Jerrod looked at Rob and Wyatt. "Carrie is home with Melody, so I can't think of a reason not to go. Can you?" He turned to Dawn. "I like to run things by these two, just in case."

"I've sent emails in response to a bunch of inquiries," Wyatt said, grinning, "and I've booked a couple of dives in July and one group in August, with backup dates. And hey, it isn't even noon."

"So, looks like I can meet the librarian," Jerrod said. "And now it's time for lunch. You care to join us, Dawn? We usually send Rob out on a sandwich run."

If he only knew how much she wanted to sit with them and be part of their group. "Don't I wish. But when the text from Marion came in, I was running some errands before my meeting at Fitness & More. I'm having lunch there." With a light laugh, she added, "No doubt some kind of salad whose main ingredients are kale and sprouts. Maybe they'll live dangerously and sprinkle on a few sunflower seeds."

Rob snorted. "Are you sure you can't make up an excuse and have a thick roast beef sandwich with us?"

"I'm sure. Besides, I've grown kinda fond of kale lately."

Rob responded with an exaggerated grimace. "Good for you."

"Should I meet you at the library?"

The light moment was over. Jerrod had already gone back to his typically serious mode.

"Sure. I'll be there a little before two."

She raised her hood again and headed out into the rain. She had just enough time to get to the fitness center. Earlier, when Marion had contacted her, Dawn hadn't been running any kind of business errands. She'd been on her way to Rock Hill on a mission for new summer clothes. She had Party Perfect's book signing and a couple of fund-raisers coming up, including an event at the yacht club that called for a dressy dress. What she wore on her day-to-day rounds needed an update, too.

But she didn't regret detouring to the marina to deliver the message in person. Disturbing or not, she'd wanted a glimpse into Jerrod's life before the terrorists had killed Augusta and Dabny. Now she had it. The radiant woman and a little girl who fancied herself a mermaid were real to Dawn now. Most heartbreaking of all, the littlest girl in the photo didn't remember her mom. *I'd keep her alive for you.*

But no one had asked her to jump in.

Fighting back confusing tears, Dawn forced

herself to drive toward Fitness & More. Unlike her best pal, Lark, she didn't shed tears easily. But sitting in the office with Wyatt staring at Augusta and Dabny, she'd had trouble holding it together. Ever since that night many weeks earlier when Jerrod and Gordon made tacos she'd been drawn to Jerrod—and Carrie—and the magnitude of the tragedy hit home.

Soon, she was inside the fitness center and her meeting with Paul and Nancy was underway. She'd long admired this couple, whose center had expanded into the storefront next door. They were one of those "have it all" couples Dawn admired, both professionally and personally. Over huge salads of greens and various kinds of seeds and nuts, Dawn went over her proposed plans for the next six months.

But it didn't take long to note that neither of them was paying much attention.

"What's up?" she asked, frowning. "You're not in the room."

They exchanged sheepish glances. "You don't miss a beat, do you?"

For reasons she couldn't explain, Dawn knew what they were going to say. Nancy was pregnant. "Anyone can see you're pre-occupied with something else."

"Okay, okay," Paul said, "you win."

"No, *we* win," Nancy blurted. "We're having a baby."

Dawn let out the best fake squeal of surprise she could muster. "When?"

"November...we think," Nancy said. "I knew even without a test. I feel awful in the morning and can't keep my eyes open past eight. I have a doctor's appointment tomorrow morning."

"Ah, I'm so happy for you." The walls closed in. Dawn powered down her tablet and stood. "I've got an appointment at the library across the street, and there's nothing that's truly pressing here. Seeing the rain has stopped and the sun is out, do you mind if I leave my car parked in your lot?"

"Not at all," Paul said, "but we're sorry we wasted your time today."

Nancy snickered. "Right now, we can't seem to focus on anything but us."

Through the glass wall of the office, Dawn could see a handful of people on the treadmills and cycles, and in another area, one of their instructors was leading a weight training

class for at least a dozen seniors. She wanted
to break into a run and go as far as her legs
would allow. "You seem to be doing fine.
Give yourself the day to bask in your news.
You deserve it."

Her clients exchanged another glance, intimate and pleased.

Assuring them she'd check in later, Dawn
gathered her things and left. The library was
across the street and down half a block. She
spotted Jerrod sitting on the front stairs waiting for her. But he couldn't see her, not if she
turned the corner to the side of the building.
When she dropped her bag on the sidewalk,
she braced her hand against the brick wall.
She stared down at her shoes and took air
deep into her lungs and let it out slowly.

Her reaction was over-the-top and she
needed time to regroup. She wasn't going to
get it. She picked up her bag and hoisted it on
her shoulder and lifted her chin. News of new
babies on the way always brought on stabs of
envy, but nothing this ridiculous.

"Dawn? Are you okay?"

She spun around to face Jerrod. "Oh, hi."
Caught off guard, she didn't have a chance
to reset her mood and fake her demeanor.

"Oh, my meeting was a little tougher than expected." She started down the street. "How were those sandwiches?"

Jerrod stared at her, looking as if he had something he'd like to say. She changed the subject fast to the meeting ahead. Back to business, her safe haven.

Once they were inside Marion's office, Jerrod took over and she stepped back, as she had during the interviews. Jerrod had no trouble talking about the topics of presentations he could deliver, from marine history to shipwrecks to the ecosystem of the Great Lakes.

Dawn inserted herself into the conversation only to talk about the usual mundane things like press releases. "Jerrod's blog will be underway soon, and he can use the educational series at the library as a basis for a post. We'll promote it on his social media, too."

"Anything you want to send out is fine," Marion said, pushing away from the desk.

Dawn knew the signal well. The meeting was over, short and sweet. That was good, because the day was pressing in on her. As Marion and Jerrod said their goodbyes, Dawn realized she had no inclination to go back to work.

Just outside the library, Dawn pointed across the park-like lawn in front of the building to a wood-and-stone pillar a half block away. "Have you seen the World War I Memorial over there?"

"I walked by it and meant to stop, but you know how that is. No time that day," Jerrod explained.

"Let's go over there for a minute. I bet you'll find it interesting."

As they walked, Jerrod chatted enthusiastically about ideas for his talks and blog posts. Dawn's mind wandered in and out. But when they stopped in front of the memorial she said, "I thought you'd be interested in this because our mutual acquaintance, Zeke Donovan, had a hand in restoring this."

The pillar was stone, but the pedestal and the base were made of wood, and the circular metal top was gleaming in the afternoon sun, obscuring the names etched on it. Two benches sat side by side at the edge of the bricks surrounding the memorial.

"What did Zeke do in the restoration?" Jerrod ran his hand down the smooth stone.

"I don't know Zeke well, but he and an architect put in a proposal to bring this memorial back to its original condition. Some people wanted to haul it away rather than fix it up. They wanted to put an engraved plaque on a boulder over by the other war memorials around City Hall."

"You're kidding? It looks like a lot of thought went into this memorial."

Dawn pointed to the list of names. "These four men died in that war." She moved around the pillar a few feet. "And these five men were injured." She reached up and tapped one name. "See this one? James Loran. My mother's great-uncle. He lost an arm and was badly burned. I didn't know him, but I heard a lot about him. He and his wife ran a little candy store here in town."

"I see. I'll bet you were among those who wanted this restored in place, right here."

"You got it," she said, running her fingertips along the engraved name. "And I wasn't alone."

She turned to take in the park around her. "For such a small town, only 13,000 people today, it always surprises me to look at the memorials and see how many men—and women—went off to the many wars."

"I didn't realize your family has such a long history here. Interesting about Zeke, too."

Jerrod asked if she had time for coffee at the Bean Grinder. "One of my favorite Two Moon Bay institutions."

"And another of Zeke's projects. He worked with the architect to restore the octagonal building, originally an old dance and music hall they used in the summer."

On any other day, she'd have jumped at the offer, been eager to go. She repeated almost those identical words. "Normally, I'd like that, but I have a conference call in an hour. I really need to get home."

Why had she lied? She had no answer, but she wouldn't find one if she went out for coffee with Jerrod.

"No problem," he said. "We can do it another time."

"Soon." She took a couple of steps toward the street to go back to retrieve her car. "I'll check in with you tomorrow."

Jerrod walked off in the opposite direction and Dawn hurried to her car. Once inside, she gripped the top of the steering wheel and rested her forehead on her hands. What had come over her? The photographs in Jerrod's office. Yes, they'd disturbed her. The unbearable sadness had thrown her off center. But then, minutes later, the news of new life on the way. Paul and Nancy having a baby. Their first.

Be grateful for Gordon. She shushed the little voice whispering that message. She didn't need that reminder. She was overwhelmed with gratitude for her son sometimes. But did that mean it was wrong to want another family, another baby?

Dawn lifted her head and lowered her hands to start her car and buckle in. She'd soon be home and drop that heavy bag of business in her office and shut the door. She was eager to leave all those confusing emotions behind.

CHAPTER SEVEN

CARRIE PEEKED AROUND the doorjamb, but didn't come all the way into the room.

"Hello, sweetie. Are you hiding?" Jerrod asked the question as he lined up his three neckties on the end of the bed.

"Nope. Just watchin' you." She moved into the doorway.

"You want to help me pick out a necktie?"

Carrie nodded and came into his bedroom holding Candy by its ear.

"So, what will it be? Red or blue? Or, how about this one, yellow-and-white striped?"

Carrie put her finger to her lips and frowned in thought.

Oh, to be able to freeze the moment when his necktie choice was the most important issue on his little girl's mind.

"I like the red one best, Daddy."

"Well, then, that's the one I'll wear." He'd been leaning toward the yellow-striped one, but what did it matter? He couldn't recall the last time he'd worn a necktie, or a sports jacket, for that matter. Turning to the mirror, he knotted the tie and tugged it in place. He assumed his navy sports coat and khakis were right for the evening.

"Where are you going, Daddy?"

"Remember, I told you this morning I'm walking over to the bookstore. Dawn invited me to meet some people who wrote a book and lots of people are going to buy copies of it at the bookstore." He deliberately avoided calling the book signing a party. That would sound like too much fun and Carrie would want to tag along.

"I like Dawn," Carrie said, climbing up on the end of the bed.

So do I. He grabbed his jacket off the chair. "She's very nice, huh? And she works hard, too." That was a safe comment, and Carrie wouldn't notice that he'd brought himself back to their business relationship. Where it needed to stay. "So, what do you think? Do I look okay?"

Carrie nodded. "Is Gordon coming to the bookstore?"

"No, honey, he's spending time with his

dad tonight." He reached out to smooth her silky dark hair, the braids loose now at the end of the day. Jerrod understood the question about Gordon. Ever since the taco dinner, Carrie had asked about Dawn and Gordon frequently. The questions were tough on him, even though he knew all his daughter wanted was another chance to spend time with people she thought were their new friends. That's what he'd called them.

She hugged her bear to her chest. "I don't feel good."

What? "What do you mean, honey?"

"My stomach feels weird."

Her almost offhand remark about not feeling good was odd. Not something that happened often. Melody was there, so he could leave if he needed to, but backing out was okay, too. Even picking out his tie he felt like a nervous teenager getting ready for a date. And that was wrong in so many ways. It wasn't only about mixing business and pleasure. That was the simple explanation. More like an excuse, he thought.

"When did you start feeling sick?" he asked, putting his hand on Carrie's forehead. It felt cool.

"This afternoon," she said.

"Did you eat dinner?" He lifted his hand and put it on her forehead again. Maybe it was a little warm. Worried now, he didn't trust himself to judge.

"A little. Melody made macaroni and cheese. Wyatt and Rob ate some, too."

Why hadn't he been there for dinner? Saying he had to work on his library presentation, he'd stayed behind, snacking on crackers and cheese in his office. The people who were the closest he had to a family were eating together and he was alone. He'd have to analyze that later. "Wait here, sweetie. I'm going to go talk to Melody."

"She's in the kitchen," Carrie said.

He went down the hall to the kitchen, where Melody was wiping down the counter. "Did Carrie tell you she didn't feel well?"

Frowning, she said, "No. We just got back from the other house. I brought mac n' cheese over there, and they made salad. Carrie seemed fine then."

"She said she wasn't feeling good. That her stomach felt weird, her word." He looked back down the hall to his room. Something didn't seem right.

"Well, she'll be with me," Melody said. "She doesn't get sick much, but I can take care of her if she does. You won't be far away."

"I know. I'm not worried about that." What was he worried about? Being gone and him needing her. "I think it's because she's *not* sick very often that I'm concerned."

He made a fast decision. "I'm going to cancel. I'll call Dawn now."

Her expression quizzical, Melody said, "Jerrod, really, you don't have to do that."

He smiled at the woman he'd completely trusted for two years. "I know she'd be fine with you, but this is something I need to do." He didn't say it out loud, but he left too much of this kind of care to Melody. Yes, she was Carrie's nanny, but he was her father. "I need to know I can."

He went back to the bedroom to get his phone and check on Carrie. She had stretched out on the bed on her side using Candy as a pillow. Her eyes were closed. No bigger than a minute, he thought, the old expression Augusta used coming back to him, seeing his tiny girl on the big queen-size bed in his room. He knew Carrie sometimes went up to Melody's room on the second floor and climbed into bed with her early in the morning. It was a game they played, with Carrie pretending she had to drag Melody out of bed.

He called Dawn and left an apologetic voice mail, but followed up with a text just to be sure to reach her. It was an important evening for Dawn, not only because of her clients' success, but because she'd planned to introduce him to people she believed should be in his network. He scoffed to himself. She hadn't said these people could be his friends, just in his network. He admired her professionalism, most of the time, but it could grate on him now and then, too. Like now.

He also couldn't deny his curiosity about what happened with her husband. Why didn't she have what she wanted? She hadn't offered an explanation and he hadn't asked. But he'd bet it was a painful chapter.

DAWN LIKED HAVING had a reason to be in downtown Two Moon Bay at night. There was a different atmosphere when most of the retail stores were closed but the Half Moon Café and the ice cream and fudge shop and the diner at the end of the block stayed open.

Starting in June, the Book Shelf kept evening hours, too, and the Half Moon Café hung strings of white lights around the outdoor patio in the back and stayed open way past midnight.

She could have headed home, but she didn't feel like calling it a night just yet. She stood by her car, trying to decide where she wanted to go. She knew, of course. She wanted to see Jerrod. But she kept trying to banish that thought. On the other hand, it wouldn't hurt to call him to see how Carrie was doing. Right? She could wait until morning, but there was no reason to put off a friendly call. Besides, the book signing hadn't been much fun without Jerrod. In her mind, it was much more of a social occasion than linked to her clients. *Oh, quit the big debate*, she scolded. She took her phone out of her jacket pocket and made the call.

"Are the festivities over?" he asked, bypassing a regular greeting.

"Yes, they are. I'm getting ready to go home, but I thought I'd call you first and see how it's going with Carrie?"

"Everything seems okay now," he said. "She's sleeping."

"Do you need anything? Soda crackers, ginger ale?" She waited for the answer.

"Well, now that you mention it, we could use some ginger ale. I already hunted up crackers for her."

That took her by surprise. A pleasant one. How strange the needs of an ill child meant her evening wasn't coming to an end after all. But wanting to see Jerrod had nothing to do with business.

"See you in a few minutes," she said.

HE STOOD ON the porch and watched her pull in behind his van.

"I always like seeing your van," she said, coming up the walk. "Somehow, the tropical aqua and yellow fish and the deep blue lettering brighten up the atmosphere."

"It looks a little like a fish out of water," he said, groaning at his own pun.

"Not bad, Captain Jerrod, not bad."

Her words and inflection sounded a lot like flirting. He admitted he'd invited her with the ruse of needing ginger ale. But no matter what he told himself, he couldn't deny his desire to know more about this intriguing, endlessly entertaining woman with her halo of curly hair and eyes that changed color so easily.

"Come on inside."

"Is Carrie in bed?" she asked, her voice low.

"She's asleep on the couch in the living room. For the moment, she's out like a light. I'll carry her to her bed later."

"So, how sick is she?"

"Well, she doesn't seem to have a stomach virus, but she had a little bit of a fever, 99.5 and 99. She munched on crackers and Melody gave her some sparkling water. Fizzy water, she calls it."

Jerrod stared down at Carrie, so peaceful now in sleep. He hadn't said anything to Melody, but he didn't think Carrie had been sick, so much as a little anxious in a quiet way.

"She looks so peaceful," Dawn said. "She's not pale. She's sleeping soundly. Kids spike fevers and fight off whatever bug they catch. A few hours later they can be good as new. I guess you'll have to wait and see what happens in the morning."

"I'm supplied with plenty of ginger ale," he said, grabbing a couple of glasses and filling them with ice. He handed them to her and he picked up a bottle of the soda and jar of nuts. "Let's go out to the front porch. We can hear Carrie from there if she wakes up. You can tell me all about the signing."

"Look at the sky tonight," she said, following him to the porch. She put the glasses down and pointed between the high oak trees where a few stars shone through on the clear, but moonless night. They settled in the two chairs with a table between them.

He sat across from her and tilted his head back. "Too much ambient light to see many stars, but for all my time on the water, I can't identify many constellations. The Big Dipper is about it."

"Lark's son, Evan, could identify them, and probably Gordon, too. He got his interest in astronomy from Evan. So, we'll have the two buddies, one a marine biologist, the other an astronomer."

She took a long gulp from the glass. "In only a week or two you won't be more or less alone down on the docks. People on sailboats and motor yachts will be having drinks and inviting each other over to their boats for parties. A resort atmosphere takes over. Some die-hards in town don't like the extra people, the traffic, crowded restaurants and every-thing else that goes with what's becoming a little more upscale tourism. They like the old fishing town atmosphere."

"But right now, the street seems dark and deserted," he said. "I like these warm early summer nights."

Dawn took another sip of her ginger ale. "Enjoy them, because they don't last long."

"Yes," he said, and left it at that. He could say that about a lot of things. Carrie's inno-cence and sense of wonder, for one thing. How much longer would that last? He'd missed too much of it already, not because he wasn't present in body, but because he wasn't paying close enough attention. As much as he'd looked forward to an evening with Dawn, he'd made the right decision to stay home with Carrie. There was a time he'd have left her in Melody's hands. She'd have been fine, but he'd have missed the chance, no matter how short, of comforting his little girl, stroking her forehead and reading stories about talking bears. That would have been his loss.

"Gordon is getting eager to go up to his grandparents' cottage on Redwing Lake,"

Dawn said, breaking their silence. "I always thought Gordon would be a fun big brother."

Jerrod frowned. Didn't Gordon have a baby sister?

"That came out wrong." Dawn swatted the air as if trying to make her words disappear. "Forget I said it."

He mumbled something about her family not being any of his business. But it sounded the wrong note and he shifted in the chair, wishing he could take back his words, too.

"I guess I walked right into this kind of awkward conversation," she said. "You've never asked, but what happened to my marriage isn't some dark secret. I'd just as soon you hear it from me and not in some gossipy way. My husband fell in love with someone else." She looked out at the street, not at him. "Bill left me to be with her, Carla."

In the dim light, he couldn't see her features, but he could guess they matched her soft tone. "I don't know what to say. I'm just sorry you were hurt."

She tilted her head and cupped her chin as if she were mulling something over. "Until it actually happened, I'd always imagined myself a warrior woman, sword in hand fighting for my marriage. No matter what. But then, when it actually happened, I realized righteous fury was futile." With a shrug she added, "Back here in the real world, Bill managed to make it work with Gordon."

Jerrod knew where he stood on that score. "I'd guess you had a strong hand in that. Sword or no sword."

She flashed a closed-mouth smile. "Thanks for that. Holding it together for Gordon was my biggest challenge during those first dreary months." After only a second of hesitation, she said, "I wasn't all that perfect at being evenhanded. I tended to grumble to other people, not my son. But no matter how heartbroken I was, I kept my eyes on the ball, Gordon."

Carrie was all that mattered, too, but especially at the beginning, he'd allowed others to step in and take care of her. Even Wyatt and Rob had picked up his slack. He'd changed that, though, little by little. Carrie was the only child he'd have and he'd needed to be worthy of her.

"I'd thought, even believed, Bill and I would have at least one more child, so that's why I said I thought he'd be a good big brother."

Another reason she'd ended up with a broken heart. She'd not sugarcoated the story. "And now Gordon has a baby sister."

"Not the way I planned it," she said. "But what do you know? Even preteen kids can't resist a baby." She snorted a laugh. "Even one name Zinnia."

He laughed along with her. "Whose idea was that?"

"Probably Carla's," she said sarcastically, but with a laugh in her voice. "Most of the time I'm okay with all this—now. But if I tell the *whole* truth, it took me a couple of years to heal. I was really bitter about losing what I considered my ideal family." She looked down, studying her hands, or so it appeared. "My pride—and confidence—got taken down a notch."

Wounded pride wasn't fatal. But she'd used the word *heal*, the same word people used when reassuring him after his losses. Eventually he'd heal, most had claimed.

"I made it sound like it was smooth, no bumps at all," she said, "but we've had to work hard to figure out how to give Gordon a lot of time with his dad. Carla hasn't always been easy to deal with on that score, especially now that she has Zinnie."

Sensing she had more on her mind, he didn't speak.

Dawn stood and went to the porch rail and leaned against it, looking at him directly now. "Family is really important to you, Jerrod. I can see how you feel. It's the same for me. Last year, when Zinnie was born, I went through another painful time. But I got my head on straight enough to encourage Gordon to enjoy her. She is his baby sister, after all."

He refilled their glasses, glad to busy his hands. If he told her how he admired her, he'd only stumble over the words and it would sound patronizing.

"Luckily, though, I got over Bill. And who knows? Maybe another marriage is in the cards for me. Maybe not. But I eventually adjusted to reality and got on with my life. And I love my business."

"That's what makes it great working with you," Jerrod said, grateful for a comment he could roll off his tongue that carried no risk. "You bring such joy to it." From the day he met her back at the hotel in Chicago, she'd struck him as a woman who was easy to be with—and look at.

"Thank you for the kind words," she said, voice soft. "They mean a lot coming from you."

Puzzled, he cocked his head.

She stood and drained her glass. "I mean because you're successful yourself, but much more important, you've survived real tragedy, Jerrod. The kind that crushes people, but here you are, starting over. Willing to try something new."

"Oh, I don't know how far I've come." He weighed the pros and cons of mentioning what he'd lost. Despite doubting the wisdom of bringing it up, his gut pushed him to go ahead. "Wyatt mentioned she showed you the photos of Augusta and Dabny when the two of you were alone in the office."

"Yes, well, she saw me glancing at them on the shelf behind her." She laced her fingers in front of her chest. "It sounds trite, I know, but seeing Augusta, so beautiful, and Dabny in all her childlike dreaminess, touched my heart more than I can say." She lowered her head. "I didn't mean to intrude on your privacy."

He waved her off. "No, no, not at all. I put the photos out after those interviews. We'd had our go-round about being more open. But I didn't think it through, so I brought the most personal pictures back."

"Good," she said. "A wise choice."

"It's one thing to have some location pictures with the crew, including Augusta and Dabny, but some were just family." His jaw tightened. "I've sent too many mixed messages, even to Wyatt and Rob. They don't know if I want to talk about Augusta and Dabny or not."

"There's something about the candid snapshots, those moments in time…"

Before she went any further in searching for words, he said, "At first I couldn't bring myself to look at those pictures, and then it was all I wanted to do. I think now I can see them with better eyes. Frankly, healthier eyes."

She nodded her understanding.

"I didn't mean to bring down the mood, Dawn."

"You didn't." She pointed to herself. "I did that when I brought up my former husband."

"Not really. You liked your life with your

husband. You felt cheated when it was taken away. That's not a crime." Knowing exactly how she'd respond, he raised his hand and quickly added, "And I'm not trying to say our situations are comparable."

She nodded again, and then gulped back the last of her ginger ale.

Wanting to get off the subject of their families, he said, "We're taking four people out to the *Franklin Stone* early next week. We have room for a couple more. How 'bout it? Want to come along and do your first dive with us?"

"Hmm…oh, I don't know. Next week is bad. I probably can't fit it in. That big planner you like to tease me about is pretty full." She left the porch rail, came back to the table and put her empty glass down. "Time for me to take off. I've stayed longer than I intended."

An abrupt refusal, he thought. "Sorry to hear you're busy, but we can schedule a dive for another day."

He followed her into the living room, where she picked up her handbag from the coffee table. She stopped to look at Carrie sleeping soundly on the couch. "Such a beautiful child," she whispered, turning to him. "I'm glad I stopped by."

"Me, too." He hadn't known how much he'd enjoy just sitting with her.

She glanced back down at Carrie, who stirred and opened her eyes. Seeing Dawn, she opened them even wider. Then she grinned. "Hi, Dawn."

"Hi, sweetie. I didn't mean to wake you."

"That's okay." She glanced at him. "Daddy stayed home with me."

He touched her forehead. It felt cool, no hint of the earlier warmth. "Dawn brought you some ginger ale, but she has to go home now. Then I'm going to take you to your own bed."

"Okay." She waved at Dawn. "Bye."

"Bye, sweetie."

"I'll be right back," Jerrod said. "Stay right where you are."

A little troubled, Jerrod walked Dawn down the driveway and opened her car door. "Can a kid her age create a fever just from being a little upset?"

Even in the dim light, he saw the change in her expression, the knowing look. "Maybe not wanting Daddy to go out without her?"

"Uh-huh? She's still kind of clingy with Melody, but I've been around more lately, and spending a lot of time with Carrie, too." He hesitated, but went ahead, anyway. "Could be she's more aware of what's missing. A mother."

"Ah, maybe she sees that in this new place you have other friends and that's shifted her world a little."

He leaned forward as if sharing a secret. "And I'd put on a sports coat and asked her which tie she liked best."

"A little too special, huh? This place you were going without her." She gave him a long, pointed look. "Not that she thought that all through, like an older kid scheming."

"No, but still."

"It doesn't sound too serious, Jerrod," she said softly, glancing up at him. "Pretty normal, actually."

He squeezed her shoulders for a casual hug, but couldn't let her go. He rested his cheek on her hair and inhaled its scent. Mint, like peppermint candy. Alive and fun, like her.

"I…uh…better go," she said, quickly lifting her head.

And almost colliding with his mouth. He wished...

She slid into the driver's seat and he closed her door.

"I'll see you in a few days, then. Meanwhile, I'll send you updates."

He lifted his hand in a goodbye gesture. "I know you will."

The engine turned over and she backed down the drive. He watched for, and got, another quick wave before she drove down the street.

Walking back to the house, he hoped she wouldn't regret opening up to him about her marriage. She'd left so abruptly. That was about diving. He was getting that now. Being busy was a habitual fallback position for her.

She'd looked so pretty that night leaning on his porch rail, staring at the sky. He'd seen behind the whirlwind-businesswoman Dawn and caught a glimpse of the whole woman. The real Dawn could show both happiness and hurt on her face.

Carrie was in a deep sleep when he gathered her in his arms and carried her down the hall to her room. When he put her down, she turned to her side and sighed. Content and probably in her dream world. He walked through the house, picking up stray toys and rinsing the glasses in the kitchen. He was curiously content, too.

CHAPTER EIGHT

"WILL JERROD GO to Nelson's barbecue?" Gordon asked, getting into the car.

Dawn didn't know for sure and said as much as she backed the car out of her driveway and onto the street. She and Gordon were on their way to the waterfront park for the Fourth of July fireworks. "Why do you ask?"

"I don't know. I haven't seen Jerrod since he was at our house," Gordon said with a shrug. "And I'm leaving with Dad tomorrow."

"But when you get back you'll be ready to go diving with him. He said you could and he won't go back on that."

Gordon nodded, but said nothing.

Dawn drove the few blocks and found a parking place on the edge of the lot at the already crowded park. As she pulled in, the likely reason for Gordon's question hit her. "Were you thinking we might be invited to Nelson's party? Because I work with Jerrod now, kind of like one of his crew?" It was easy to see why Gordon could get the wrong impression.

Nelson threw an annual July Fourth marina party. He cooked burgers and hotdogs on the grill for his marina regulars and boaters just renting a slip for a night or the weekend. The marina customers brought salads or chips and made it a real potluck meal. Dawn had never been to one of Nelson's events, but she assumed Jerrod and his crew would be among this year's crowd.

Gordon shrugged. "I guess so. I mean, the two of you hang out. Kind of."

"He's my client, honey. Sure, I check in with him often, and I go with him to interviews or meetings. But that's not the same as hanging out."

He grabbed the door handle, but didn't make a move to get out of the car. "It seemed different with him. Not like your other clients. You're friends, right? He was at our house."

"Business friends, yes," Dawn said, reluctantly, but firmly. "He and Carrie were at our house for dinner that one night because of my accident."

"I thought he'd, you know, maybe start being around more."

So, that was it. "You thought we'd start going out together. On dates."

"I guess." Gordon didn't wait for an answer. He opened the door and got out, and then pulled the folded camp chairs and cooler out of the backseat.

Her spirits spiraling down, Dawn got out of the car, too, and scanned the park looking for an empty spot on the grass. As it was, the Fourth of July had arrived with little fanfare. She'd been preoccupied with helping Gordon pack to go up north with Bill and Carla and had hardly thought about the holiday other than going through the motions of their usual routine. She'd made them thick roast beef sandwiches, Gordon's favorite, and packed the cooler with cold drinks. Taking a picnic to the waterfront fireworks on the Fourth was a given every year, just like Gordon spending the rest of the month with Bill was part of their summer schedule.

Watching Gordon, a tall and athletic teenager now, Dawn knew the same old thing, watching fireworks in the park with Mom couldn't work much longer. Even this year,

Gordon was acting like a hard-to-please teenager. Yesterday at breakfast he said he couldn't wait to get up to the cottage with his dad, but by lunch he was grumbling about the clothes she suggested he take along. They were all wrong. By dinner, he announced he didn't want to go at all.

When she reminded him he and his dad were diving, he shot back a response. He could get certified with Wyatt and Rob at a local pool. She had no answer for that, other than to remind him it was his regular time with his dad. Not to mention seeing grandparents who'd doted on him all his life.

Dawn took a deep breath. "Let's be clear. Jerrod isn't interested in going out with me." Avoiding his gaze, she pointed to an empty spot and picked up the chairs and started walking to it. Gordon grabbed the cooler and followed her. "You know he lost his wife and daughter."

"But that was a long time ago."

"Not really. Two years isn't that long to get over that kind of loss." Her resigned tone even surprised her. Her son had no idea how much she liked his scenario. If it had been up to her, Jerrod would have invited them to join their group at the barbecue. She'd much rather enjoy festivities on the docks, too.

"I admit it's a little strange to be by ourselves this year," she conceded. "I guess this is as good spot as any." She gave the first chair a push to let it fall open. Last year they'd been with Lark and Miles and their kids. This year Evan was camping with his dad in Michigan, and Lark and Miles were away, too.

"Evan didn't even want to go camping." Gordon put the cooler down and took out a can of cola. "He wanted to go away with his mom and Miles." Resentment had seeped into his voice, and the vein in his temple pulsated as he popped the can open.

She set up the second chair, annoyed by the direction of the conversation. Somehow, it was hard to feel too sorry for either of these boys, Evan or Gordon. Camping, diving, seeing grandparents. Poor kids. "You're right on the edge of sounding angry. Is this about Jerrod? Or are you telling me you don't want to go up north? Tell me, what has you in such a grumpy mood."

"Nothing."

"Right. Nothing. Then lighten up. Okay?"

His expression finally sheepish, Gordon nodded. "Let's eat."

Good. She sat down and unwrapped their sandwiches and handed Gordon one, along with his own bag of chips. Sulky or not, he all but inhaled their dinner, and there was still a lot of time before fireworks. Meanwhile, laughter rising from groups all around them reminded her of what she wanted in her life— and didn't have. Inside, she was as grumpy as Gordon.

"You don't have to stay here with me and wait for the fireworks," Dawn said. "Take a walk. You might run into kids you know from school. Really, go ahead. I can see you're restless."

"Okay, but I'll be back when it gets dark." He hesitated only a second before taking off.

She watched him weave through the groups of people at picnic tables and grills before moving closer to the beach.

Watching her son disappear, Dawn hoped he'd bump into kids he knew. Anything to improve his mood. But she blamed herself that they'd ended up alone in the park. Why hadn't she come up with a better plan? She had friends and neighbors she could have invited to come with them. Or why hadn't she asked Jerrod and his crew to join her and Gordon?

She couldn't shake the idea that Gordon saw through her. Yes, Jerrod was a client, but she spent more time with him than the others, and talked to him almost every day. They often called each other when they could have emailed or texted. Apparently, her son had noticed.

Her thoughts drifted to the night they'd sat on Jerrod's porch. Getting personal. Oh, they had a thing, the two of them. Dawn was sure of it. Call it chemistry or something else. They had an understanding that didn't need words, like recognizing a kindred spirit. As different as they were, that bond was there, hanging between them, whether Jerrod thought he was ready or not.

WITH WYATT'S HELP, Jerrod secured *Wind Spray*'s dock lines and adjusted the fenders until he was satisfied the boat was snug in the berth. Raising his hand overhead, he signaled for Rob to turn off the engine. The end of a good trip with three divers, a couple and their college-student daughter. After saying goodbye to his guests, he watched them head toward the office with Wyatt to gather their things and be on their way.

It wasn't an easy path to the office, not with dozens of people hanging out at the potluck table and the grill. Nelson himself was serving the burgers and hotdogs. A few of the marina regulars had told him about the marina's annual July Fourth party, and it seemed to be living up to its reputation. Carrie and Melody would be coming down soon. He hadn't talked to Dawn specifically about it, but he assumed she and Gordon had already arrived.

Lost in his thoughts, he started when he heard Rob calling out to him. "Hey, Jerrod, turn around."

He spun on his heel to see Rob in the wheelhouse pointing out beyond the dock. Whoa... a sailboat, a twenty-five-footer at least, was drifting with its half-lowered mainsail flapping. And it was heading toward *Lucy Bee*, whose bow was in its immediate path.

Jerrod ran down to the end of the dock and, cupping his hands around his mouth, he shouted, "Hey, hey, what's the problem?"

A man on the bow pointed to the sail. "The

engine cut out on us. Now the sail is stuck," he yelled. "We can raise it, but we can't lower it."

They were running out of time, too. Sometimes the only way to stop a crash into another boat or a dock was to physically fend it off until somebody could get it under control.

"Turn the wheel to port," Jerrod shouted at the helmsman. "You might catch enough breeze in the sail to shift your direction."

"I'll get a runabout and go out there to hook up a towline," Rob said as he jumped off *Lucy Bee* and ran down the dock.

"Let Nelson know what's going on," Jerrod shouted after him.

Meanwhile, though, the breeze died down, and turning the wheel worked only to keep the sailboat dead in the water for a matter of seconds. When the boat began drifting again, the guy at the helm shrugged helplessly. Apparently, he had no idea what to try next. If Jerrod had been on the boat, he might have raised the jib to at least attempt shifting direction. But that wasn't an option now. At that moment, Jerrod needed to be two places at once. On the dock and on the bow of his tour boat. He could fend off the out-of-control boat from either place.

Fortunately, the sailboat was drifting slowly, making it easier to hold off if it came to that.

Suddenly, a voice came from behind. "I can help. What do you need me to do?"

Jerrod didn't immediately recognize the voice, but when he turned around, he knew the boy. "Hey, Gordon." He quickly explained the situation. "You stay here. I'm going aboard *Lucy Bee*." He put his hand on Gordon's arm. "Don't even think about getting any closer...got it?"

Gordon snickered. "Oh, okay, but I could push the boat off the dock if I had to."

"Maybe you could. But don't."

With that, he boarded the tour boat and positioned himself on the bow with his legs over the rail and the boathook in hand.

"Sorry, man," the helmsman called out, only a few yards away now. "We'll push off using your hull for leverage and stay off your bow."

"Someone's coming with a towline," Jerrod shouted. He could practically reach out and shake hands with the guy.

The seconds ticked by, the boat was inching closer to the front of the dock. He glanced down. Gordon stood in a wide stance, ready to put all his weight behind his raised hands and force the drifting boat to stop in its path. The chance of Gordon getting hurt was small, but that was irrelevant. It wasn't the boy's job to muscle around a boat. "Gordon, back off now," he yelled. "It's okay. I've got it."

Gordon glared at him, but did as he was told and moved back a couple of feet from the end of the dock. He planted his hands on his hips. The kid's angry look didn't surprise him. Jerrod knew exactly what it was like to be thirteen and yearn to jump in and lend a hand. He'd been raised on the water and hung out with other boys who helped their dads in situations exactly like this one.

When Nelson motored up to the sailboat, Jerrod stayed put until Rob positioned a towline. As Nelson eased the boat the short way to the fuel dock, Jerrod got off *Lucy Bee*.

"It's all over, Gordon." Jerrod pointed to Nelson's crew positioning the boat while the two sailors began securing the lines to cleats on the dock. "And thanks for offering to help.

How long have you been here? Were you having one of Nelson's burgers?"

Gordon frowned. "Uh, no. My mom and I had sandwiches over there in the park." He waved to the crowded waterfront beyond the marina. "We're waiting for the fireworks. I just felt like going for a walk and wandered down here."

"Are you with other people in the park?" Jerrod asked, puzzled. "Will you be coming over here later?" He'd been looking forward to seeing Dawn.

"No. It's just us." Gordon gestured to the shore and to people on boats. "Mom said Nelson's party is for the people on the boats. You know, Nelson's customers. You gotta have an invitation. You can't just show up."

He needed to invite Dawn and Gordon? "Wow. I should have asked how this gathering works, Gordon. I assumed you'd be here because you and your mom know Nelson. She's down here a lot because of me. I had no idea…" He didn't know how to finish the sentence.

"I could go get her," Gordon said eagerly. "I mean, she'd like to come, I think."

Jerrod thought for a minute. He could send

Gordon on his way, but that wasn't good enough. "No. I'll go get her myself. If you don't mind, keep an eye out for Carrie. She's coming down with Melody for the fireworks."

"I don't mind," Gordon said.

"Okay, go find Wyatt and Rob and introduce yourself. We all planned to watch the fireworks from Wind Spray."

Gordon's face broke into a big smile. "Okay."

"I'll get your mom."

Jerrod set out for the park, more eager than he should be to find Dawn. In his mind, he'd had it all arranged. As soon as the dive was over, he'd planned to find Dawn and invite her and Gordon to come aboard the boat for the fireworks.

Funny, he thought, he hadn't needed Gordon to save *Lucy Bee*, but without knowing it, the kid had saved the day.

CHAPTER NINE

DAWN PAID FOR the two iced lattes and led the way out the door to one of the few empty tables on the Bean Grinder's brick patio. The warm June day made it nearly impossible to stay inside if she didn't have to.

"I email and text Jerrod every day," Dawn said. "We chat when we need to, but until the Fourth of July fireworks, I hadn't seen him since the night of his presentation at the library. That was a week prior. But I'm going on the tour later this week."

"Miles called to sign up for his training later this month. He's eager now to see the two shipwrecks."

"That's great. Jerrod's season is truly underway. He's so busy." She rubbed her hands together and whispered. "Ah-ha, my master plan worked, you see, and he has customers. What do you think of that?"

"My first response?" Lark asked, playfully. "I guess I'd say, 'So what else is new?'"

True, her campaign had raised a flurry of interest in Jerrod. Dawn was dividing her time between other clients, including the merchants' association in Two Moon Bay who were planning their annual sidewalk sale, Stroll & Shop.

"I've been working to drum up interest for Stroll & Shop," she told Lark. "The bead shop and the art supply store have given our downtown another boost."

"And what about diving?"

Dawn groaned. "That again."

Lark lifted her hands in a show of mock helplessness. "You never give me a good answer, so I have to keep asking."

"I know, I know. Jerrod mentioned it again, but I begged off successfully. So far." She held up her left arm, the immobilizer gone. "Too bad my sore wrist excuse won't fly anymore."

"You knew that would have a limited shelf life."

Dawn faced the fact that she hadn't told Lark the whole truth about her aversion to diving. More than aversion. *Fear.* "I know it seems irrational, but I'm embarrassed about my fear of diving. I don't like admitting I'm afraid of anything. That's why I haven't simply told Jerrod I'm not interested. He might ask too many questions. It's about my foolish pride."

"Oh, please. He surely knows not everyone shares his passion."

Dawn shrugged, frustrated with herself. "On the other hand, my enthusiasm about the boat tour is completely genuine. I'm looking forward to hearing his spiel." She frowned at her own word. "Spiel. Not the right word. It minimizes the history, and he takes that seriously."

"From what you've said, he takes everything seriously."

"So it seems," she said. *Enough about Jerrod.* She and Lark had other things to hash over. She riffled through the pages to get to her monthly planning notes and tapped the page as if to refocus.

"Where did your good mood go?" Lark asked.

Tired of avoiding the truth, she looked Lark in the eye. "I think about Jerrod way too much."

"Uh-huh. I get it. And now it's bothering you. I know what it's like for a man to start taking up space in your head. It's not all bad. But are you really *so* worried about mixing the personal with the professional?"

Dawn shook her head. "No, I could handle that. I'm worried that he's on my mind all the time." Her mind drifted back to the moment of surprise when she'd seen him wandering around the park. She saw him before he spotted her. And when he did, his face had lit up. She'd no doubt looked the same way. He'd apologized for not understanding that he'd need to invite her to Nelson's gathering. The whole night had been festive and fun. When he'd walked them to her car, he'd even seemed a little sad to say goodbye to Gordon.

She ran her hand over the open page of her planner. "I can be creative about his business and excited about interviews and booking talks for him. But I can't get him off my mind. I'm way too happy about seeing him later this week. I look forward to every call, every visit." She held her cup close to her mouth and said, "He hugged me. Twice. The night I went to his house we almost kissed. By accident. I moved, he moved." She laughed at how silly it sounded.

Lark's eyes sparkled. "And?"

"And I liked it. We might have made that connection again on the Fourth, if Gordon hadn't been with me." She batted her hand toward Lark and gulped back a mouthful of her latte. "Stop looking so amused."

"Can't help it, my friend. Besides, you're making my point."

"Which is what, exactly?"

Lark folded her arms on the table. "Maybe he can't get *you* off his mind."

Dawn's first instinct was to protest, but she didn't. Instead, she said, "I don't know. That's the thing. Sometimes I feel…" she put her hand over her heart "…there's something there. It's as if it swirls in the air between us. But then I think, no, it's only my imagination." She clenched her fist in front of her chest, almost shocked by the intensity of her inner turmoil. "That's why it's better that I don't see him so much."

Lark stared at her for a few long seconds. Finally, she said, "Meanwhile, Gordon is gone. I imagine you miss him."

"Well, I don't miss the grumpy teenage

stuff." She guffawed, glad for the diversion from the tightness in her body. "You know what I mean."

"I do. Evan is easier to deal with when Brooke is with us. She likes to hang around him. It's like he's her hero, so he tries to live up to the image."

"That's probably the way it will be with Gordon and Zinnie. She's toddling around now," Dawn said. "The other day I told Gordon that no one would ever view him with such uncomplicated adoration than his baby sister." She paused. "I wear my heart on my sleeve too often. I even told Jerrod I'd wanted more children."

"You did? How did that come up?"

"When we sat on his front porch the night of the book signing and talked. It ended up being personal. I told him about Bill leaving me. And about how I wanted more kids." She threw her head back. "What a dumb move."

Lark tapped Dawn's hand. "Stop saying things like that. It wasn't dumb. You want what you want. You've been open about that for as long as I've known you. You love kids, you enjoy your family. You shouldn't feel bad about saying it."

Dawn squared her shoulders. "Right you are. But I also wanted Jerrod to know that I'm grateful for what I have. My thwarted little wishes are nothing like what happened to him. Besides, most of the time I'm okay... even happy."

Lark gave her a sidelong look. "My opinion only, but Jerrod seems like the perfect match for you. It's why I bring him up, and not only because he's your client. Ever since you broke things off with Chip, you've said you wanted to find a man with more depth. Someone who would intrigue you."

"Did I say that?" Dawn mocked.

"You did, my friend."

"Next time I start talking like that, shut me up." But yes, she recalled expressing that exact thought to Lark. It was her statement of resolve not to hang on to relationships that her gut told her wouldn't work out. "Jerrod is nothing if not deep and intriguing. And not available."

Dawn swallowed a mouthful of her drink before patting her page in the notebook. "Let's get down to the business of the Art for Life fund-raiser."

"Right. Now that's going to be a great event," Lark said.

"I hope so. Any group trying to fund arts and music education in our schools is fine with me. I'm proud the people of Two Moon Bay have gotten together to act on their own behalf." Budget cuts had forced the issue. The town had a healthy—and growing—arts and crafts community and a budding community theater company. Firing art and music teachers didn't sit well.

Grateful for the distraction, Dawn worked with Lark for the next half hour on the wording for the program for what had become an annual event. And a glamorous one, at least by Two Moon Bay standards. Once again, the yacht club donated its space and the Half Moon Café agreed to provide a buffet.

"I'm predicting this event will be even bigger than last year's," Dawn said, gathering up her things to leave. Lark did the same and after clearing their table, they headed toward their cars, both checking messages on their phones.

"Anything interesting on those screens?" a male voice asked.

She knew that teasing tone. Jerrod. When

she lifted her head, she saw Carrie walking alongside him.

"Hi, Dawn," Carrie said. She rocked up on tiptoes, then back on her heels and all but bounced in the air with a young kid's energy.

"Well, hello there." She turned to Lark. "This is Carrie, the special little girl I was telling you about."

"Oh, *that* little girl," Lark said, knowingly, "the happy one with pigtails and a big smile."

Dawn acknowledged Jerrod, but addressed Carrie. "So did you walk here for your favorite treat?"

"Yep," Carrie said. "Next time I'll ride my bike. Wyatt and Melody taught me to ride. No training wheels."

"Really?" Lark said. "I'm impressed."

Jerrod beamed. "She caught on right away."

Dawn laughed. "Such a proud dad. I can see it all over your face."

"I guess I am." He pointed with his chin to the patio. "I suppose you two were getting some work done."

"As a matter of fact, we were." Feeling awkward, maybe because Lark was making no attempt to hide her curiosity as she looked on, Dawn filled in details about the annual

Art for Life event she helped publicize. "It's quite a gala." She cocked her head. "We even dress up."

"Sounds like a worthy cause, too," Jerrod said.

"We'll be happy to sell you a ticket—and for your staff, too," Lark said. "You might enjoy meeting some new people. Supporters come from several towns around here."

"Real subtle," Dawn said, rolling her eyes at her friend.

"I'm just saying…networking and all that."

"I'd like to come to the dinner," Jerrod said eagerly.

Carrie reached out and tugged on Dawn's hand. "You know what Melody said? She said I might get a new mommy one day."

"Hmm…did she now?" Dawn fidgeted with her necklace at her throat.

"So, we should go, little girl," Jerrod put his hand on Carrie's back as if to encourage her along.

"Could *you* be my new mommy?"

Dawn drew in a breath, her cheeks heating up, probably turning bright pink.

Jerrod laughed nervously. "Hey, little one.

You can't just go around asking people questions like that."

Not trusting herself to look at Jerrod, Dawn leaned forward and cupped Carrie's chin. "Becoming somebody's mom can be more complicated than it seems. But anybody would be really lucky to have you as her daughter."

Carrie didn't say anything, but she tapped her chin where Dawn's fingers had been.

"We'll be on our way," Dawn said, finally laughing.

"Let's go to a table, honey. You said you were hungry," Jerrod said, shaking his head.

"Yes… I…am." Carrie emphasized each word with a hop.

Keeping her gaze on Carrie, Dawn said, "You have fun."

"We will." Another hop.

Lark waited to burst out laughing until they got to their cars and well out of Jerrod's earshot. "What were we just saying about you and Jerrod?"

"I'm officially embarrassed." She smiled sadly. "But you can see for yourself she's a precious little imp."

"You handled it beautifully," Lark said.

"All kidding aside, much better than Jerrod. He had trouble getting words out."

Dawn caught her breath, affected by the question more than she cared to share, even with Lark. "Enough with that. What are you up to? I feel like we're in high school, scheming to see our favorite guys."

"I'm not up to anything."

"Oh, your innocent face! Give me a break. You basically strong-armed him into coming to our fund-raiser."

"It's a fun—and dressy—night," Lark said defensively, "and if he's really going to become part of the community, then why shouldn't he be invited to fund-raisers and other kinds of events where he can meet people?"

Dawn shrugged. "I know you're right, but it seemed like you were finding a way to get the two of us together."

"Oh, maybe I was. A little." Lark paused. "He likes you, a lot. So why not go with it?"

"You know that for sure? You're a psychic now?"

"I'll ignore your sarcasm." Lark stared at the gravel in the lot, apparently gathering her thoughts. "Okay, I get it. You're skeptical.

But I'm sure. I saw his eyes go soft when he looked at you. The man is a member of your fan club. Get used to it." She jingled her car keys in her hand. "By the way, why didn't you invite him? As your date."

Dawn felt a familiar fluttering in her stomach, more from anxiousness than excitement. What if Lark was right? The other night, the way he brushed his cheek across her hair, his mouth so close to hers. She'd let her head rest on his shoulder long enough to know she liked it. "I suppose I could have."

Before Lark could respond, Dawn changed the subject. "I've got my eye on a spectacular dress for the fund-raiser. I haven't made up my mind yet, but maybe early next week I'll go have another look at it."

Lark's face showed her delight.

"I knew you'd like that," Dawn teased. "Your smile tells me exactly how you feel."

"That's because I like to see you enjoy your success," Lark insisted. "Jerrod or no Jerrod, you've earned a great new dress."

After exchanging a quick goodbye hug with Lark, Dawn headed toward home with her mind still on Jerrod. Who was she kidding? Of course she liked him. A lot. It was true what she'd told Lark about wanting a man with depth. Jerrod was certainly that, and he'd appealed to her from the first day she'd met him in the lobby of the hotel. That day his smile seemed like a rare reward for something—she just wasn't sure what.

She thought ahead to the Art for Life fundraiser and the dress she'd picked out of a crowded rack of new summer clothes. Sleeveless and fitted, it fell just above the knee. Simple, elegant, expensive—and not on sale. She loved good clothes, but almost always waited for a bargain. This time, maybe not. Why was she waiting to buy the perfect dress? Dawn made a left turn at the next corner and drove onto the street that would take her to Rock Hill and the boutique where a cocktail dress the color of peaches was waiting for her to come and whisk it away.

Dawn sighed. Treating herself to a new dress was fun and easy. But innocent and irrelevant or not, Carrie's offhand question wasn't so easy to laugh off.

WYATT WAS EVERY BIT as capable as he was of delivering the tour script with flair. She kept the passengers entertained so skillfully that for the last couple of years, Jerrod often asked her to take on that role. His passengers sure took to her. And why not? Not only was she friendly, she looked the part of being more comfortable on the water than behind a desk. With her short, practical haircut and a sturdy, petite frame, Jerrod often thought of Olympic swimmers or platform divers. Rob could have done the tour narration, too, but he was shyer than he first seemed and preferred to hide out in the wheelhouse.

Lately, some of Jerrod's best hours were spent hanging out in his office alone while Wyatt and Rob did routine maintenance on the boats or took an afternoon off. Taking advantage of the solitude, he completed paperwork, worked on presentations or pored over his history books. On some days, he took over for Melody and he and Carrie went out for lunch or to the park. He'd had a couple of diving excursions cancelled at the last minute, something that usually left him grumpy. But he'd salvaged his day by taking Carrie to the Bean Grinder.

Now, waiting for Dawn to arrive for a day tour, Jerrod had another passing thought about how she sometimes reminded him of

Augusta, but not in the sad way he might have assumed. Maybe it was like playing a home video of images that fit together into a treasure box of their life. A snippet of a remembered day when Augusta patiently taught Dabny to tie her sneakers was as vivid now as the day it happened. Caught on camera. Or maybe it was her good-natured laughter when Carrie clamped her lips together and refused to eat the vegetables Augusta pureed into baby food herself. Didn't Dawn's eyes soften when she spoke to her son? Or even to Carrie? Wasn't Dawn always switching hats, smoothly going from mom to professional and back again? "Jerrod?"

He started at the sound of his name. "Yes? I was…uh, lost in my thoughts, I guess. What do you need, Rob?"

"Just the pre-boarding count. We have ten confirmed and paid. Not including Dawn."

"Ten." His tone was flat. "Okay, then, it's a go. Nelson told me it really picks up around here after the Fourth of July. Zeke over at the marine store said the same thing."

"I'll bet it does," Rob said. "There haven't been many warm days."

Jerrod looked up at the scattered clouds

in the sky. "I hope this weather lasts for the next few hours. This is the first time Dawn will see our show." He'd hoped for a full boat when Dawn was aboard. More people usually meant a festive, party-like atmosphere.

"Here comes Dawn," Rob said. "In cool shades and big straw hat. No sun damage for her."

"She's so fair-skinned she probably burns pretty easily," Jerrod said, realizing as soon as the words left his mouth he'd taken Rob way too seriously.

"Ahoy, *Lucy Bee*," she called out. "Permission to come aboard and all that."

"Let's see. Are you a dangerous pirate after our gold?" Rob joked.

Dawn held up her phone as she stepped onto the deck and down the two stairs into the passenger well. "No, I'm only dangerous with my phone camera. I can't resist and I never know which shots will be perfect for your blog or your website."

"You're the first to arrive," Jerrod said. He twisted his mouth in a show of disgust. "Not that we're overrun today."

"Don't worry about that. It's early in the

season." She adjusted her sunglasses and stared out at the lake.

That didn't make him feel any better. It was a good thing that he'd decided to leave the Key West crew in place and run the dives through the summer. That might end up carrying this new location, and he'd invested heavily in it. No telling when—or if—the effort would pay off. But the slow start was on him. He'd barely allowed time to place the first ad in the first paper.

Wyatt led Dawn into the space behind the ladder-like companionway to the wheelhouse and answered her questions about their itinerary.

Leaving Wyatt with Dawn, Jerrod busied himself checking the bins for life vests, although he knew Rob had already handled that job. But he'd been jumpy all morning knowing Dawn would be coming along. Only when he saw a group of six people arriving could he relax and focus on what he did best. Even Augusta used to say he was a good host.

He stepped off the *Lucy Bee* onto the dock. "You're here for the tour?" he asked just to confirm they weren't tourists randomly wandering the docks.

"We are," a woman flanked by two children said. "We've got a couple of kids eager to go for a boat ride."

"Then you came to the right place. Follow me." When he stepped back on the boat he spotted Dawn holding up her phone to catch the scene of the family of four and two grandparents coming aboard. She'd have them ready to post on his blog, whenever he managed to get it underway.

She'd lobbied for blogging as a way to tie together the two parts of his business, tours and dives, and even had a name for it: "Something to Treasure."

Jerrod soon greeted the remaining four pre-signed guests and two additional people who signed up at the dock. The tour business equivalent of "walk-ins." Wyatt got their information, processed a credit card from her phone, and then, with Rob in the wheelhouse, they were off.

As if she were a regular guest, Dawn took a seat at the end of one of the side benches and pulled a small notebook out of another blazer pocket. So, she could be separated from that humungous shoulder bag, at least for a few hours, anyway. Maybe she would simply relax and enjoy the tour.

They soon left Two Moon Bay behind and headed out to the site of the *Franklin Stone*. "For many years, my primary business has been running diving excursions. I've taken people out to discover the treasures that exist beneath the surface of the ocean, and now the Great Lakes," Jerrod said. "And though diving isn't for everyone, a day spent on the water always offers a unique experience in its way. The trip you take today won't be an exact duplicate of the trip we took a few days ago and it won't be the same as one a few days from now."

Looking at the two kids on the tour, he took them to be in that middle part of childhood, around age ten or eleven. "Why do you think that is?" Jerrod asked.

"It could rain that day." The girl of the pair spoke in a voice so earnest it sent a ripple of light laughter through the group.

"Right you are," Jerrod responded quickly. "Weather changes everything." He pointed to the shore. "All the landmarks look different even when the sun disappears behind the clouds." He asked her name.

"Bonnie." She used her thumb to point to her brother. "He's Mason. He's almost ten. I'm eleven."

He'd always enjoyed talking to kids old enough to soak in information, but still not so self-conscious they were afraid to speak up. Keeping his focus on Bonnie and Mason, he said, "Not so long ago, the five Great Lakes were like superhighways. They brought people coal to heat their houses, food to cook, and machinery to build things. They even shipped Christmas trees to cities so folks could have them in their houses. One of those ships left Michigan but never showed up in Chicago with its load of trees. Even today no one knows what happened to it. They call it a ghost ship."

He glanced at Dawn, amused that she was listening and not scribbling notes.

When they reached the site of the sunken freighter, he filled in the history and on his computer, clicked on the grainy photo of the ship and the newspaper accounts of it sinking. All eyes went to the projected image on the mounted TV screen, and Mason's hand shot up.

"I like questions," Jerrod said. "Go ahead."

"What was inside the ship when it went down?"

"Coal. It was loaded with coal and headed for Chicago."

"Where did all the coal go?" Bonnie asked.

"When I take people diving, we can see pieces of coal on the bottom, so some of it is still there." Jerrod brought up the image of the lake bottom with what looked like black clusters and dots strewn about.

From there, a couple of the adults tossed out questions as Rob motored away and headed up the coastline toward Sturgeon Bay. He pointed out towns and piers and prominent steeples of old and historic churches whose names he'd learned himself only weeks ago. His dry runs had paid off. He also mentioned more shipwrecks when they passed near various sites. In the distance he saw a boat about the size of *Wind Spray* and explained the red-and-white flag indicated where diving was going on at other shipwreck sites, some more famous and thoroughly explored than others. His own presentation reinforced his belief that divers could spend a lifetime exploring and documenting all the ignored shipwrecks in Lake Michigan alone.

"Hundreds of ships were built for the military during World War II, and many were built here in Sturgeon Bay," he said, before filling in more detail. They soon docked *Lucy Bee* at the Jacobson Marina, their designated lunch stop on full-day tours. That day, it was warm enough to eat at a long table on the outdoor deck. Wyatt and Rob led the guests to the restaurant, but Dawn hung back.

"This is so much more than I expected," she said, her features animated and her eyes more light brown than green. "Now I'm doubly glad you want me to keep scheduling presentations and interviews. You're good at this."

She had no idea how much it meant to hear that coming from her. But a part of him winced against that thought, more personal than professional. He had a really hard time separating himself from Dawn on so many levels. If he thought about the business, she came to mind; if he thought about Carrie, she came to mind; if he thought about walking on a local trail or trying a restaurant, she popped into his mind again. And it could never work between them. He was still haunted by the past. His memories were like ghosts. They would always get in the way.

He dipped one shoulder to the side. "Nice to see you're not listing to port with that heavy handbag hanging on your shoulder."

Laughing, she lifted her arms to the side and flapped them like they were wings. "And doesn't it feel great to be free of it for a day." She flicked her hand toward the harbor where motor yachts and sailboats were heading either out to the lake or the other way to the bay side of the peninsula. Small runabouts and fishing boats went up and down the channel. "It's a work day, too. How lucky can I be?"

His heart sank a little hearing her bring work into it, but that was foolish. She wasn't riding along just for the fun of it. "Let's get some lunch." He couldn't resist adding, "We need a break from all this grueling, back-breaking labor."

She rolled her eyes. "Okay, okay, point taken."

Teasing her was such fun. It was new for him to be lighthearted and able to joke around a little. When had that last happened?

Once seated on the deck, Jerrod gave his

guests a fuller explanation of the reasons Dawn was aboard that day.

"This is my first trip on *Lucy Bee* with Jerrod, Wyatt and Rob," she said. "I took a few photos I'd like to have posted on the website, but I'll only do that with your permission. I'll show them to you first."

Mason chimed in right away. "We don't mind." He looked at his parents and Bonnie. "Do we?"

"I think we can handle it," the mom said.

"We'll include the whole family," Jerrod said.

Having Dawn to interact with put him even more at ease.

Jerrod found himself in a conversation with the grandpa of the family group about the man's childhood on a Michigan coastal town. Swapping stories of being kids building bonfires on the beaches was the type of small talk he could handle.

On the rest of the tour, Dawn alternated between taking some notes and talking with the guests, specifically asking what had made them sign up. How had they heard about the tour, and what had lured them into making a reservation? As he listened in, he learned his outreach methods all played in. He looked on as Dawn jotted down their answers.

When they docked *Lucy Bee* he thanked the guests for coming, and the small group broke into applause. When he lined up with Wyatt and Rob to say goodbye to their guests, he spent a couple of extra minutes with the kids.

"Seems like you enjoyed yourselves," he said, "and now you have things to write about on those essays you'll be assigned when school starts."

"I'm going to write a story about diving to the wreck," Mason said. "I remember what the picture looks like."

Why that touched him he couldn't say. "Why don't I send a copy of that picture? Then you'll have it to study when you write your story."

The boy's expression showed his pleasure—and surprise. He nodded vigorously, and Jerrod said he'd send it by email to his mom or dad.

"Probably my dad," he said. "He checks his phone even more than my mom."

"It's a deal, then."

Within a few minutes they'd finished up and he stood with Dawn while Rob and Wyatt went through the routine cleanup.

"So what did you learn from your questions? Anything important?"

She nodded. "Mostly good news about how they found you and the business. Another positive, they believed they got more than their money's worth."

"I can't complain about that response," Jerrod said.

"It's a small sample. But all of the passengers found the photo of the *Lucy Bee* with the three of you very appealing. So, you and your crew are winners. But we already knew that."

He followed Dawn off the boat and they walked toward the parking lot. "You'll enjoy a dive just as much. We're taking new video all the time to get the kind of clips you want for the website."

"Good, good," she said, taking a few steps toward her car. "We can talk about that later. So, I'll see you at the fund-raiser next Friday. Don't forget."

She didn't wait for a response but mumbled something about needing to be on her way, and a minute later, he was watching her pull her car onto the street. Going into his office, he couldn't shake the sense she'd been a little too eager to get away.

CHAPTER TEN

WAS SHE ACTUALLY carrying a clipboard? Yes, and she was wearing a dress the color of apricots—or maybe peaches. Dawn had the clipboard tucked in the crook of her arm. Lost in her own world, or so it seemed to Jerrod, she was studying side-by-side buffet tables.

Smiling to himself when she shifted her weight from one foot to the other, he anticipated her self-mocking complaints about the occasion demanding not only a dress, but high heels, too. But at the moment, with her teal reading glasses in place, she appeared preoccupied with her lists or whatever was on those pages, while his attention was fixed on how incredible she looked. She probably smelled like vanilla or maybe spring rain. The other night, her hair had given off the distracting aroma of ginger or cinnamon.

Forcing himself to face the truth, it scared

him to think how often he found himself watching her. Doing ordinary things like scribbling furiously fast in her notebook, or observing her way of focusing all her attention on the person she was talking to. Who wouldn't enjoy seeing how she treated Carrie and other kids not as nuisances, but showed they mattered?

He closed his eyes as if that would block his memory of holding her against him for those fleeting seconds. Now, he looked on as she reached out with her free hand to gently adjust a couple of flowers in a vase.

Useless observations, feelings that could go nowhere. You would do nothing but disappoint her. She wants children, and you can barely do right by your one child.

Jerrod had walked over to the yacht club, arriving early. The shingled white building had long narrow windows with blue-and-white stained-glass fan-shaped transoms. So much of Two Moon Bay had been built in a more modest time, but this building was new and spoke of a town on the rise. Rather than coming inside from the lot, which was starting to fill up with cars, he'd walked to the room-size verandah in the front and looked at the view on the balmy night before entering the club.

Standing just inside the double doors, he'd found a vantage point where, at least for the moment, he could stand back and observe Dawn doing her work for the event.

Sooner or later, Dawn was sure to sense she was being watched, so he stepped into the room. "Hello," he called out as he took a few steps to approach her.

She glanced up and looked over her glasses. His gut jolted just a little at the way her face lit up.

"Your big night has arrived. You look…uh, ready." He'd almost used a different word. *Gorgeous* had come to mind. Her subtle frown told him she thought it odd he'd stumbled over such an ordinary word.

"I am ready—*we are*, I should say. It took a ton of volunteers to make this happen. The Half Moon Café crew pulled up to the side door of the kitchen a few minutes ago, so I wanted to be sure the centerpieces were in place."

"They look great," he said. "And the room looks like there's a party about to happen. Much different from the setup they did for my talk here." Instead of a center aisle separating rows of folding chairs, the room now was filled with clusters of round tables, some tall and meant for standing and others with seating for four. The verandah was arranged similarly. The bar was near the door and offered a couple of kinds of Silver Moon wine, local beer and flavored iced tea.

Dawn leaned in closer. "I'll let you in on a secret. It's a lot of fun to come over here in the midst of a winter storm. Bill and I used to bundle up Gordon and drop by. They board up the glass walls right after their New Year's Eve open house and open them up again the first day of spring—unless we're in the middle of a March blizzard, which has been known to happen."

He stared at the lake, relatively flat in only a light breeze on the late July evening. Hearing her talk about winter brought to mind the decision he had to make, and soon. Only recently had he begun to consider the possibility of staying in Two Moon Bay through the winter. The town was growing on him and he wasn't sure he even wanted to head back to Key West when his summer season was over. Could be he'd see the lake in its winter wildness. Then again, maybe not. So far, he'd kept this dilemma to himself. It was his choice to make, no one else's.

"And when the waves hit the rocks in front of the verandah, the spray covers everything," Dawn was saying. "You can find photos on the internet of Two Moon Bay in the dead of winter and the brave souls who come to take pictures."

"Nelson said the yacht club might stay open year-round," he said. "They're thinking of creating a wine bar with music on the weekends."

"Listen to you, already up on the local gossip." The lilt in her voice bordered on intimate. "Well, if I had a vote, I'd be all for it."

"I always enjoy hearing you talk about this place you love so much." Before she had a chance to respond, he looked past her at the two women rolling carts through the door. "Looks like they're putting the food out."

Dawn glanced behind her, but quickly turned back to him. "Tara from the Half Moon Café is in charge of that, so I don't have to give it a thought."

"You mean the whole world isn't on your shoulders tonight? Is that a first?"

She narrowed her eyes and lowered her head—mighty flirtatiously, at least her expression struck him that way.

"Isn't that something? I can take a breath. The crowd is arriving and the food and drinks are underway. The Art for Life board will take over now."

"If that's the case, can I buy you a drink?" He hadn't heard that tone in his voice in a long time. When it came to flirting, he could give as good as he got.

"Yes, you can," she said, grinning. "I'd love a glass of Silver Moon chardonnay. Everything is local tonight."

After getting their drinks at the cash bar they went out to the verandah and sat at a table for two next to the knee-high brick wall that sat on top of the slope leading to the stony beach.

"A quiet night," he said. "Out here, that is."

"It's an interlude for me," she said. "This fund-raiser is one of my main summer volunteer projects. Then later the sidewalk sale needs my attention, too. And then I'm done organizing this kind of event for a little while." She took a sip of her wine. "But for tonight, I can be an attendee like everyone else."

"I imagine you'll see lots of old friends," he said, already a little envious of her familiarity with almost everyone whose path she crossed.

She didn't respond in words, but saw something out of the corner of her eye and then she waved Nelson and Zeke over to their table. Jerrod was secretly glad he'd led Dawn to a table with only two chairs. The two men could stop by, but they likely wouldn't stay.

"Here are a couple of old friends now."

"New friends for me." He stood and shook hands with both men. Remembering Zeke's dad, he asked if Art had come along.

"Nah, thanks for asking, but he wasn't feeling up to a party." Zeke flashed a lopsided grin. "Besides, he thinks the yacht club is a bit too highfalutin."

Dawn let out a mock groan. "Some people around here can't stand a little sophistication."

"That's my dad," Zeke said. "Give him a broken-down building and add some buckets and bins and call it a store."

"That old argument about progress aside, you did a nice job here, Dawn." Nelson looked inside the room. "The line is shorter now, so I'll go and get myself some of that food before it's gone." Glancing at Jerrod, he added, "It's good see you here."

With Zeke and Nelson gone, Jerrod remarked about how easy it was to deal with businesses in Two Moon Bay. "It isn't that way everywhere. Rob said the other day that people around here assume the best about a person, not the worst." He grinned. "We've dealt with all kinds of troublesome people in a few locations. None as friendly as the folks here."

"I love hearing that about my hometown." She tapped her temple. "Oops, I almost forgot to mention that Gordon will be home soon," Dawn said. "He asked about diving with you. As long as there are openings. He's got his certification now." She seemed to hesitate, but then added, "I think he wants to learn from you, hang around and watch how you handle a boat. He got so much out of being with all of you on the Fourth. He's interested in both wrecks, but it really goes beyond that. You made quite an impression on him."

"He did on me, as well. And my Carrie took a shine to him."

For a few more minutes, they sipped their drinks quietly and without interruption. But suddenly, a woman appeared in the doorway, raising her hand in the air to get Dawn's attention.

"I'll be right back," she promised, soon disappearing inside.

Jerrod moved from the table to an empty spot against the verandah wall. He wasn't alone for long before a man joined him, introducing himself as Miles Jenkins.

"At these events in town, I'm Lark McGee's husband," Miles joked. "I'm a newcomer like you. It's my first time at this event," Miles said. "Lark enjoys volunteering for it. Dawn sure works hard for Art for Life."

"I guess she does that for all her clients." Oh, no. The words were okay, but his grudging tone was all wrong.

Miles jerked his head back, laughing in surprise. "Isn't that a good thing?"

"Of course... I didn't mean that the way it sounded. I wasn't dismissing what she does..."

"Because all her clients get the same five-star treatment?" Miles asked, still amused.

"Exactly." Miles accurately picked up on

his petty wish that Dawn would view him as special. It was time to steer this conversation in another direction. "Is Lark with Dawn now?"

"Yes, she's helping Dawn and the event's emcee juggle the program," Miles explained. "Apparently, one of the teachers scheduled to speak on behalf of the schools' art and music programs had to pull out at the last minute. Her replacement is on her way from Bratton."

"A fire to put out," Jerrod remarked.

"I see a lot of this last-minute stuff in my work," Miles said. "Nobody puts out more brush fires than an event planner, and I work with many of them."

"I'm less dependent on people than I am on the weather," Jerrod observed. "But I've been lucky so far this year."

"I wish I could be home more to enjoy it, but I'm also glad to land new consulting clients and speaking gigs, even if they mean leaving on short trips." Miles pointed at the buffet tables. "We probably shouldn't wait to get in the buffet line. I don't have a long history of being the guy on Lark's arm at these affairs, but my limited experience tells me Lark and Dawn might be gone awhile. I don't think they'd want us to wait for them. They'll catch a few bites of dinner when they can."

"You're the escort, huh?" Jerrod joked as they went inside. It sounded as if Miles was giving him some advice, one man to another. And what did it hurt that Miles thought Jerrod was Dawn's date?

Something about hanging out with Miles made him feel included as a local in a way he hadn't been, even in Key West. He didn't blame anyone for that. With a few exceptions, he and Augusta had made little attempt to become part of the year-round community. Maybe because they were busy with the girls, and their crew of four to six or even eight at times was like a big extended family. They also were on the move a lot. But here in Two Moon Bay, Nelson was more than his landlord, and Zeke wasn't only the guy who ran the marine supply store. *And Dawn was more than the paid PR consultant.* A friend. A good friend, he insisted, as if debating the point with himself.

Jerrod and Miles filled their plates with roast beef and salmon and various salads and went to the verandah when the program started. They could see the podium and the

VIRGINIA McCULLOUGH

speakers using the mic allowed them to hear the series of impassioned speeches about the value of keeping art, music and theater in the schools.

When they were done, Miles said he hoped they raised a ton of money. "The district puts plenty of money into sports, and that's fine. Brooke and Evan both play sports. But I don't like the idea of taking away any chance to play an instrument or sing in the chorus, too." Miles paused long enough to take a breath. "I know I'm letting my disgust show."

Jerrod chuckled. "Hey, you'll get no argument from me. I'm just impressed by the kind of energy Dawn has for these things. Clearly, Lark shares that trait."

Miles's expression turned curiously tender when he said, "That's one reason I admire both women."

It was nearing dusk when the Half Moon Café's van drove off and Lark left with Miles, leaving Jerrod to banter with Zeke over the current state of tourism. According to Zeke, Two Moon Bay was on the upswing, along with Door County and the whole region. Maintaining his cheerful mood to the end, Zeke said his goodbyes and headed home.

"You hung around?" Dawn said, surprised.

He was at a loss to explain why. Instead he mentioned something about wanting to see if she needed help.

She tilted her head and seemed to study him. "Uh, if you have time, there's a spot only a little way down the shore I'd like to show you. It might be a good place to bring Carrie for a picnic."

Now? She wanted to go for a walk now?

"I suppose I have the time. Carrie is home with Melody." He pointed to her shoes. "Can you walk on the grass or the stones in those?"

"Don't worry about that. I've got flats in my car."

"I might have known."

Saying she'd be right back, she spoke to a couple of people on her way out. He stepped out the side door and waited by the shore for her. What kind of place would she want to show him when it was nearly dark?

DAWN SHOVED HER feet into flats. It was a warm night, so she decided against bringing her sweater. They wouldn't be out that long. When she came back to join Jerrod, the cleanup committee was starting to turn off the kitchen lights. A few guests lingered in the parking lot, talking. She was feeling emboldened by…what? Not the grand success of the event or even Jerrod's presence there.

She thought about the flashes of tenderness in his expression when she caught him looking at her earlier that evening and on *Lucy Bee* the other day. And they'd had moments. The delight she saw in his face when he found her in the park. Her face probably showed the same happiness. They'd had a couple of embraces that weren't easy to label. Except that she could barely breathe. But then, neither could he.

In her mind's eye, she remembered how his face brightened when she and Lark had happened to run into him at the Bean Grinder. It wasn't her imagination. He wasn't only surprised—he was happy to see her. Later that day, when she'd carried her new dress out of the boutique, she'd decided she'd no longer question why he dominated her thoughts. She'd go with it and see what happened.

He was her client, true, but their feelings most likely wouldn't harm their working relationship. Besides, the risk was worth it.

When she reached him, she said, "Follow me," in a feigned mysterious tone.

"It must be quite a place."

She led him away from the yacht club and toward the lakefront park. "I'm taking you through the woods, well, a little patch of forest, anyway."

"Whatever. You've succeeded in making me very curious."

They soon left the beach behind and crossed over a small footbridge to a wooded area that looked like the end of the natural walking path along the lake. "Even locals sometimes stop here, but there's more to see."

"The shore here is beautiful at dusk, isn't it?" Jerrod remarked.

"I know—the sunset colors to the west sometimes tint the water and the trees a pretty shade of pink. It makes this place even more special."

The woods gradually thinned out until they reached a strip of land that jutted into the water and then curved around the shore. Still walking, she pointed to the single maple tree standing alone. A picnic table sat under its protective branches. "There it is, the perfect tree in a nearly secluded spot."

"It seemed to appear out of nowhere, as if it's not connected to the woods we just came from."

"Exactly. I don't know why, but for as long as I can remember, the tree has stood here by itself. The city owns the land. It's basically the end of the Two Moon Bay waterfront. Beyond this point and over another footbridge cottages dot the shore for about another half mile."

"Oh, those are the cottages I see from *Lucy Bee*." He grinned. "I'll bring Carrie down— or perhaps invite the whole crew and take a picture and write a blog post about it. My PR consultant is always encouraging me to do that sort of thing."

"Yep. It would be something different. Most of all, I had a feeling you'd like it." She looked at the picnic bench and knew she'd miscalculated. No way could she sit down on it in her brand new dress. "I was going to suggest sitting, but it's too dirty."

"Let's walk a little way down the beach, then," Jerrod suggested. "I'm game if you are."

Good. He hadn't suggested going back. It bought her a little time to gather her courage.

"I have something on my mind. I want to talk with you about it. That's my ulterior motive for suggesting a walk."

"Oh, what's that?"

"I'll bet you can guess," she said, leading the way across the second narrow bridge and onto a patch of sand and weeds.

"Ah, no. Is there something wrong? A problem we need to address?"

"It's personal, Jerrod." She stopped and turned to face him. "It seems like one of us has to acknowledge the proverbial elephant in the room, and it might as well be me."

The flicker in his warm eyes revealed surprise.

Without adding to her preamble, she blurted, "I like you, Jerrod. I get the sense you like me, too. Maybe we should acknowledge this *thing* between us?"

His head jerked back. In an instant, the air around her changed. The sound of the waves lapping the shore grew louder. The slightly fishy smell in the air intensified.

Jerrod grimaced, as if in pain, and looked past her, gazing out into space. What happened? She couldn't have been that wrong. She hoped.

"Say something, will you?" Was he going to leave her standing there feeling like a fool?

"I don't know what to say except *I'm sorry.*" He took a couple of steps away from her. "You don't want to like me in any way other than as a client and friend. Good friend."

In for a penny and in for a pound. In an instant that old saying had popped into her head. Why? Maybe because she was trembling inside and wasn't thinking straight. But the adage fit. She'd taken a chance and might as well commit to it all the way. "Is that so? Well, then, go ahead, tell me. Why is that?"

"Because I'm no good to anyone." He puffed out his cheeks and exhaled in obvious frustration. "Coming here to try out a new location for my business is the first sub stantial step I've taken in two years."

"Since the awful tragedy." Her tone was matter-of-fact. She'd understood that. He didn't need to point that out.

"Yes. But a few moves in the right direction don't mean I have anything…uh, anything to give you." He planted one hand on his hip, and widened his stance. "This is all wrong. You have so much to offer the right person.

You should find someone who can freely take what you want to share. You're a special—"

"Don't you dare patronize me with empty flattery." Her voice rose on each word.

"I'm not." He lifted his hands in the air, appearing helpless to find the right response. "I'm not going to apologize for saying what's obvious to anyone who knows you."

"Yeah, well, my ex-husband told me how *special* I was as he tossed his clothes in a couple of suitcases and carried them out the door. I was still so special when he shoved them in the back seat of his car and drove off to Carla's house." She paused and in a lower voice added, "I'm not kidding. And the next time I saw Bill he still went on about how smart I am and how he'd fallen *so* hard for me. Oh, and by the way, we built such a *great* life."

"Dawn…please. I'm sorry."

She pretended he hadn't interrupted and kept on going. "But he fell in love with someone else all the same. So, forgive me if I don't want pat reassurances about how terrific I am."

Jerrod shifted his stance. "I know you won't like to hear this cliché, but it's not you, it's me. I'm the one who's emotionally numb—dead. You're a woman with enthusiasm for life—you understand joy. I give all I can to be any kind of a dad at all. To my *one* child. I've got nothing left over to give."

Defeated and drained, she let her shoulders slump forward. "You're a really good dad, Jerrod," she whispered. "Don't sell yourself short." She could be such a fool sometimes. Here she was, reassuring him.

"It's easy to say that now, because that's what you see. But if you asked Rob and Wyatt, they'd tell you the truth about me. For the first six months after Augusta and Dabny were killed, my precious little three-year-old had a nanny—and lucky for her, Rob and Wyatt and others on my staff were a substitute family." He kicked at the stones on the ground. "I was barely able to function."

"Maybe so, but from the outside, it seems you're doing really well now." She took a few steps back and raised her hands, palms out, her way to create an even wider boundary separating them. "I completely misread the signals." Not really, she thought, but no matter. She had to take the blame and escape.

"Forget I said anything. Write it off as my mistake."

She managed to glance at him, but quickly looked away. "We should go." She rubbed her bare arms. "It's cooling off and it could get buggy, too."

"Dawn, really, you need to trust me on this." It sounded like a plea. "I don't know that I'll ever get past what happened to my family. But except for the way I am with Carrie now, I'm like a stone inside." He lowered his head. "That's all I can say."

He wasn't a stone when he'd had his arms around her. His eyes weren't stone, either. She squared her shoulders and lifted her chin. "Okay. It's over and done with. We'll go back to having a friendly consultant-client relationship."

Still gathering her thoughts, she turned toward the path back to the yacht club. Keeping her voice even, neutral, she said, "My son admires you, and I enjoy working with you."

"I don't want anything to change, Dawn. Not in the least."

"Then let's pretend we never had this conversation." Or act as if he's never gazed at her—more than once—with soft, hungry eyes. The near kiss, the intimate conversation. That had fueled her stupid idea of laying her cards on the table. Maybe he'd meant nothing by the kind of attention he gave her, but he was still wrong to deny it.

She gave herself credit for putting on a good display of how well she could handle rejection. Wasn't that part of being so special? Correction, it wasn't rejection, only a misunderstanding. A much nicer word they'd both use now by silent agreement. But she fumed inside as she led the way on the path, an obvious departure from their earlier side-by-side stroll. When they reached her car she didn't trust herself to say much more than a quick good night.

"I'll see you next week for the radio interviews," she managed to say in a reasonably normal voice. "We're meeting at nine in your office to do some prep for them."

"I've got it in my calendar," he said quickly. "It's a tour day, and I'm letting Wyatt and Rob handle it. And you were going to let Gordon dive with us next week. Is...well, is that still okay?"

"Absolutely," she said, head held high. "Like I told you, he admires you. I would never interfere with that." She opened her car door and waved. "See you."

He waved back. She put the car in Reverse and backed out of the spot. Wow, she thought, pulling onto the street. When she made mistakes they were almost never insignificant little nothings. No, not her. This was a real whopper.

Her emotions surprised her, though. She might have been really hurt—oh, she was bruised, all right—but wasn't humiliated or in pain from rejection.

Maybe because she didn't believe him.

CHAPTER ELEVEN

"YOU'RE GETTING YOUR local start with a trip to the *Alice Swann*, a hardworking schooner in her day," Jerrod said as Rob motored away from the dock. "Sleek, too. She was considered a beauty."

"I saw the picture on your website. You've got a lot of good stuff posted." From their spot at the rail, Gordon glanced around *Wind Spray* and nodded approvingly. "It's really cool. I didn't expect to be out with you and Rob by myself."

"We didn't expect that, either," Rob said with a laugh. "You got this lucky because we didn't have guests scheduled this afternoon."

"We don't have that many free days," Jerrod explained, not wanting to sound like they were wanting for business. "The weather's been so good we haven't had to hand out too many rain checks."

"You're getting the platinum trip," Rob

called out from the wheelhouse. "Besides, I'm not diving. Someone stays with the boat, even when we're close to shore in shallow water."

"I could be on boats all day," Gordon said, his eyes lighting up. "I kayaked a lot up on Redwing Lake when I was staying with my dad. We went out almost every day. Sometimes my friend Evan and I put our kayaks in the water right in front of his house."

"Kayaking will build your muscles. Do you play football in the fall?"

He shook his head. "Mom is too afraid for my head… I mean my brain. She thinks about concussions way too much. That's 'cuz her friend Lark wrote a bunch of articles about kids and head injuries and now my mom worries about that." He smirked. "Like she worries about everything."

"I don't blame her," Jerrod said in Dawn's defense. "I thought you were a hoops guy, anyway."

Gordon nodded. "That's right. I never liked football much. I'm into chess. Evan and I started a club." He tightened his mouth. "Some of the guys on our basketball team call us nerds."

"Ah, let 'em. I got those labels slapped

on me, too." Jerrod felt for the kid. He was smart, maybe a little gangly, but he was showing signs of growing into those long arms and legs and being a tall young man. "But I was the one who got a scholarship to Penn State. Without that, I'd have had to take out big loans."

"What did you major in?" Gordon asked.

"History. US history was my favorite." He'd been a loner as a young person. Bookish, not a team sport kind of kid. Maybe a little too quiet. Gordon seemed sort of the same, but with more friends, which was good.

"Those guys are just talkin'. Don't mean anything by it."

Good to know, Jerrod thought, jumping ahead to imagine Carrie at thirteen when everything was more complicated. Reaching that far into the future had the power to bring on heavy dread, even in his imagination. But he couldn't freeze time. He glanced at Gordon standing next to him, leaning on the rail, staring back toward the shrinking shore.

Rob reduced their speed as they approached the site. Jerrod was almost sorry to move on to the next thing. He liked talking to Gordon. He was bright, for sure. But more important, curious. Like his mom, and maybe his dad. Jerrod couldn't say anything about Bill. Well, except that he'd hurt Dawn. When she put the facts out of how he'd left her, her emotions had been raw. Like the other night. She was pretty raw, then, too. Jerrod couldn't stop the vague feeling that she'd seen right through him.

Suddenly, Gordon said, "So how did you get into diving?"

"I'd already been a recreational diver for years. I had a buddy in high school whose dad liked to dive and he taught me. Later, I worked as a commercial diver during summer breaks. But during my short stint in commercial diving, I saw some strange things."

"Like what?" Gordon asked.

"Well, I once went down with a team to examine a railroad car." He laughed, recalling the sight of that rusted relic. "The thing had just rolled off the tracks when it derailed and it kept going until it was in pretty deep water. It had junk metal in it, so it was a pile of rust. I've seen the corpses of old refrigerators and washing machines sitting on the bottom in the sand. All kinds of stuff like that."

"Weird. Like dumping toxins in the water or something dumb like that," Gordon said.

"*Your* generation is smart enough to know that," Jerrod said. "My parents' generation was *beginning* to figure that out."

"Maybe there's going to be a need for marine biologists...you know, in the future. We had a guy come in to talk to the science class about Lake Michigan and all the things that could change it. And not in a good way. Knowing how to dive might be good for a scientist."

"Good thinking. You'll see one of those hazards today." Jerrod filled in a little background about how he and Augusta started their diving business when he was a commercial diver in Milwaukee. "Early on, we realized we didn't want to spend our lives in regular jobs. You know, doing the same thing every day."

"I get that. That's what my mom says about her business. She's her own boss and gets to do different fun stuff. And she never liked the idea of being stuck behind a desk."

An amusing picture came to mind of Dawn getting in and out of her car many times in the course of a day and checking her phone and scribbling in her notebook, doing research on her tablet. "I got that impression the first day I met your mom. When my wife and I went to Florida we got regular jobs only long enough to save our money to start our own business."

At one time, Jerrod choked on the words when he tried to recite the most basic facts of their story, but not so much anymore. As he'd grown closer to Carrie in the last few months, the memories of Augusta and Dabny weren't erased, not at all. But they were easier on his heart. He couldn't explain any of it. He'd hoped the change of location would help, but he hadn't anticipated feeling so at home here. He'd told Dawn he was emotionally dead, like a stone inside. But here with Gordon on the boat, at the yacht club with Dawn, and making small talk with Miles, he'd been present, as alive as anyone else.

"Our dream grew from there," Jerrod said, eager to finish the story, "and our girls eventually came along."

Gordon lowered his head and stared at the cockpit floor.

Jerrod sensed he'd said too much, been too personal. Jerrod wasn't even sure how much

Dawn had told him about what happened to Augusta and Dabny.

"Let's get the anchor down," Rob called out. He circled *Wind Spray* to put the bow into the wind and shifted the engine to neutral while Jerrod lowered the anchor. Following Jerrod's hand signals, Rob put the engine in slow reverse to increase its hold. They were in only about eighteen feet of depth and just behind the outer edges of the wreck.

Rob put out the diving flag on a buoy line. They were already in wet suits, but before they finished getting into the rest of the gear, Jerrod said, "I know this is going to sound like a history buff talking, but every wreck, no matter where it is, Thailand or right here in Lake Michigan, is its own time capsule. It's what hooked me in the first place."

"A time capsule? I like that," Gordon said, nodding.

"It's true. A wreck is like a museum that puts on display a little part of what life was like a long time ago. And in this case, nine people survived and two died when the *Alice Swann* capsized. We're like marine archeologists when we explore a site to see what was left behind, not either salvaged or destroyed.

Nowadays, we don't bring any of the treasures back up with us. Wrecks are preserved, not pillaged, if you know what I mean."

"I hadn't thought about people dying here, but I guess they did."

"I don't mean to be morbid about it, especially because most survived the capsize that sent the schooner to the bottom. With the other site we explore, the *Franklin Stone*, the men had a chance to get into lifeboats and start heading for shore. Some people on land came out to help. The ship burned up and sank to the bottom, but all the men made it home. When I look at a site, I also like to remind myself that so many things we take for granted weren't invented the day this schooner went down. On the other hand, we still use a compass and anchors and line."

"My grandpa tells lots of stories about when he was a kid," Gordon said, looking like he was trying really hard not to laugh. "They didn't even have their own phone in the house. There were, like, five TV channels."

"Hard to believe, isn't it?" Jerrod feigned an astonished expression before adding, "Hey, my dad told me all those stories, too." He guffawed. "Tell you the truth, I used to groan when he started one of his anecdotes. They were like mini lectures."

"My dad's not too bad that way. Just Grandpa Keith." Gordon shrugged. "He's really old, but he tells funny stories about sneaking out of the house at night and diving in some quarry where they weren't supposed to go. He claims he only got caught once, but I don't know."

"Oh, right," Jerrod said sarcastically. "Trust me, old men always say they did dangerous stuff and nobody ever got caught. Or hurt. And they came back with huge fish, bigger than any of us have ever seen. They don't even *make* fish that big anymore."

Gordon started laughing. Jerrod had to admit it felt pretty good to make a young teenage boy react like that. Carrie was easy. She giggled if he made a funny face. But older kids? They could be a tough audience.

They finished with all the gear—the weight belt, the buoyancy devices, the tanks, regulators, dive computer. Impressed with how smoothly and respectfully Gordon managed the equipment. Jerrod's confidence in the thirteen-year-old went up a notch or two.

This boy had the ability to handle himself on a dive with adults.

"Only one more safety reminder," Jerrod said. "We don't touch anything, and not only because we don't want to disturb this archeological site, but because sites can have broken glass and jagged sharp metal edges. Especially with the zebra mussels covering things up, you don't really know what you'll find. I don't want anyone getting hurt. No trips to the hospital for tetanus shots." He almost said, *especially you*.

"Got it," Gordon said. But he started to pull at his suit and fidget with the dive computer.

He needed to stop talking and get the kid in the water, Jerrod thought.

Preparations done, masks in place and fins on, he signaled and they jumped off the side and began the descent, adjusting the pressure as they went. Jerrod pointed to his own ear, his signal to Gordon to make sure he wasn't feeling a squeezing pain in his ears. Gordon gave him the A-OK sign back. He watched Gordon closely, signaling to stay close and follow him.

The rudder on the bottom came into view first in the midst of a mix of mussels and clumping underwater plants swaying in rhythm with the water. It was as if it had been waiting for Gordon to see it. *Alice Swann* had been loaded with shingles and cord wood, but much of that cargo had been salvaged.

Curiously, the masts and booms, and even the bowsprit, were intact. For Jerrod's money, these functional, but still sleek pieces were the treasures of this particular dive. They wouldn't be salvaged now, or Jerrod would have wanted to see them assembled in some kind of replica. It remained a mystery why these pieces had been abandoned on the bottom for almost one hundred and fifty years.

He'd told Gordon about the ship's two anchors, pointing to the rusty one deep in the sand, set apart from the other pieces. The other anchor was on display in a park in town, along with pieces of the hull. Gordon had probably seen it but not known what he was looking at. Now he would.

Jerrod watched as Gordon lingered over the anchor with him and knowing time was short, pointed back to the large pieces of the intact hull where small fish disappeared and then suddenly reappeared. Some of the ship's planking had fallen in a pattern that created tunnellike spaces that played to some instinct in the fish that led them to dart through these passages as if chasing each other in a game of tag.

Through the mask, Jerrod saw Gordon smiling as he pointed to the booms as they passed, but then frowned as he called attention to the colonies of invasive mussels. Today's kids knew nature wasn't static. Nothing stayed the same for long. Gordon already understood more about toxins and threats to the water than Jerrod had learned in four years of high school.

Jerrod signaled it was time to ascend, and they soon climbed back on the boat and began removing their gear.

"So what did you think?" As if he didn't know. Through his body language and calling attention to what he saw, Jerrod could see Gordon was fascinated by this underwater world.

"Cool. I like it. Can I go out with you again? I don't mean alone. I know you usually take a bunch of people."

"Sure you can." He held his hand up and paused. "I'll rephrase that. It's up to your parents, but as far as I'm concerned, you can come out whenever we have space. Looks like you had a good instructor on Redwing Lake."

"Oh, yeah, my dad asked around and checked the guy out. My mom talked to him, too."

"Well, good. We're glad to have you."

Later, when they'd gone back to the office, Rob immediately left to pick up an order at Donovan's Marine. Jerrod was ready to tackle some paperwork, but Gordon hung around like he was reluctant to leave. He was tempted to ask what was on his mind. Instead, he waited.

Finally, Gordon shifted his weight from one foot to the other. "Do you ever need any extra help around here? Like, maybe I could clean your boats or help in your office. I could maybe post things on your website. I'm good with tech stuff." He spoke fast, but finally had to stop to take a breath. "See, that way I could pay for my diving. I go to my dad's house on weekends, but I'm with my mom during the week until school starts."

Jerrod really liked this boy. His parents might be divorced, but however they'd handled it, the good result stood in front of him. "I think we could arrange something." He ticked off a few of the jobs that had to be done, pushing back worries about how Dawn would feel about her son hanging around him. "We get a few walk-ins and if we're out on the boats we can miss them. They usually text or call, but maybe you could give them brochures, take their names—talk about what we offer."

"Sure, I could do that."

"I bet you'd be good at doing what marketers call 'selling the experience.'"

The way Gordon nodded, it was clear he liked that compliment and nodded without any trace of false modesty. "I know how to talk to people…adults." He shifted his weight from one foot to the other. "I mean, I can learn."

"Wyatt handles the website and posts my blogs and does all the social media. She's probably at it right now. She's a pretty fine tech person herself, but she might welcome a little help."

"That'd be cool."

"So, I'll ask your mom," Jerrod said, the specter of awkward conversations popping up again. "If she says yes, we'll work out a schedule. Come to think of it, we can find plenty for you to do. We can work in some barter, but I'll pay you for the hours you put in."

"Okay…when…"

"I'll call your mom a little later today," Jerrod assured him. "Then I'll let you know."

Apparently satisfied with that answer, Gordon wheeled his bike out of the storage room and through the front door. He called out, "See ya," before letting the door close behind him.

Jerrod stared at his phone.

Calling Dawn should have been easy, a pleasant break in his day. But telling lies had a way of messing things up, and he sure hadn't been honest with her. He'd wanted to pick up the phone more than once in the last few days. Brave man, he was. So brave he'd held his phone in his hand a couple of times, but never punched the number.

Thinking about that night on the point was like having twenty-pound weights attached to his feet. He got nervous every time her words came back to him. Words about the elephant in the room, and his empty self-effacing talk. And most of all, her anger at his flattering her. Exhausted, he rubbed his eyes and dragged his hands down his face.

He was alone now and could make the call. It wouldn't be long before Rob came through the door and Wyatt would be around later. They'd be on their computers comparing notes and he'd run his blog ideas by them. The days would pass one by one, and then, when the air was chilly and smelled of fall, he'd button up his boats for winter storage and be on his way to Florida, season one on Lake Michigan over. That's the way it had to be.

That painful exchange with Dawn had convinced him he couldn't stay in Two Moon Bay. No, going back to his familiar routine in Key West was the right choice. But he'd never feel good about what happened, and not just because of Dawn driving off in her car, making as clean a getaway as possible. Most likely she was second-guessing herself. That's what he found so hard to live with. Especially because he'd wanted to take her in his arms and tell her she was right. Emotions he thought he'd never experience again had snuck up on him.

SHE OPENED HER eyes that morning, wishing she'd never met Jerrod Walters. Feeling more cynical than she had in a long time. "The show must go on," she murmured. Right. After a quick breakfast and shower, Dawn dressed in casual khakis and a crisp white shirt that would probably wilt as the temperature climbed into the nineties. Then she stared at her image in the mirror while finger-combing her damp hair to fluff up the curls. Sunscreen, mascara and lip gloss were next. Done. Time to go.

Feeling more than a little foolish, she added one more step. She looked into her eyes in the mirror and said, "You'll breeze into his office, cool as can be. Not a hint of stress. It's as if the conversation never happened and nothing has changed. He'll do his three interviews, you'll keep him on track, and then you'll leave. That's it."

She was glad Gordon wasn't around to hear her talking to herself. But she'd read about affirmations and how saying something out loud added power to the thought. Glorified positive thinking, or maybe it was only a case of mind over matter. On that particular day, she was madly in love with the idea that acting like a situation was cool would magically make it so.

Bracing her hands on the sides of the sink,

she sighed in disbelief. After these last months, she never anticipated her gut closing tight at the prospect of seeing Jerrod. She took the blame for it, of course. She climbed way out on that shaky limb marked with a hazard sign: Personal—Hands Off. All she accomplished was making their professional dealings—and friendship—awkward. Now she had to face him…she checked her watch…in twenty minutes.

"Speaking of personal," she muttered to herself, she still couldn't bear to admit how stunned and upset she was by what happened. Ever since Bill left her, she'd had trouble trusting herself when it came to men. But this time she'd been so certain. It was small comfort, but Lark didn't believe Jerrod, either. Looking up into the mirror to check her makeup one more time, she said, "Yeah, and that and fifty cents…"

Once she was in her car and underway, her thoughts turned to Gordon. He'd been excited after diving with Jerrod and Rob. There was nothing like it, he'd said. Nothing. Something good had come from working with Jerrod, after all.

Knowing Gordon had benefitted from Jerrod's expertise made the situation more tolerable, at least a little. She had good news for Jerrod, too. Still, she wasn't exactly feeling breezy cool, and tried to conjure up a bit of nonchalance. She had to laugh at that notion. As Bill used to quip, nonchalant wasn't in her repertoire.

As she parked the car and approached the office door, it opened and Wyatt and Rob came out.

"He's waiting for you," Rob said. "We're doing the tour, so we're out of your way."

"Not that you'd be in the way," Dawn said.

"He can be a little self-conscious doing interviews with us around," Wyatt said, "so he'd send us to the boats, anyway. He's never let us come along to hear his speeches. Augusta got to go because he couldn't say no to her."

By the time she went inside, she was restless, jumpy. She thought she hid her internal turmoil well when she said hello and sat down across from him at the desk.

"Hey, how are you? Big day for Adventure Dives," he said, a big phony grin on his face. "Once again, your work paid off."

His voice was shaky, so she chose to overlook the patronizing praise. She'd give him a break on that since he wasn't the picture of cool, either. For the sake of the interviews ahead, she trusted this was only a temporary case of nerves.

"I bring more good news."

"Is that so?"

"It's your blog. People are noticing it," she said, her tone bright. She filled him in on some interest he'd stirred up in Two Moon Bay and other towns. Planning boards and conservation groups had inquired about his business and programs. "I gathered the information. One event is in late August, so it fits in your time frame. I assume that's true, based on your text about going back to Florida in October." Back in the spring he'd been vague about his fall plans. Apparently, that had changed.

He nodded. "Nelson and I finalized a deal for this same dock space next year. We'll be back in May."

"That's good." She wondered about Carrie starting kindergarten in Two Moon Bay, then moving to a new school in Key West. Or maybe she'd stay with Melody in Florida. Oh, why was she even speculating? Either way, it was none of her business.

"We're doing better than I anticipated. But the Florida location needs attention, too."

"I imagine so." So polite, so stiff. She cringed at the sound of her own voice. "As I mentioned, the first interview is seven minutes, and could be broken up for teasers throughout the day. You can use your minutes to talk about the diving, specifically the two wrecks."

Managing a looser tone, she filled some minutes talking about how often she'd worked with the Green Bay news station with other clients. It could sound like bragging, as if he needed convincing. She shut herself up as abruptly as she'd started. She'd learned something from this episode with Jerrod: she needed a life. Other than Gordon and a few short relationships with unsuitable men, she'd lived and breathed her business.

"The public radio interview is different." She reminded him the hour was going to be all about local attractions and how they fit into the big picture."

She looked up from her notes and he glanced away, pretending something on his desk was of great importance. Was he even listening to her? "You'll be on long enough to field anywhere from two to three questions from callers."

"I understand," Jerrod said, rocking the office chair forward and back and making it squeak with every move. "I listened to that program in the car the other day, so I know what to expect."

She wished he'd stop with the chair. The squeaks were getting to her. Okay, he was nervous, but being there unnerved her, too. "Once the interviews begin, I'm going to move my chair away from the desk, so there won't be any noise." She pulled out a roll of tape and a sign she'd written on yellow construction paper: Interview in Progress. Reopening at Noon.

His eyes widened in surprise. "You really do think of everything."

"Not really. But you don't want Nelson coming around to say hello—or my son. He can't stop talking about you."

"Gordon is smart," Jerrod said softly. "He catches on to things, seems to know what's important. I see a great future for him."

He sounded like he was leaving his parting

thoughts. Maybe he was. Once he got back to Florida he might think twice about ever coming back. "He told me all about your commercial diving days," Dawn said, "so now he has it in his mind he'll see a plane or rusty old appliances someone threw overboard."

"Underwater junk." He smiled. "But no one needed to tell him that practice was harmful. Very smart that way, your son—and most of his generation, I suspect."

She checked the time on her phone. "You can call in now. The producer is James, not Jim, Mantz. And my phone is off." Relieved, she stood and pulled her chair away from the desk and closer to the door.

It took only a minute or two for James to transfer him to the interviewer, Lacey, a woman Dawn had worked with many times. She closed her eyes and listened to Jerrod, his voice strong, upbeat but modulated. He was a gifted speaker and radio guest. Not just okay.

In those few minutes, he'd sold the diving trips, repeated his website URL twice and used the phrase "mysteries beneath the surface of the familiar lake we often take for granted." They'd worked on the wording until he was satisfied with the message. It invited questions.

The only glitch in the public radio spot was the lengthy caller going on about the dangers of diving. Dawn tensed when the man talked about not being able to breathe during a dive. Jerrod did the best he could in the couple of minutes he had to talk about safety and preventing accidents. Unfortunately, the interview ended with Jerrod responding to a host's question about decompression sickness, the biggest risk in diving. He had only one minute—Dawn timed it—to explain it, but he was clear. He also added that he'd rarely seen it in his twenty years of diving.

When the call was finished, Jerrod swiped imaginary sweat off his forehead. "I'm glad that's over. But that's not how I like to end interviews. You know, finishing up with all the scary stuff."

"But you managed to direct them to your website for more safety information."

"That guy sure had a bad time of it, huh?"

She scoffed. Then in an instant she realized she had no reason to hide her experiences. What difference did her fears make now? "The man will probably never dive again. Like me."

"What?"

She flicked her hand at him in dismissal. "I didn't mention it before because it's not really important, but some people have bad experiences that make diving out of the question."

"That's how you feel?" Jerrod asked. "And you're just telling me this now?"

Dawn shrugged. "We shouldn't get into it. Besides, we don't need to have this conversation at all."

"It's just that I've asked you to dive with us. I've mentioned it more than once. And each time you've avoided an answer."

It was an accusation, Dawn thought, and she supposed he was owed an answer. "Okay, you're right. I guess I thought you'd drop it, maybe sense that I wasn't a fan of the sport, even though I'd been on a diving excursion with Bill years ago." She repeated what she'd told Lark about not being able to breathe, flailing around, and the panic...all of it.

"I wish you'd told me." He spoke with gentle reproach.

She wouldn't be thrown by his kindness. "It wouldn't have mattered. I would have eventually said something if you'd kept pressing me." In a light voice she added, "I guess the cat's out of the bag now." Her handbag sat on the floor at her feet and she playfully tapped it with her foot.

"The nightmares were the worst part. They went on for a couple of months. The fear of suffocation is natural, I get that. But the terror of the dreams had me thrashing and calling out in the night. Not normal. For the first time in my life I was afraid to fall asleep."

"That's terrible," he said with a frustrated sigh. "Panic is the biggest risk of diving, at least in my experience. I panicked once as a teenager. But I'd already had good experiences. I wish..."

"You need to call the station now," Dawn interjected. "The producer is Kay, Kay Carlson."

The next fifteen minutes passed quickly. Dawn watched Jerrod's expression change from pained back to neutral as he skillfully took on the knowing tone of a local. He got in a couple of good plugs for the tours on the *Lucy Bee* and also responded to a good question about the huge numbers of well-preserved wrecks in the lakes—thousands of shipwrecks, mostly unexplored. Dawn was more than satisfied with how he'd done. He'd made the most of placements that weren't easy to get.

He patted the edge of the desk a couple of times. "Two fairly solid, one a little shaky. Not so bad."

"You did fine. Don't sell yourself short." She stood and moved the chair back to the desk. Picking up her bag, she headed for the door.

"Do you have to run off?" Jerrod asked. "I thought, well, maybe we could have lunch."

"Sorry, I have a lunch date. A committee meeting at the merchants' association." She kept her tone even, matter-of-fact without being unfriendly. "The sidewalk sale is coming up fast."

Jerrod stood and awkwardly rested his fingertips on the desk. "I need to talk with you. The sooner the better. Could you stay for a few more minutes?"

He's a client. She fought off the strong urge to run and instead put her handbag on the floor and sat down again. "What's on your mind?" *Please, please, nothing personal. I'm not ready.*

"Uh, I need you to know…what I mean is… I wasn't happy with the way we ended things the other night."

He just had to get into it, didn't he?

His halting voice was such a contrast to that of the relaxed radio guest of a few minutes ago. "You don't need to explain," she said, her weariness showing. "I get it."

"I do need to explain, and no, you don't get it."

She lowered her head in a slow nod, but stayed on her feet, ignoring the chair at her side. "Okay. I'm listening."

"You were right about me, Dawn. About a couple of things." He rubbed his forehead as if he had a headache. "My feelings for you aren't a figment of your imagination." He shook his head. "You didn't get the wrong impression. Not at all. I sent the messages." He paused and looked her in the eye. "But I shouldn't have."

If he'd said nothing else, she would have walked away with her spirit a little lighter. Maybe her pride fully intact.

"Everything I said about you is true. You're smart and easy to be with. I admire how you put your son first and came back from your losses." He frowned. "I'm searching for the right words. I think you handle yourself and your business with a great energy."

"Thank you for that." She was grateful. No question. She also knew a "but" was coming around the corner any second now.

"All that's true. But the good things about you don't make up for what's missing in me."

He was honest. No wonder he would have done just about anything to avoid this conversation.

"I said I don't have anything to give a woman now. But that's only a part of it." He pointed to himself. "There's something missing inside me. I'm thankful I've got Carrie, but she deserves more than she's getting."

"That's the one thing I'll argue about," Dawn said, convinced what she had to say had value. "She's surrounded by love. That's because of you. And Melody, Wyatt and Rob. The other night I told you not to sell yourself short as a dad. And I meant it."

The muscles in Jerrod's face relaxed. "So we can go back to the way we were with each other before? I don't want a wall between us."

"That's it? I said you were a good dad, end

of story. We're never supposed to talk about it again?"

"You see me with Carrie *now*. But you didn't know me before. I hired Melody for Carrie and hid out alone with my grief. I didn't do right by her."

"You're doing right by her every second." She was close to yelling at him. "That's what I mean when I tell you you're a good dad. So, you weren't always perfect. So what? It's who you are today that counts."

"But I'm only finding my way now as a dad." He rested his palms on the desk and dropped his head. "The thing is, Dawn, I can't do it again. Not ever."

Dawn stared at her shoes, gathering her thoughts. She could turn around and walk out the door. He'd said his piece. It cost him, too. She wouldn't make him pay an even bigger price.

"You want another child, a new family." His voice softer, he said, "You've been honest about that."

"I know, but…"

"You're entitled to someone who can give that to you." He looked at her directly, not avoiding her eyes. "You're young and beautiful and like I said, you deserve more than a man haunted by ghosts from the past. You deserve more than I can give."

She had no words. What would she say? That she was wildly attracted to him, even knowing it was futile? And why? Because of his heart? His mind? Jerrod thought of himself as cold and numb. No matter what he said, she saw him as engaged with life and his child. So maybe he wasn't animatcd all the time, but he was present.

"Dawn?"

She glanced up. "Sorry. My thoughts are racing. I take everything you said seriously. And I want to be friends, too." She paused before adding, "But I don't like hearing you run yourself down. You're not perfect. Big deal."

She smiled and slung her bag over her shoulder. "But I really do have to go."

"We're good?"

With a quick laugh, she said, "We're good." She left and didn't look back.

CHAPTER TWELVE

JERROD SPOTTED CARRIE skipping across the parking lot, with Melody following behind. She had the hood of her jacket pulled up over her head and tied to keep it in place. The rain was only a warm, gentle drizzle, but if the forecast was correct, they were in for a third straight day of rain. That meant cancelling a tour and rescheduling two diving excursions. No business dependent on tourists welcomed rain on the weekend. His was no different.

Jerrod was on the way to meet Dawn at the chamber of commerce building a few blocks away. He hadn't expected to run into his Carrie out that Saturday morning.

"Hi, Daddy," she said. "Are you going somewhere?"

"Well, sweetie, I have a meeting with some people Dawn wants me to talk to."

"Can I come?"

"Not this time, honey." When Carrie's

mouth turned down it felt like an indictment. "It wouldn't be any fun for you. Just grown-ups discussing stuff."

"I still want to go." She sounded whiny. Notable in itself. She almost never showed that kind of pique.

"Here's the thing. This is something I need to do, and I can't take you along. But I'll be back in time for dinner." He glanced at Melody, who was standing quietly a few steps back while he handled the situation. "I'll make your favorite spaghetti and we'll share it together, just you and me. We'll give Melody a night off. How about that?"

"I want Melody to be there, too."

Jerrod let out a quick laugh and looked at Melody, who nodded. "Okay, I'll fix dinner for you and Melody."

"Promise you'll be back? Promise?"

"Absolutely." Curling his fingers into a loose fist, he held out his hand for a quick fist bump to mark his promise. Carrie started that little ritual. She'd picked it up at school and it was her favorite thing. When he touched his big hand to hers, he sealed his own resolve to get home on time. "But if I'm going to be on time for dinner later, I better get moving."

"Okay." She ran a few steps toward the office door. "I want to see Wyatt and Rob. And Gordon."

"I'm sorry, honey, but he's not here today. He's with his dad for the weekend."

"But I wanted to see him." The whiny voice was back.

"Sorry, sweetie, not today." He missed Gordon when he wasn't hanging around the office. Just like he missed Dawn when he didn't see her.

With an unhappy expression, Carrie disappeared inside the office. He asked Melody why she'd brought Carrie to the dock. They usually didn't stop by randomly.

"She wanted to come down to see you. I told her you were probably busy. I actually thought you might be gone already," Melody responded, her voice slightly exasperated. "Then she would have had her visit with Rob and Wyatt and we'd have gone home. I called Heidi's mom to see if she'd bring her over this afternoon, but they're going to some kind of family thing."

"Is it all this rain?" he asked. "Is that why she's restless?"

"I suppose." Melody folded her arms over

her chest. She looked away for a second before answering him. "I'm not sure what's going on with her today, but she's seemed out of sorts for a few days. She's been talking a lot about school. A bunch of the kids at her preschool are starting kindergarten at the Lincoln School a couple of blocks from the house."

"I know the one you mean."

"Carrie asked me a couple of times if she'll be going there with Heidi," Melody said, "but I've been noncommittal and have tried to change the subject."

"You don't know what to tell her," Jerrod said. "How could you? I haven't finalized the plan yet." That was a hedge. He'd made up his mind to leave Two Moon Bay in the fall, so why couldn't he just say so? But every time he started to let the others in on his decision, something held him back. He wasn't being fair to Carrie, but this was no way to treat Melody, either. Or Wyatt and Rob. This free-wheeling life of the last couple of years was probably reaching its expiration date.

"This is my fault." He looked up to the sky for no particular reason other than the change in the rain. It was coming down harder now.

"You need to get out of this rain, and I need to go. But tell me this. Are you okay either way? If we stay here or if we go back to Florida?"

She hesitated, but not for long. "I'm fine with both places. You know I love Carrie and I don't have other plans right now. But I'd like to know if we're packing up in a few weeks. It feels unsettled," she said, her tone pointed. "If it's like that for me, the uncertainty probably affects Carrie, too."

"You're right. I need to make a decision."

"Okay, then, we'll see you later." She narrowed her eyes as if warning him. "Don't forget about that spaghetti."

"I won't. You can count on that." Fixing an easy dinner was all well and good, but it wasn't hiding his apparent indecision as well as he thought. Normally, he'd have walked to the chamber meeting, but it was raining too hard. When he got to the building, he pulled the van into a parking place next to Dawn. She quickly left her car and climbed into his passenger seat.

"Good morning," Dawn said in her usual cheerful way.

He grunted. "I guess."

"What? You don't like this weather?"

"Now you're just baiting me," he said with a cynical laugh.

"Oops. I'm sorry. You really are in a bad mood. I was just joking around."

The rain hit the windshield and the roof, rapidly turning into a heavy downpour.

"Don't apologize," he said. "I'm in the midst of mishandling my life once again. Well, really, it's Carrie's life I'm talking about."

"What brought that on?"

"It seems like I only drove my van into town with Carrie a couple of weeks ago. I've barely settled into the house. The business is just getting off the ground." He was going somewhere with the conversation. Or maybe he was only rambling and wouldn't come to any conclusion. "Now Carrie's friends at pre-school are all excited about starting kinder-garten."

"And you don't know if you should enroll her? Is that it?"

"In part. Sure." He stared out the window at the rain-blurred cedars that formed a fence between the chamber building and the Victo-rian B and B next door. It was so hard to picture himself packing up and heading to Key West for an entire winter season.

"Carrie has friends in her preschool, so she probably expects to go off to kindergarten with them," Dawn said.

"That's what's weighing on me." He thought back to the darkest days after he'd left Bali to come back to Key West with Carrie and the crew. Would he ever stop regretting his inability to come out of the shadows and take care of Carrie himself? An old friend had sent Melody to him. She'd opened her arms—and her heart—to *his* child.

Lately, he'd begun questioning some of the assumptions that had dominated his thoughts and influenced his actions. Why did he continue to cling to the idea he was too wounded to be a father again? Too flawed to deserve a real life? Even thinking in those terms was beginning to sound hollow, even to him.

"Without fully realizing it, Melody pushed me to begin acting like a real father again. Now she'd like some answers about *her* future. Imagine that?"

Dawn kept her eyes on the windshield, but smiled when she said, "Gordon gets a big kick out of Carrie when he sees her around the office and the dock."

"She was very disappointed when I told her he wasn't in the office today."

Dawn sighed. "That makes two kids. Gordon wasn't particularly happy when his dad picked him up last night."

"No? Why?"

"He's only been helping you in the office for a few days, but he likes being around you and Wyatt and Rob. I think he feels grown-up when he's working with Wyatt to update the website or the blog. This weekend arrived like an interruption."

"I'm glad he doesn't feel exploited," Jerrod said, pleased. "If you can keep a secret, Gordon is a little…uh, awestruck by Wyatt. He seems sort of tongue-tied around her."

"He talks about her a lot. She's very cool." Dawn laughed. "Especially her name. He thinks she's pretty, too, but is shy about saying so. Instead, he goes on about how brilliant she is. That's his new word, *brilliant*."

"Wyatt is fond of him. She treats him like one of our company family now." That was a stupid thing to say, but he couldn't suck the words back in his mouth. Gordon wasn't part of their vagabond crew. He'd be left behind when Jerrod packed up and took off.

His thoughts turned to the meeting a few minutes ahead. An active chamber of commerce, Dawn said they were laser-beam focused on the future. How ironic. It was struggling with thoughts about the future that left him jumpy and tense.

"Do you have questions about the meeting?" Dawn asked. "I believe they're expecting about a dozen people."

"Not really. But I do wonder if it makes much sense for me to be in a meeting like this." He heard frustration in his tone. What did he have to offer the Two Moon Bay Chamber of Commerce, anyway? He wasn't even feeling very sociable. "Maybe it would have been better to wait until next spring. Here it is August and there's not much left of the season." Now he was acting as if leaving was a sure thing. He confused himself.

Dawn fell silent and turned away, but not for long. Her jaw rigid, she tightened her grip on her handbag. Tension built in what now seemed like an awfully small space.

"Look, Jerrod, let's clarify something. When I set this up, I told you the chamber was looking for local business owners interested in future development in town and the county." She peered intently into his face. "It's a task force meant to generate ideas to help the chamber plan for the next ten or twenty years."

"I am interested," he protested, immediately regretting his attempt to defend himself, but resenting her implication that he didn't understand what this group was about.

"But the series of weekly meetings starts in the fall," she said. "When I first talked to you about this, you assured me you were staying through October and would be back next spring—May first. The seasonal businesses like yours are included in this project because they're essential to Two Moon Bay."

She relaxed her jaw and exhaled. "If you're not going to be here then, please tell me. I convinced the organizers to include you because everyone wants the outdoor businesses represented."

"That's smart, too," Jerrod said. "I get it."

"You're a big picture kind of person with a concern for what makes the area special in the first place." Impatience still colored her tone. "I sold you to them because you have a grasp of the past. Let's just say I was a pretty strong advocate for including you."

"I know."

Glancing at the clock on the dash, he also knew he was cutting it close on time. It was unfair to Dawn all around. She took commitments seriously.

"What do you want to do?" she asked with a scoff. "Short-term, I mean."

He almost winced against the unmistakable edge in her voice. But she'd put her reputation on the line over this chamber task force.

"I'll stay at least until early November." He'd enroll Carrie in school, which would make her happy. If he ended up moving everybody to Key West, she'd adjust to a new school. But maybe he'd end up staying after all. He had an idea or two about what he wanted to do in the off season, but he wasn't ready to talk about it. "And yes, I intend to be back in the spring."

She put her hand on the door handle. "Okay, then, no ambivalence?"

"I didn't say that," he said dryly. "Ambivalence lives in every cell in my body, but I'm making a decision. I need to talk to Melody and the rental agency for the two houses. I'll work out arrangements for Wyatt and Rob to go back to Key West a few weeks ahead of me."

Dawn smiled but shook her head, almost in disbelief. "I have to say I'm relieved. I didn't relish the idea of showing up only to pull you out of the group."

"I'm sorry. I've been going back and forth in my head, stay, leave, stay, leave. Put Carrie in school. No, wait until we're in Florida. Give notice on the houses. No, wait."

"You could have fooled me," Dawn said. "You seem to be going along fine day by day. You—and your crew—seem happy here. You fit in."

If he said what was on the tip of his tongue, he'd be sending the wrong message—again. But on some days he chalked up all the good things that had happened to him because of Dawn. If he was managing, it was because of her.

WHEN THE TWO-HOUR meeting ended, Dawn had begun to wish she was a member of the task force. She'd been born in the area, so she had as much at stake as anyone sitting around the long conference table. And that included

Jerrod. Despite her reassuring words about appearing happy, she was right to call out his indecision about his plans, immediate and future. But once in the meeting, she understood why his audiences took to him.

"You endeared yourself to your colleagues in that meeting," she said, standing in the shade of the building. The rain had stopped for the moment, but the air was muggy.

"I'm glad you were there."

"Not that you needed me. But it was understood I'd sit in on the meeting," she said. "They might need me this winter to help explain the task force to the public."

"So much for the sidewalk sale being the end of your volunteer work for the year."

She laughed. "I was only kidding myself. This happens all the time. I'm sure you understand why this task force is important to me."

"I do. I feel a lot better having made a decision for the next few months."

Reminding herself it was none of her business, she kept quiet. She'd been putting effort into pushing Jerrod out of her mind except when the issue was relevant to his business.

"Let's get some lunch," Jerrod said. "If you have time?"

"Sure. Let me think of a place you haven't been yet." There were so many good places to choose from.

"I've been meaning to go to the Half Moon Café."

"You still haven't tried out one of our best all-around lunch and dinner spots?" she asked, surprised he hadn't been there with Rob and Wyatt. But maybe he didn't socialize with them after working together all day. "Then that's where we'll go." She couldn't resist adding, "You still have a lot to see in the next couple of months."

"I know you're teasing," he said. "but I don't have to see everything this year. I'll be back in the spring."

Maybe, maybe not. When it came to Jerrod, she'd become a skeptic.

They left their cars and walked down Bay Street, chatting about the meeting and the naturalist, Morton Price. Along with his wife, Morton ran a not-for-profit center that offered programs to local schools.

"Morton has turned so many of our kids into conservationists," Dawn said. In his eighties now, Morton had singled Jerrod out as the kind of leader the task force needed to preserve the character of Two Moon Bay. Unlike some folks, he didn't care that Jerrod wasn't born there.

Dawn knew the head of the tourist information center, and a resort owner, and the principal of the high school, who had a role, too. "So many stakeholders in a project like this."

"I'm glad they see this task force as the beginning, not the end," Jerrod said.

If nothing else, Jerrod had her thinking more deeply about the place she called home. Even Gordon was becoming more attuned to the world he lived in, no longer taking the lake for granted. Diving with Jerrod—and working for him—had made becoming a marine biologist seem even more exciting, and way cool. Pretty much everything her son liked fell under the umbrella of either cool— or now, brilliant—including Jerrod and his crew.

With a laugh in her voice, she said, "Have you noticed my son's limited vocabulary? How everything is way cool?"

"It's his favorite phrase," Jerrod responded. "It's my dad's favorite phrase, too."

"My mom's, too. That's why I thought it

would have been retired...replaced. But no end in sight."

"I suppose Carrie will pick it up soon." He laughed, but said, "I don't know why I find this so funny."

"Me, neither, but I do."

They were still bantering back and forth about it when they went inside the café.

"I'm glad to be indoors," Jerrod said. "I'd just as soon not run into Carrie and Melody. I promised I'd make her and Melody my favorite spaghetti for dinner, but I'm happy to have an adult lunch."

"Me, too."

From the looks of things, the lunch crowd was thinning. At her request, the hostess seated them at a booth in the back. A nice quiet spot, Dawn thought. The little jump in her stomach was like a warning flag. She shouldn't be happy about sitting in nice, quiet spots with Jerrod.

Jerrod scanned the room, his expression amused.

Dawn thought the Half Moon Café used the theme of the town's name in a tasteful, fun way. In addition to wooden beams and trim, wainscoting covered the lower sections of the walls, so the flocked wallpaper with its silver moons and stars didn't overwhelm the space. The theme carried through the menu and the great food kept bringing the crowds back.

"I can read your mind," she said. "It's filled with quips about the moon and stars."

"I plead guilty."

Keeping her voice light, she warned, "Make fun if you will, but you'll sing a different tune when you taste the food."

"Okay, I trust you. No jokes, at least not yet."

"They have great dinner fare, too," she said, picking up the menu, "but when I come here for lunch I usually get a salad or a burger. And today, I can't wait to bite into a juicy burger. I'm really hungry."

"I'll have the same thing," he said. "I suppose you're in a hurry, anyway."

Puzzled, she said, "Uh, no, not particularly. Are you?"

"No, no. If I'm home to fix dinner for Carrie, I'll have kept my promise. But I've noticed how busy you are, how you seem to make the rounds on days you're not working from your office."

"It's that obvious?"

"Pretty much."

"Well, not today. I don't have anything else scheduled." She cocked her head, feeling happier than she had in days. Maybe it was her resolve to work on her own life, find some balance. Although Jerrod had made himself off-limits, he'd been part of her drive to break out of the rut she'd created for herself.

"This was a big day for me, actually. It was sort of like finding my way to do my civic duty—for lack of a better term."

"It fits," he said thoughtfully, as if he'd tried out the idea in his head. "Until I was in the meeting I thought of it more as a chamber promo plan for the town. But it's much bigger than that. I'm glad you were there," he added, "so I don't have to explain what went on."

When the waiter came to the table, they each ordered a burger and he quickly returned with a pitcher of raspberry iced tea and two glasses and hurried off. Dawn didn't know quite how to phrase what she wanted to say next. It could sound personal, but she meant it to be business related. She pulled together her thoughts while Jerrod filled their glasses.

"Since we have this unplanned chance to talk," she said, "I'm wondering how the summer is shaking out. *Really*." She paused. "Since I'm not good at beating around the bush, I'll just ask if you believe this move was worth it. Would you go through all this trouble again?" Confident her reputation wasn't affected one way or another, she didn't lose anything by asking. Her curiosity was more personal than professional.

Avoiding her gaze, Jerrod used up more than a few seconds opening a packet of sugar.

Oops, she might not want to hear the answer. "I didn't realize that might be a difficult question."

"I didn't say it was," he said. "It's just that it isn't so clear-cut. When Nelson said that the immediate area could use a tour boat, I listened. But I sure didn't think that part of the business would take off as fast as it has. I thought we'd have way more interest in diving. But that hasn't materialized." Frowning, he absently stirred sugar into the iced tea. "I expected the diving to be our major focus. I planned around that."

"But you have full tours. I've seen that for myself from the large numbers of people gathered on the dock." She would have thought the day tours would have been considered easy income.

"For so long I've had the notion that everybody who tried diving would be like me—and Gordon, for that matter. Wyatt and Rob also love being underwater." He leaned against the back of the booth. "When I dive, nothing else matters other than the demands of that world."

His hands were in motion as he spoke about breathing, moving through the water, staying alert. "It's as if I've adjusted to the surroundings so well, they become my home for those minutes every bit as much as having my feet on dry land."

Dawn believed him, but in the abstract way she might believe there's a thrill in walking a tightrope. Still, she had no idea how to explain why she couldn't see herself ever feeling that way. She was spared from any kind of response when the waiter brought their burgers.

The burger sat untouched on Jerrod's plate, but Dawn was too hungry to wait. She was chewing the first bite when Jerrod began finishing his thought.

"That was a roundabout way to answer your question, or to maybe avoid answering it," he said. "Given how I feel about diving, it's a little disappointing that we don't have more people in the certification groups. Or have more qualified people going out to the wrecks. But then there's another side to being here."

"What do you mean?"

"It's complicated because it has very little to do with the business."

That aroused her curiosity. "Tell me more."

"I like being part of a community, a neighborhood," he explained as his expression brightened. "Earlier at the chamber meeting I felt at home, even though I've been here for such a short time."

"Two Moon Bay is like that. You've met a lot of people. Folks at your library talks, for instance, and the next thing you know, you're running into them at the Bean Grinder or the ice cream shop," Dawn said. "I see you as pretty well connected."

"That's because of you."

"And you. But thank you." Ignoring her lunch, she rested her chin in her palm and threw out another thought. "You haven't answered the question, not exactly. Are you really saying it's a mixed bag? That you're happy with your decision, but because of the diving numbers, you're not?"

He shook his head. "No. I'm happy with my decision. I like the quality of life here. I haven't been in a traffic jam yet. No horn blasting, no rude people, either."

"Hey, that's good to hear," Dawn said.

"With the tours carrying us, the business is in fine shape. The Key West office is doing okay even in the off-season." A faint smile appeared on his face. "That's why I agreed to stay and why I said I'd be back."

"Gordon will be thrilled with that news."

For the next few minutes they both finished their food while they rehashed the issues raised at the task force meeting. When she glanced up and scanned the restaurant, it was mostly empty and the staff was setting up for dinner. "We had a long lunch. It was nice, though, and as your consultant, I needed to find out how you felt about the season so far—your first season."

Dawn insisted on paying the bill, calling it a client lunch, and then they walked to the sidewalk through the drizzle that had begun while they were inside. They hurried back to the lot where they left their cars.

"Will you follow me to the office?" Jerrod asked. "There's something there I want to show you."

Since he sounded almost somber, she put thoughts of laundry and cleaning aside and agreed. The rain picked up along the way and the two ran from his parking lot into the office. It was as if the rain had settled over all of Northeast Wisconsin and was planning to stay.

She laughed at the spectacle of trying to stay dry with her raincoat over her head. He was laughing, too.

"Have a seat," he said. "I won't keep you long."

She fluffed up her hair and ran her hands up and down her arms. "So, what is it?"

Jerrod took a key out of the top drawer of his desk and opened the bottom drawer. He pulled out a pile of yellow legal pads and put them down on the desk with a thud. "I've been working on a project. It's something I've wanted to do for a long time."

She pointed to the pile. "Looks like you've been writing."

"You're the first person I'm confiding in

about this. No one else, not even Wyatt or Rob, knows what I've been up to."

"It's a book, isn't it?" She splayed her fingers across her chest. "I'm honored." Touched was more like it. Her heart beat faster. She sensed how important this book was to him. "When did you find time to start working on it?"

"Some nights I walk down here after Carrie's asleep, but mostly, I'm letting Wyatt and Rob run a few of the tours, and sometimes even the dives. That frees up time."

"Your reward for having such a great crew, huh?" She laughed. "I don't know exactly what the book is about—it doesn't matter. I'm still excited."

"It's my take on Great Lakes shipping. Shipwrecks tell tales and most people will never see these relics firsthand, but I'm trying to tell the stories of an era. I want to bring the past alive through the wrecks. But I also want to talk about the value of the Great Lakes today."

"And the threats to them, I suppose," Dawn added.

"That, too. That's why I hope the book will speak to young people. Gordon understands the fragility of the Lakes more than I did at his age."

"I hope you'll let me help promote it when the time comes," Dawn said, her business wheels already turning.

"Let you? I'm counting on it. This is the first of three books I have in mind."

"Do you write everything in longhand?" she asked. "Talk about old school."

He nodded. "I'm getting ready to put it all on the computer, though. This is only my first try."

"I'm happy you confided in me," she said, getting to her feet. She reached out to pat the stack of legal pads. "Your secret is safe with me."

Jerrod stood, but didn't come out from behind the desk. "Speaking of secrets, will you tell me yours?"

That was a shock. "What? What secret?"

"It's obvious you don't want to dive with us. I've invited you more than once and you always change the subject or run off."

Her stomach dropped with a thud. This was the big question? Did her face show her disappointment? She was annoyed enough to put it all on the line. "I'm not sure why you're asking now, but if you want an answer, here it is."

He pulled his head back, a look of surprise crossing his face. "Whoa. I wasn't attacking you. I'm curious what's holding you back. If it's lack of interest, you can just say so. No pressure."

"I already told you how terrible it was for me," she said, still standing on the opposite side of the desk. "Panic. Terror. Awful nightmares." She told him everything, all the details that she'd shared with Lark.

"I'm so sorry you had that experience, Dawn." His expression matched the sadness in his voice.

For a few seconds they stood quietly. She heard only the rain hitting the window, but it was curiously comforting.

Feeling antsy and uncomfortable, Dawn went to the window and crossed her arms over her chest as if protecting herself. The rain had stopped at last and the sun was breaking through the light cloud cover. She felt exposed now. And in a bad way. In her head she understood how ridiculous that was, but her emotions hadn't caught up.

"I wish you'd trusted me enough to talk this through."

Not able to suppress a mocking laugh, she lowered her voice and said, "Well, I did have a sprained wrist."

"But the truth is out now."

She lowered her head, her face heating up. *Like the truth had come out about what was between the two of them.* "I better be on my way. You have fun with Carrie."

"You're welcome to join us. She likes you so much." Then he hedged, "Well, it's true she might be even happier if Gordon was joining us."

"Thanks, no. I've got plans for this evening." A lie. She grabbed her rain jacket and stuck it over her head. Then, as if remembering her manners, she said, "Maybe another time. See you next week."

He stood, but stayed behind the desk as she left.

On the drive home she thought about her lie. Plans? She didn't have anything scheduled for this Saturday night. What? Maybe slice some fruit and have it with cheese and crackers for dinner. Then she could visit her favorite online movie site to find something entertaining to watch. How about a romantic comedy? Ha! She'd live on the edge, maybe even consume a big bowl of ice cream and a couple of cookies. So exciting.

So, why hadn't she accepted the invitation? She could have gone, had some fun.

What a joke.

She didn't trust herself to sit at the kitchen table and watch Carrie color a picture or tell stories about her stuffed bear. She couldn't afford to indulge in the pleasure of helping Jerrod fix the meal, offer to make the salad or heat the rolls. She liked that kind of cozy cooking too much. A long time ago, she and Bill had liked chopping and shredding and mixing side by side. They'd entertained their little boy with hip bumps and teasing.

Dawn closed her eyes and saw herself offering to read Carrie her bedtime story. Little pieces of the life she wanted would only leave her disconnected, hurt, because they weren't part of a whole life. With Jerrod. She seemed powerless to keep herself from falling more deeply in love with him.

HOURS LATER, WHEN it was dark and the movie was over, she poured herself a glass of chardonnay and went out to the deck off the kitchen, where she could see the moon rising. She couldn't view the lake from her house, but she knew what it looked like hanging out over the water, even on a cloudy night.

When her phone on the kitchen counter signaled an incoming text, she went back inside to see who it was from. Hmm… Jerrod. *Forgot to talk about the plan for end of season dinner at the yacht club.*

As if on autopilot, she began to compose an answer, an acknowledgment that he'd brought up this idea a while back. But she stopped herself in time. Supposedly, she had *plans*. She was busy. If she texted back, she'd expose her fib. She'd never played these kinds of games before, and she wouldn't do it again. It was long past time to actually have plans. For herself. If she wanted more children in her life, she could make that happen. Jerrod or no Jerrod.

Groaning, she turned off her phone. Tomorrow morning was soon enough to answer a message that wasn't the least bit urgent.

CHAPTER THIRTEEN

JERROD WAS SICK of feeling confused. Not only did he often confuse himself, he unfairly confused Dawn, as well. After a pleasant day, despite the rain, he invited her to dinner. It seemed like the most natural thing in the world. In his blindness, he was stunned when shc'd said no. That's how messed up he was. He spent so much time denying his feelings he forgot how to deal with the real ones.

And sending that text? How self-indulgent could he get?

If he was thc kind of man he wanted to be, he'd hope that Dawn had wonderful plans with someone, a man who was good enough for her and wanted the same things she wanted. He'd root for Dawn as a caring friend. Instead, he stared at his phone, willing her return message to pop up on the screen. He held his head in his hands, embarrassed by trying such high school tricks.

Carrie was sound asleep. Melody was out at the Silver Moon Winery with Wyatt and Rob. And he couldn't stop himself from checking his phone one more time before he went to bed.

An hour later, after hearing Melody come in, Jerrod pulled on jeans and a clean T-shirt and went into the kitchen. He scribbled a note to Melody and left it on the counter. He'd let her know he'd gone down to the boat for a while. He didn't say why. He didn't know. But sleep wasn't coming easily, and he doubted it would.

He left the house and walked the couple of blocks to the waterfront. A smattering of people still sat at tables in the park. Citron candles burned and the scent of charcoal from earlier cookouts lingered in the air. He got to *Wind Spray* and stared out at the water.

Why am I here? Trouble sleeping. Something that didn't happen often since his days were more satisfying now and he was more content than he'd been in a long time. In a town that felt more like home every day. He glanced at the marina building with its unpretentious square addition, his office. More

than that, the new Wisconsin headquarters
of a business he'd spent most of his adult
life building. He chatted with Nelson almost
every day. Art and Zeke were as friendly with
Wyatt and Rob as they were to him. He and
Carrie made their rounds through town, going
from home to the Bean Grinder or to the market or library. Carrie knew her way around
the waterfront like she'd lived in Two Moon
Bay all her life.

Jerrod pulled a bottle of water out of the
refrigerator and walked to the bow. The half
moon was bright white, leaving its reflection
on the lake. It would travel its path across
the sky and the lake would be dark again in
a few hours. From the first day he'd driven
into town, Jerrod had a plan to leave, spoken
or unspoken. With the logical deadline coming closer, he'd found a way to avoid a decision. Now he'd committed to a time frame
that allowed him to serve on a community
task force, something he'd never done in Key
West.

It was all well and good to give himself a
rundown of reasons he wanted to stay, but of
course, it was really all about Dawn. When

he told her only a few weeks ago that he had nothing to give, that was only partially true.

He took out his phone, and even knowing it was futile, he checked his messages. No emails, no texts. *She had plans.* He laughed to himself. A couple of hours earlier he'd lectured himself about wishing Dawn well, as if he could send her off into the arms of another man. Not so fast. She belonged in *his* arms.

As unbelievable as that would have seemed even months ago, he'd fallen in love with her.

And he had to tell her. He only hoped it wasn't already too late.

STILL IN HER NIGHTGOWN, Dawn took her coffee out back to the screened-in porch. It had taken her a while to fall asleep, but she was feeling good now. A free day stretched out in front of her. Gordon wouldn't be back until much later, and she intended to walk downtown when the bookstore opened and browse until she found a novel with sun and sand and blue water on the cover.

No work for her. Not that day. She rested her bare feet on the porch railing, resolved to put self-examination on hold. But it was so hard to shut off her busy mind always mulling over this or that client and project. Thoughts of Jerrod were never far away, and she'd answer his text after breakfast. No need to rush.

She sipped her way through a couple of cups of coffee and was about to fix herself breakfast when her phone buzzed. A text. Could be from Gordon, so she didn't hesitate to have a look. But no, it wasn't. It was from Jerrod. Will u meet me at the 1 picnic table by the point...

Should she meet him? Probably not. Would she meet him? She set her jaw and stood a little taller. Hadn't she already decided how she was going to spend the day? And why had he chosen the picnic table at the point? She didn't have the best memories of the last time she was there. With him. Had he forgotten that? But maybe the crew was already in the office and Melody was at the Bean Grinder with Carrie.

Oh, what harm could it do? She could go downtown after she met him.

She texted back, what time.

A minute later, his reply: 30 min.

She looked at her nightgown, ran her hand

through her messy hair. No, too soon. She typed in her reply: 45 min.

She stared at the screen until okay popped up.

Curious now, she put on jeans and sneakers and a sleeveless tank top suitable for the hot day and her own later trip to the bookstore. Something she wanted to do. No work involved, or Jerrod, either.

About the time she slathered herself with sunscreen, doubts set in. What did he want that couldn't wait? There was a time—weeks ago—she'd have speculated that he was finally going to open up about his feelings for her. The elephant in the room that pushed her to put her heart on the line.

Even the possibility made her jittery as she drove to the yacht club parking lot. Hers was the only car. Jerrod's van wasn't there. Odd that he'd be late, since he called this early morning meeting.

Dawn took off down the path, picking up speed with each step. She crossed the footbridge and there he sat. He was on the bench with his back to the table and his legs stretched out in front of him. No one else was around. "Hey."

He stood and walked toward her. "I'm so glad you agreed to come."

"I was heading downtown later, anyway. I'm taking the whole day off, after our meeting, that is."

"No business meeting, Dawn. Not today." He touched her cheek, running his finger down to her jaw. "I have so much to say. I only hope I'm not too late."

Too late? Was it possible he brought her here because…? No speculating. It got her into trouble before.

She caught his hand and squeezed it. "Explain, Jerrod, please."

Holding her hand, he led her to the picnic table where they sat side by side facing the lake. Only the sound of a distant car on the road and a barking dog broke through the peaceful silence that morning.

He lifted her hand to his mouth and kissed it. "I'm just going to say it, Dawn. I'm in love with you."

She raised her gaze, met his eyes. And waited.

"I've known it for a long time, and ever since we were here the first time, I acted against what I knew to be true. It gave me a mental swift kick and I've questioned everything about my life. Certainly all my assumptions about what I do or don't deserve in my life."

"What do you mean? Spell it out."

"None of this is going to matter if I'm too late."

"Too late for what? You're not thinking of changing your plans?"

"No, I'm here to stay." He looked down at their laced fingers. "When we were here before, you opened up to me, told me what was in your heart. And I've already told you I wasn't honest with you then."

She nodded, her whole body tingling now.

"But I suspect you knew that. You saw right through me. The truth is, you are the one person who could heal my heart. And you did."

She covered her mouth with the fingertips of her free hand, unable to speak, but eager to hear more. And more.

He kissed her hand again. "My heart was so closed off that I couldn't admit to myself that I began falling hard for you way back in the hotel lobby in Chicago."

Her chest filled with the kind of joy she

hadn't known for a very long time. "Way back then, huh?"

Laughing, he said, "The thing is, I've watched you be you. That's all it took. You didn't do or say anything to make me fall in love with you. The more time I was around you, the more irresistible you became. I finally realized I *could* love again because I already *am* loving again."

Jerrod let go of her hand and wrapped both arms around her. She rested her head against his chest, feeling the warmth of his arms around her. When they broke the embrace, he kissed her once, then again, and one more time. Quick, teasing kisses perfect for that moment when she was dizzy with the newness of him.

Breathing hard, he pulled away, searching her face and kissing her again. He drew her head against his shoulder. "I'm glad I know your son. He's such a great kid."

"And I'm pleased that Gordon knows you. And I think Carrie's so special," she said, lifting her head. "But we can't confuse them."

"Being in love isn't only about us," he said. "I understand that. We'll take it a step at a time, get them used to the idea we're going to be a family."

"We have time…lots of time," she whispered.

"You and all that's ahead for us, for me, is so much more than I thought I would have again."

"Me, too," Dawn said, shaking her head, the air still buzzing around her.

"The thing is, if we're going to have a family of our own, we can't wait too long. We need to get these kids used to the idea and—"

"Wait a minute," she interrupted. "Slow down. Do you really want to have a child? Our baby?" She stepped back to look into his eyes.

He took her hands in his. "That's what I said. It's what I want. But only with you."

She didn't trust herself to drop every barrier, believe in the whole fairy tale. When he opened his arms, though, she leaned into them and lifted her face for more soft kisses. His arms tightened around her and for a few minutes, she relaxed. "What do you want to do now?"

"Right now?" he asked, puzzled.

"Today." She purposely put on a challenging tone.

"I don't know. I hadn't thought about it." He peered into her face. "Was there something you wanted to do?"

She nodded. "As a matter of fact, there is. Let's go. I'll tell you about it on the way." She held out her hand and he took it. "You're really going to like this."

It was like a switch had gone on in her brain, Dawn thought.

On the way back to her car, she explained their first step was picking up Carrie. Then, only a few hours later, the three of them walked out of the Book Shelf with a full bag, including Dawn's beach read and two books of fairy tales for Carrie.

"I planned to stop for ice cream, too," she told Jerrod as she winked at Carrie. The three of them got on the trolley and headed down Bay Street. Soon they sat on a bench outside with cones.

"Next stop, shoes," Jerrod said.

Dawn was happy to help Jerrod buy new shoes for Carrie. That meant another trolley ride to the indoor mall on the main corner. This was like having her cake and eating it, too, Dawn thought. Because the man she'd wanted for months now wanted to be with her.

"Come on, Carrie," Jerrod said when they went inside the children's shoe store in the mall, "let's go find those ballet flats you've been talking about for school."

A little girl…school shoes. She could hardly believe it. She'd been tingling and buzzing for hours and hours now. "I might look for some new shoes, too," Dawn said.

"Can we ride the trolley again?" Carrie asked.

"I'm sure we can," Jerrod said. "We'll make the loop and have it drop us off at the park."

"Okay." Carrie skipped ahead and stopped to wait for them to catch up.

"So this was the plan for yourself today, huh?"

She lifted her shopping bag from the Book Shelf as proof. "Everything except the trolley. I knew Carrie would get a kick out of it. It was my no work, all play day."

Jerrod laughed. "This is how it's going to be, huh? A summer Sunday in Two Moon Bay."

"It's one of our choices, if you don't have

divers scheduled or a tour." Dawn was feeling kind of smug about going to pick up Carrie and making their private special day into something ordinary in the most wonderful way.

"Just checking. Wanted to see what I was signing up for."

Dawn squeezed his hand and grinned. "This, and so much more."

Jerrod laughed again. "I like the sound of that."

CHAPTER FOURTEEN

DAWN AND LARK stopped at a vendor and bought papers cups of lemon gelato to eat while they wandered down the center of the street on a hot, hazy afternoon. It was the second day of Stroll & Shop.

"I could almost do a tap dance right here on the street, or maybe hum a little happy tune."

"Is that because of the weather, or the crowd?" Lark asked, her tone teasing and light.

"Mostly it's the size of the crowd," Dawn said, pretending they actually were talking about the sale. "It always lifts my spirits when the shop owners consider the sidewalk sale a great success. But maybe I'll shout for joy over the weather, too."

"Between the tap dancing, humming and shouting, you'll be making a fair amount of noise." Lark cast a knowing glance at Dawn. "You don't have to be so cool and calm."

"Who, me?" Dawn joked.

"I'm thrilled for you. It's good to see you so exuberant."

"I'm almost afraid to believe it myself."

What had happened at "picnic table point," as she and Jerrod decided to dub it, had changed everything for them personally. But Dawn still found it difficult to explain how it felt that he'd been accepted, even warmly welcomed into planning the vision of the future for Two Moon Bay. "You know how it is around here. People who moved to town thirty years ago are considered 'from away.'" She scoffed. "Okay, not everybody is like that, but some people still are."

Dawn stopped to browse a table of brightly colored cloth handbags, some quilted and a few with foot-long fringe hanging from the bottom. Not that she needed a new purse.

"Those handbags aren't nearly big enough," Lark pointed out.

Dawn bent to the side. "Jerrod says I list to port with my usual bag on my shoulder."

"That's pretty funny." Lark laughed. "For such a serious guy, he has a good sense of humor, doesn't he?"

"Oh, he can be funny, all right." She

glanced at Lark. "When I first met him, he rarely smiled. He's more at ease now and enjoys bantering with Nelson and Zeke. And you know he likes Miles a lot. He's different. Happier. And it's because he's found his new home."

"Namely you," Lark said. "You're his new home."

Dawn stopped walking and took in a deep breath. "And he's my home. Just think, I'd longed to fall in love again. When I first started dating after my divorce, I even thought it would be so easy to find someone wonderful."

"Have you spread the news?" Lark asked. "I mean beyond Miles and me. What does Gordon think? I bet he's happy. And I think we can all guess how overjoyed Carrie is going to be."

"No, no, we haven't talked to the kids yet," Dawn said as she started strolling toward the jazz band at the end of the street. "There's plenty of time for that. And it will be an adjustment for Gordon, too. We want to let Carrie get used to the idea of me. It's all well and good when it's a little girl thinking about a new mommy, but the reality could be different." She grinned at Lark. "See? It's like we're still trying on our relationship. Like adults. So far, it fits."

They walked on, and just ahead of them, two hanging racks were filled with what Dawn estimated to be at least two hundred scarves in silk and cotton in colors and patterns of every description. They billowed in the breeze that was picking up now. After a day of unmoving air hovering over the town, a break in the heat would be welcome.

The gelato gone, Dawn and Lark tossed their cups and spoons in the recycling bins. Looking at the crush of people on the street, she could claim with confidence that her publicity efforts had worked. The merchants' group had drawn people to Two Moon Bay from all over the area.

"There's something about Stroll & Shop that signals the end of summer," Lark said wistfully. "Doesn't it feel like another season is winding down, even though it's still August?"

"And hot and sticky," Dawn said. "It's a good day to be out on a boat. Gordon is getting all the diving in he can before school starts. It's hard to believe he's old enough to ride his bike to the marina to help Jerrod clean up the boats and post his blogs."

"Miles is out with Jerrod today, too. It's his second trip," Lark said. "On his first dive, he saw the schooner that's close to the shore, but this time he's going out to the bigger wreck in deeper water. I can't remember its name."

"Franklin Stone." Dawn playfully elbowed Lark. "Who would have imagined that the two of them would end up diving together? Who knows? Maybe Jerrod will offer Miles a job, too." She moved her arms back and forth as if swiping an imaginary mop. "Can't you see the two of them swabbing the decks?"

"It's good he has a backup in case his public speaking career doesn't pan out?" Lark deadpanned. But she quickly admitted she worried about Miles diving. "Odd, but I feel a little better knowing Gordon is with him. It sounds ridiculous, but I can't help but think of Miles as safer with Gordon along."

"That's pretty funny considering neither one of them is very experienced—and Gordon is thirteen," Dawn said. "But to be fair, Gordon dives about twice a week. This first summer, the diving excursions have been slow. The day tours have kept them afloat… pardon the pun."

"You're forgiven," Lark joked as they walked past bins filled with running shoes on sale and approached a display of hand-made toys from an upscale kids store.

Dawn was about to steer them to the jewelry shop, but a strong gust of wind sent the scarves at the boutique flapping. Loose note cards blew off a table and skittered across the pavement. Taylor, the owner of the card shop, hurried out to gather them with help from her teenage daughter. Dawn knew Taylor from the sidewalk sale committee and was about to run over to help, but the cards were soon safely gathered and anchored down.

Lark pointed to the west, where clouds had suddenly gathered—and were rapidly darkening. "I don't remember hearing thunderstorms predicted for this afternoon."

"Only that standard line they always repeat when it's hot and humid." The temperature had dropped fast. Dawn wished she could exchange her tank top for long sleeves.

Looking at the scene around her, Dawn saw the crowd of shoppers slowing down, some watching the sky, many checking their phones, as Lark was doing.

When Lark looked up from the screen, she pointed to the sky. "Those clouds aren't so distant anymore, are they? Now there's a storm warning for the area."

As if by instinct, Dawn turned in the direction of the lake, where the sky was clear. "I guess the excursion out to the *Franklin Stone* will be cut short. Or maybe they're already back."

"I'm sure Jerrod and the others keep a close eye on the weather," Lark said.

As Lark spoke reassuring words, the wind increased and the sky darkened. Lightning broke through the cloud cover in the distance.

"We have to assume everyone is okay out there. You're right. And Jerrod and his crew have been doing this for years." Dawn looked up and down the street, where the stores owners were busy pulling bins to protected spaces under awnings, if they had them. Not that many stores did. Most were exposed to the wind whipping down the street, and nothing was going to protect the merchandise from the coming downpour.

"I'll help Taylor drag those tables inside,"

Dawn said. "Then let's see who else might need help." She took off across the street and grabbed a corner of a wooden bin that Taylor was struggling to pull through the door. Between the two of them they were able to angle it to get it back inside—fast. Taylor's daughter followed with her arms loaded with boxes of cards. Dawn went out to scoop up more off the folding table.

Glancing across the emptying street, Dawn spotted Lark closing and stacking shoe boxes. The fudge shop had acted fast and already had cleared its outdoor display baskets and closed the front door. The owner was helping the jeweler next door clear his display.

For the next few minutes, Dawn went from store to store moving merchandise or bringing folding chairs inside and helping employees break down displays. Lark was doing the same on the other side of the street.

The sound of rolling thunder preceded another sharp rise in the wind whooshing down the street, sending signs swinging and even the streetlights swaying. A maintenance crew took down sawhorse barriers and chased the orange cones that had been used to create the no-drive zone downtown. Many had blown over and were rolling down the street. Along with dozens of other people, Dawn and Lark ducked into the indoor mall.

"I just sent Miles a text, but he didn't respond," Lark said, her voice higher pitched than usual.

Dawn put her hand on Lark's arm. "That could be for all kinds of reasons. Cell service isn't that reliable on the water. Jerrod has said that many times."

"Maybe so," Lark said, "but they shouldn't be on the water."

No argument there, Dawn thought. "I'll text Gordon and see what happens." She pulled her phone out of her bag and sent a quick text: are you okay? She left it at that. Despite her resolve not to worry, she and Lark stared at the screen waiting for a reply. Looking out the window, a streak of lightning lit up the nearly black sky, followed by a piercing crack of thunder that sent a shudder through the building.

They continued staring at the phone. Finally, Dawn couldn't stand it another minute and went outside to look toward the lake. Even the end of the street was now obscured by the rain. Gusts of wind pushed small tree branches into gutters and along sidewalks. Cars in the distance were stopped and flashing their hazard lights.

She went back inside. Lark was sending another text.

Thoughts of the *Wind Spray* offshore with Gordon and Miles—and Jerrod and his crew—raced through her mind. When Lark looked up at her, it was through frightened eyes. Her friend had never been good at hiding her emotions and they were on open display now. Dawn put her hand over her heart, vainly thinking it would quiet the thumping in her chest. In itself that wild beating was urging her to do something. Take action. She couldn't stand there and wait for a message.

"Let's go down to the marina, Lark. It's not that far. I parked my car there when I dropped Gordon off, anyway. You walked here, too."

Lark nodded. "I thought of that, but I tried to convince myself I was overreacting."

"Maybe we are, but let's just do it," Dawn said emphatically. "I've got a couple of sweaters in my car and a beach towel. We'll dry off when we get there."

Dawn pushed against the wind to open the mall's heavy glass-and-metal door. Once outside, Dawn led the way around deep water-filled dips in the pavement. They jumped over a few too big to skirt. The storm drains couldn't handle the rain fast enough, leaving the winding narrow street that led to the winery and the Bean Grinder mostly underwater. They hadn't seen a storm like this one in several summers, Dawn thought. A disquieting fact when she pictured Jerrod and the others caught unaware.

Dawn slowed down and caught her breath, looking behind her to check on Lark, whose hair, like her own, was flat against her head. Their clothes had soaked through and standing still, Dawn shivered. So did Lark. They had to keep moving.

"I know this sounds irrational," Dawn said, "but as drenched and miserable as we are, I don't really care." She gestured to her right. "We could take the path—well, what we can see of it—to the Bean Grinder and wait it out there, or we can keep going straight to the marina."

"Let's get to the marina. If the office is locked, we can warm up in your car, like you said."

They broke into a jog again, but the blare

of a siren immediately brought them to a stop. Dawn looked behind her and through the wall of rain saw the blurred flash of red lights. Both the siren and the lights got closer by the second.

"It's coming this way," Dawn said. A wave of nausea hit hard. "It's probably going somewhere else. Maybe to the Bean Grinder."

"It's an ambulance," Lark said. "Not a fire truck—someone is in trouble."

"Let's go." Dawn forced worry aside. If she gave into the feelings coming over her, fear would paralyze her. Her legs were already wobbly.

They were half a block from the marina when the ambulance passed them and pulled into the lot. Dawn didn't know she could go any faster, but she picked up her pace and Lark matched it. When they finally reached the parking lot, Dawn stopped next to the ambulance and bent almost in half. With her hands across her thighs above her knees, she finally caught her breath. A couple of feet behind her, Lark was in the same stance. An EMT in rain gear ran to them.

"What are you doing?" the man asked.

"Why are you here?" Dawn asked. "Who called you?"

"We got an emergency call from a dive boat, the *Wind Spray*. Someone's hurt. It sounds like a head injury."

"Who?" Lark demanded, her voice loud. "What's his name?"

"We don't know. It's a boy, a teenager."

Dawn reeled forward, her legs barely holding her weight. Only Lark's hands on her shoulders kept her upright. "Decompression sickness? Could it be that?" In her mind, she recalled each of the hospitals equipped with a hyperbaric chamber. One was Northeast Memorial. Only ten minutes away.

"Uh, ma'am, that's not what they indicated. The captain would have said as much. They tell us, so we're prepared. I don't believe they were diving when it happened."

"Where are they?"

"They're coming in now."

Nelson, covered head to foot in yellow rain gear, approached them. "We got the message on the radio."

"I texted Miles," Lark said. "Dawn tried to reach Gordon and Jerrod. No response."

"They were either busy or in a dead spot.

Happens all the time." Nelson stared at them both. "Come on, follow me. I opened Jerrod's office when I saw the ambulance pull up. You can wait inside."

"It's Gordon," Dawn said. "I just know it is. How many teenagers would Jerrod have on a typical dive?"

Nelson didn't contradict her, but urged her along toward Jerrod's office door.

"Miles is on the boat, too," Lark said. "We don't know who else. It could have been another young person with them."

Nelson didn't offer any piece of information that left open that possibility. Dawn detoured to her car and pulled out the towel and sweaters. Lark searched her purse but realized she hadn't brought her spare key to Miles's car.

"No problem, Lark," Nelson said, "I've got whatever you need to dry off and warm up."

"Cold or warm, I don't care. None of that matters now," Dawn said, going inside but positioning herself by the window. Lark put the towel around her.

Nelson and Lark exchanged a pointed look—Dawn saw it clearly. Neither one looked calm—or hopeful.

"Here it comes, the boat," Lark said.

Dawn pushed past her and was the first out the door. She started running, but Nelson followed and cupped her shoulder in his palms to hold her back. "Stay here, Dawn. Let the EMTs get to the end of the dock. They can work faster if we stay out of the way."

"You're right," she hollered over the wind. "I know you're right."

Everything that followed happened slowly, or so it seemed to Dawn. Rob steered the boat to the dock, Wyatt jumped off and secured the lines. Miles and a woman Dawn didn't know were in wet suits when they stepped off the boat. They hurried up the dock, but Miles stayed where he was at the end.

"Is a boy hurt?" Dawn yelled at the woman as she went by.

"Yes, yes," she said, "but he's awake. Are you his mom?"

Dawn nodded, keeping her eyes on the EMTs in their rain gear rolling the stretcher down the dock. "Did he hit his head? Was he diving?"

The woman shook her head frantically. "We never went down. It all happened pretty fast. Your boy tripped and fell. The captain,

Jerrod, took care of him. We couldn't bring him back right away, because of the storm. Jerrod told us it was safer to ride out the worst of it."

Dawn was vaguely conscious of Lark draping a rain jacket around her shoulders and murmuring reassuring words. She wanted to break away, run to the end of the dock, but even she, despite her panic, saw she'd only complicate things in the narrow space.

It took only a minute for one of the EMTs to board the boat with a backboard. After what seemed like hours later, Dawn saw the EMTs maneuvering the board, with Gordon on it, off the boat and onto the stretcher. They covered him in a waterproof casualty blanket and rolled him down the dock. Jerrod was only a couple of feet behind the EMTs, but Wyatt and Rob stayed on board.

Dawn broke free when they rolled the stretcher toward the ambulance. "Gordon, Gordon," she shouted over the wind. She grabbed the edge of the stretcher and walked along beside it.

"I'm okay, Mom," Gordon said. "Don't worry."

"It's not a diving accident," Jerrod said,

looking her squarely in the eye. "He tripped and fell in the cockpit when the boat pitched in a strong gust."

"The woman who came down the dock told us you canceled the dive." That only got one worry out of the way.

Jerrod went to talk to the EMTs, but Miles stayed with her. "Jerrod saw changes in the weather before the storm began. But the wind came up fast and we had to ride it out."

Dawn searched Miles's face. "But why would Gordon fall?" She heard her own tone, accusatory, angry.

"It just happened," Miles said. "An accident. He lost consciousness for a few seconds, not very long."

She touched Gordon's shoulder. "But you can talk?"

"Yeah. I'm okay." He closed his eyes. "I'm kinda tired, though."

"He's going to be checked out," Jerrod said, coming to her side. "That's why I got on the radio with Nelson and made sure the ambulance was here. It's possible he has a concussion, probably mild, if at all. But—"

"He didn't answer my text. Neither did you."

"I'll check my phone later," Jerrod said, putting his arm around her, "but we didn't have reception during the storm."

The EMTs collapsed the wheels of the stretcher and transferred Gordon into the body of the ambulance.

"I'm going with him," Dawn told the EMT, who then helped her step up inside.

"I'll follow in my car," Jerrod said.

For the first time she noted Jerrod's mouth was not only frozen in a grimace, his skin looked as gray as his eyes. He probably blamed himself. But that made sense. She blamed him, too.

"Then I'll see you there," Dawn said tersely.

"We'll bring you dry clothes," Lark called out just before they shut the doors and drove away.

Dawn looked down at her white jeans, the bottom edges muddy from the run to the marina. Her yellow tank under the huge rain jacket clung to her skin, and her feet were almost numb with cold in her sneakers. Only now, looking at her son's face, knowing he wasn't in a coma or worse, did she allow relief to ripple through her.

"I think I'm hungry," Gordon said.

"That's a good sign," Dawn said, squeezing his arm.

Gordon grunted. "I don't like all this fussing over me, Mom. It's just a bump on my head. Like you had in the car accident."

Dawn looked up at the EMT sitting where Gordon couldn't see the woman's face. She was trying very hard not to smile. "That remains to be seen. Let's leave the diagnosis to the professionals. That's what I had to do when I showed up in the ER. As for the fuss, that's too bad. You'll adjust."

"Ha ha," Gordon said. "Very funny."

"It's the best I can do when I'm cold and dripping wet. And scared out of my mind that something happened to you."

"Uh, do you think Jerrod will let me dive with him again?"

"That's not up to him," she said firmly. "It's up to me, and I'm saying no." Since Gordon took his diving and working for Jerrod seriously, she was prepared for words of protest.

"Anyone can fall on a boat, Mom."

"Anyone didn't fall. *You* did." She couldn't help the rising fury at herself for letting him go. She'd taken her son's interest in diving way too casually. He was a kid, thirteen. But most of all, she was angry with Jerrod. Even worse, she realized with a jolt, that she didn't trust him. It was like a blow to her chest.

She looked up as they pulled into the ambulance bay at Northeast Memorial. "We're here." The hospital never looked so good.

JERROD CHECKED IN at the desk, but wasn't surprised when the intake clerk asked if he was family. He almost blurted *not yet*. Instead, he explained that Gordon Larsen was on his boat when the accident occurred. And when that freak storm had happened. He called it that because of how little warning there had been. No predictions for it, either. The barometric pressure dropped and he could almost detect the peculiar scent of an oncoming thunderstorm. That's why he'd cancelled the dive.

"I know the boy's mother well," he added, eager to see Dawn to know how she was doing. It was always easy to write this sort of event off and say no one was to blame. Technically true, Jerrod still accepted responsibility. It went with the territory of his type of business. But even more so, it went with being a dad, and now loving Dawn—and Gordon.

"And your name is?"

"Jerrod Walters."

The woman disappeared and Jerrod wandered around the waiting room, impatient, still worried that his hunch could be wrong. All signs pointed to Gordon having, at worst, a mild concussion. No matter how mild, he'd never forget seeing the boy lose his balance when the boat pitched. He'd crashed into the wood trim of the companionway ladder. Ironically, Gordon had been trying to soothe the woman who Miles later helped off the boat. A new diver, like Miles and Gordon, the storm upset her, but instead of being honest about it, she tried to hide it—at first.

When fear took over, Jerrod understood everyone was apprehensive, including Rob and Wyatt. Boating of any kind meant accepting a degree of risk. Finally, when the woman admitted she was afraid, Gordon paid attention, and when a wave hit the boat he tried to move closer to her, intending to steady her. That happened fast, before Jerrod could intervene. The teenager forgot to protect himself, and Jerrod didn't step in fast enough.

"Jerrod."

He knew that voice. "Dawn, there you are. How's Gordon?" He crossed the room to hear the answer.

"We're waiting for him to have a scan. They're concerned because he doesn't feel well. Kind of sick to his stomach."

"That doesn't necessarily mean he has a concussion, though."

"Of course not," she said, her voice tinny. "I know that, but they still have him on an IV."

"Could be he got a little dehydrated," Jerrod offered. "It was hot before the storm and I don't remember when he last drank any water."

The look she tossed his way wasn't pleasant. Did she think he should know when Gordon had finished off a bottle of water? "I'd like to see him. Can I come back and wait with you?" He was going to be this boy's stepdad, after all, as well as the person in charge of the boat.

She hesitated, but then shook her head. "Not just yet, Jerrod." She turned to walk away. "Why don't you go update Lark and Miles?"

"Dawn, I really would like to see him. I'm upset about what happened, too."

She shook her head. "Maybe so, but I'm... let's just say I don't feel good about this. He's the only child on the boat. He's the one who gets hurt." She took a few steps back. "We can rehash this later."

"Wait, wait," Jerrod said, "Obviously, I take responsibility for this, but you're acting like I let him get hurt out of carelessness."

Her hands flew to her flaming cheeks. "We were just talking about the possibility of having a child. You and me."

"I know." He frowned, taking a step closer. "You aren't saying..." He grabbed the back of his neck in frustration and groaned. "What are you saying?"

She stared at him, her eyes light brown just then, and filling with sad tears. "I don't know you well enough, deeply enough. I've been paying attention to all the wrong things. And you warned me. You told me how long it took you to fully be a father to Carrie. But I didn't listen."

"*Dawn. Stop.* You can't mean this." He put up his hands in surrender. "You were right earlier. We should discuss it later."

"There's actually not much to say." She wore Nelson's oversize rain jacket, which made her look small and vulnerable, even as she crossed her arms in front of her chest. "You told me yourself you let someone else take charge of Carrie for a whole year before you stepped up again."

Slam. Another blow. "I can't believe you're throwing this back at me. That's low. I've confided in you about what happened to my family. You know I blamed myself."

"But Jerrod—"

"Let me finish. What happened to Gordon was an accident. *Accident.* Don't pretend I haven't been up front about the risks of diving." He paused, opening and closing his jaw in frustration—and disbelief. "I was honest with you about having nothing to give. And then, because of you, I opened my heart again. I fell in love with you."

When Dawn glanced around her, he became conscious of being in a hallway, where any minute people could be coming and going.

Jerrod stared at her, determined to fight for this. Did she think he didn't understand what it was to be so scared she'd lash out at anyone close by? But when she nodded grimly and turned away to walk through the doors back to the examining room, he had no choice except to wait. But he meant it. He would fight, maybe not today, but he wasn't letting this go. Or letting her go.

In the lobby, Jerrod faced Lark, Miles and who he assumed was Evan coming toward him. Miles carried a duffel, presumably with clothes for Dawn. When they met, Miles introduced the boy.

"Is Gordon going to be okay?" Evan asked.

"It looks that way," Jerrod said, addressing the concerned boy. "He's having a head scan, though, just to be sure. He scared us all. You're his good friend, aren't you?"

Evan nodded.

"Gordon's told me how the two of you started the chess club. I guess you do a lot of things together, huh?"

"We play basketball." Evan grinned. "He really likes diving with you."

"Are you leaving?" Lark asked, strain showing on her face, especially in her eyes.

"No, no. I'm off to the cafeteria to get Dawn something to eat. Gordon has an IV in and can't eat yet."

"What? An IV?" Evan looked at Lark. "Isn't that serious?"

"Not necessarily," she said, patting his shoulder.

"Dawn says he doesn't feel very good and needs some fluids," Jerrod explained, "but after the scan is done, I imagine they'll let him have some food."

"Then you saw him?" Miles asked, frowning.

"No, no. Uh, Dawn wanted me to wait." He hated the way he sounded, like he was stammering and unsure of himself.

"Can we see him?" Evan asked.

"Why don't we wait?" Lark suggested.

Jerrod had a strong feeling Dawn would welcome her old friends, even though she'd sent him away. "It wouldn't hurt to ask if you can say hello before they take him up for the test. No guarantees, but they might bend the rules a little for his best friend."

"Well, then, let's be on our way," Miles said. "We'll see you later, when you come back with the food."

"Well, actually, I'll leave it at the intake desk," Jerrod said, giving them a quick wave.

"I'll see you all later." He walked away, knowing he'd left Miles and Lark puzzled.

On the walk to the cafeteria, he couldn't stop thinking about the irony of what had happened. Dawn had nixed football because of the risk of a head injury. Her biggest fear about diving had been the potential for a brain injury from decompression sickness. Jerrod had gone over that risk with her, being honest, but able to ease her fear. But in a split second the teenager was hurt in an ordinary fall. On *his* boat.

Jerrod ordered a sandwich for Lark and bought her a large coffee to go with it and dropped it off at the desk in the ER.

When he got to his van in the lot, he climbed in but didn't start the engine. The wind had picked up again. Another storm was developing. Meanwhile, there he was, alone, haunted by the memory of Gordon going down, the *thwack* of his head hitting the wood, Jerrod's own gasp. The looks on the faces of everyone on the boat, including Miles, were painful to recall and could never be erased. Gordon could have been badly hurt.

But then, he knew it too well. Anything could happen to anyone.

GORDON LOOKED PALE and tired, but he perked up when Evan came into the room. Dawn's heart lifted a little seeing him, too, especially because Lark and Miles followed behind.

"I'm glad you're all here," Dawn said, hugging Lark. Miles leaned down and gave her a quick kiss on the cheek.

"Hey, Miles," Gordon said, "how's Jean?"

"Jean? Who's Jean?" Dawn asked.

"The woman who got off the boat with me," Miles explained. "She was kind of panicky in the storm." He pointed at Gordon. "He started talking to her, trying to calm her some. Right, Gordon?"

Gordon nodded. "We were all a little scared, except for Jerrod. He and Wyatt were positioning the boat to keep her from rocking too much. I just figured I'd help out by talking to Jean."

"Oh, Gordon," Dawn said. "That was Jerrod's job. Not yours."

"Jerrod came to talk to all of us, too," Miles said. "It wasn't like he was off somewhere. He was seeing to the boat. But at one point, a gust of wind sent the boat lurching, and Jean was kind of thrown sideways and Gordon went to help her."

Who was he trying to convince? Dawn found this explanation missed the point.

"We just saw Jerrod, and he told us you were awake and talking," Lark said. "Just the news we wanted to hear."

Gordon groaned. "Everyone is making way too much of this. It's a bump on my head. It was a storm. I can't wait to go diving again."

"Oh, please. Give me a break, my friend." Dawn sent a withering look to Gordon. "It isn't up for discussion at the moment. No one has ruled out a concussion. I don't care how mild they think it is." She hesitated, but because she wanted Gordon to understand, she said, "And Jerrod isn't equipped to have kids on his boat."

Dawn picked up on the look Lark and Miles exchanged. Did they believe she was wrong? It didn't matter. She was sticking to her guns on this.

"It was an accident," Miles said in a low voice. "Gordon was quick to respond. He was trying to help."

"That's what scares me the most," she said.

It wasn't Gordon's job to help Jerrod keep everyone else safe. She wanted to trust Jerrod, but she couldn't. She couldn't trust him with her thirteen-year-old. How could she trust him with another child—their child? It was impossible.

CHAPTER FIFTEEN

WHEN HIS OFFICE DOOR opened and Dawn appeared, Jerrod felt a familiar catch in his chest. Right on schedule, his heart beat a little faster. To say he was surprised to see her was an understatement. Over a week ago, she'd had the courtesy to send him an email with the diagnosis, a mild concussion. Emphasis on *mild*.

Meanwhile, Labor Day had come and gone, and the change in Two Moon Bay was already visible. All their communication had taken place through text and email, no wasted words. She'd sent a text asking him when he was leaving town. Why would she think he'd run away? He'd replied immediately, I'm not leaving.

That had led to a couple of quick exchanges in which he told her he signed the lease for the house he, Carrie, and Melody lived in, and in October Wyatt and Rob would head to Florida for the winter season. His last message was about enrolling Carrie in school.

"Dawn. I didn't expect to see you." He pushed back the chair and got to his feet. "You look wonderful…rested, I mean. Relaxed." He'd keep babbling about how great she looked if he didn't stop himself. "Have a seat."

She looked at the chair, as if she wasn't sure she should sit.

"Please, Dawn."

A slight nod, and then she sat. "Gordon is fine, and says hello. He's with Bill overnight. School started yesterday."

"Carrie started, too. She's very excited, as you can imagine." Dawn was supposed to be sharing in that exciting day with him. Fortunately, they hadn't told Carrie, or Melody, about their plans. They'd agreed to wait a little longer. Only Miles and Lark were privy to what was supposed to be their special secret. "Uh, Bill must have been very relieved to learn Gordon wasn't seriously hurt."

"I'll say. But by the time Bill arrived, even Gordon had adjusted to the reality of the concussion. The word itself is scary, but I'm glad the doctor explained it." Dawn paused. "But maybe some good will come of it. Maybe he'll remember to wear his bike helmet every time. A little fear isn't always a bad thing."

"No, it isn't." Were they going to simply talk all around this? "I believe Gordon has a healthy amount of fear. He's not reckless. Not even a little bit." He paused. "And neither am I."

As if she hadn't heard him, she reached into her bag and pulled out a file folder. "I stopped by for two reasons."

She had that "I'm on a mission" look he'd come to expect. It usually meant she had good news, business news. "Two reasons? Is this a business call?"

Ignoring the question, she said, "I'll get the bad news out of the way first." Her voice was ominously low.

"Bad news?"

She nodded, but didn't look up. The file still sat in her lap. "Do you recall back in late May, I set up a phone interview with a staff writer for the outdoor magazine *Sun, Sand & Surf*?"

"I remember. It's a national magazine and the offer was too good to pass up, even if the piece had a long lead time."

"It was a round-up piece, specifically about Great Lakes diving."

How did all this add up to bad news? "So why is there a problem?"

She took some clipped pages and folded the first two back and passed them across the desk to him with the opening lines highlighted in yellow. "They opened their piece about you with this."

Walters opened his Great Lakes office two years after he and his family were victims of a terrorist attack while living in Bali, a popular diving destination. His wife and eldest daughter were killed in the incident. Until recently, Walters refused to discuss the attack, but continued running diving excursions in Key West and now in Two Moon Bay, Wisconsin. Rumor has it he's enlivened the boat tour and diving scene in the popular tourist town.

He lifted his hands and shrugged. "So? You thought I'd be upset?"

"I guess so. We had an argument over this very thing. For some reason, the local writers mostly steered clear of the past."

"But, Dawn, that was months ago. I was wrong then. *You* set me straight." It was true. "I used to think that if anyone wrote about

Augusta and Dabny, they'd just be two anonymous victims. And like I said to you, I'd be the poor guy who lost wife and child."

"And you're aware that I've never thought of them that way."

Her coldness took him aback. "Yes, of course I know that. And I'm over all this." He didn't get it. Why would this be an issue between them now?

"So, tell me, why are you staying in Two Moon Bay?"

"Because I became myself again," he said without hesitation. "I made friends. *Someone* even got me on a local task force to help create a vision of the future. I enrolled my child in kindergarten. *I fell in love with a wonderful woman here. Why would I leave?*"

She stared at her shoes. "Those are some major reasons."

"You think?"

She worked the stretchy band on her watch, avoiding his eyes. "So."

"So," he said back. "Nothing has changed, Dawn. Not as far as I'm concerned."

"I was unbelievably upset when I saw EMTs rolling Gordon down the dock. It was one of the worst memories of my life."

"Of course it was."

She abruptly stood and wandered over to the photo shelf, now filled with more recent pictures of families sitting together on benches on the *Lucy Bee*. She'd taken one on her tour showing Wyatt chatting with Jerrod, their elbows propped on the rail. She picked it up and turned it so Jerrod could see it. "What a lovely day that was."

"Yes," he said simply.

"And this one," she said, picking up another picture.

One of Jerrod's favorites. Dawn and Lark had taken Brooke on one of Jerrod's short morning trips, too. Brooke liked the idea of being on a "girls only" day with Melody, Carrie and Wyatt.

"That day reminded me about what Lark had said about addition, not subtraction when it came to her family. The same is true for me. This summer brought more people into my life, but hadn't taken anyone away."

"It was a special tour day for me, too," Jerrod said, "watching all of you in a group."

She put the photo back. "We had another day like that with Carrie downtown. How she loved the trolley."

It made no sense holding back. He loved her, and he didn't think she'd simply fallen out of love with him. "One of the happiest days of my life, Dawn, start to finish."

"But when Gordon was hurt, that was one of my worst."

"I know. What I said holds true. I take responsibility for it, and his safety was always on my mind. Everyone's safety was." Defending not just himself but Rob and Wyatt, he added, "We handled the boat as well as we possibly could to safely transport all the passengers back to shore."

"But that didn't happen."

A storm, especially a freak storm with winds much higher than a typical lake squall, was part of the risk. He couldn't pretend otherwise. "What happened to Gordon wasn't about neglect or carelessness. It was about risk. If I had to do it over again, I would have told Gordon specifically not to move. He thought he was helping, Dawn. Remember that."

Dawn nodded, but picked up another photo. "Gordon sure looks happy in this one." She handed him a photo he recognized.

"We always take a photo of everyone on

their first dive with us," he said, smiling at Gordon's image. "Look at that grin. He was so proud of himself that day. He was our only diver. I recall remarking that he'd been very well trained up on Redwing Lake."

Jerrod stared at Dawn, who was picking up one photo after another. Watching her, all he wanted was to hold her, caress her face and tell her he loved her with his whole heart. He'd never been more sure of anything else in his forty years. But he couldn't push, make demands or force the issue. But he could listen and make his case.

"I like the idea of a wall of photos," she said, turning and pointing to the opposite wall with very little on it. "It needs some paint."

"I'll say." He laughed in spite of the situation. "I don't think Nelson would object if I rolled some paint on the walls in here."

"Or corkboard," she offered, a smile tugging at her lips. "Then you just rotate the best pictures from Two Moon Bay and Key West."

Like any of this was about photos and walls. "What else, Dawn?"

With a long sigh, she said, "I couldn't stay away. I said some things I didn't mean."

It wasn't that simple. A simple apology, either way, wasn't going to cut it. "I think you did mean them."

She spun around to face him. "No, that's not true. I was scared, ready to blame anyone. Do you know that just yesterday Gordon walked me through your every safety rule and guideline?" She gestured expansively as she spoke. "He told me about how you watch out for your divers. He said he never felt scared out on your boat. He knew you were watching him."

"That's what every passenger gets. Because of his age, Gordon got a little more of it, a little more often." He laughed lightly. "I know he got tired of it."

"I suppose he did," Dawn said.

"I would never lie to you, Dawn. And I wouldn't be foolish and assure you that nothing could ever happen to Gordon. You know that." He considered his words before saying them out loud. "Something could happen to Carrie, or to me or to you, or to the new baby we have."

She looked down at the floor. "I don't like that we wasted even a week, but because of my stubborn streak, we did."

She was coming back, and they would pick up, but not where they had left off.

Folding her hands over her chest, she said, "The reason I'm here is that in my fear I forgot to be grateful that this was a minor, very minor injury. And in the end, when I thought it all through, I was grateful he was with you."

"Thank you for that."

She stepped toward him and he took her into his arms and held her tight. "Maybe we can stay like this the rest of the day," he said, laughing. "Or at least until the kids come home."

Then the sound of the door opening grabbed his attention.

"Hello," the man said. "Are you Jerrod?"

"Bill?" Dawn took a half step away. "What are you doing here?"

"I was on my way to pick up Gordon and bring him to your house. Thought I'd stop in to introduce myself to Jerrod."

Jerrod held out his hand. "Well, surprise or not, it's nice to meet you."

Maybe check out his boy's boss, too. Especially after the accident. That was fine. He'd do the same thing.

Bill looked around the office, stopping to focus on the poster of the *Franklin Stone*. "Gordon even told me about that poster. He's thrilled about this place."

Jerrod noticed Bill glance at Dawn. "He's afraid you'll take it away from him."

"Don't worry about that," she said with a groan. "I'm coming around. Jerrod and I were just discussing what happened."

Bill looked from Dawn to Jerrod. "I suppose it's not any of my business, but how serious is this between you two?"

Jerrod wasn't touching that. That was Dawn's job.

She laughed. "Did Gordon give you the idea Jerrod and I are a…couple?"

"He implied it." He looked at Dawn expectantly.

"First, it is your business, more or less, because it affects Gordon. And second, yes, it's very serious, Bill, but I haven't told Gordon yet." She pointed to Jerrod. "We're taking that part slow. We won't disrupt his life. Nothing with our arrangements will change."

Bill smirked. "Well, you two, I'd say something pretty soon. I think he's already figured it out."

Jerrod didn't doubt that, but he had something else on his mind. "Did you have questions about Gordon's accident? I'm happy to talk about it." So far, Bill had been friendly enough, but he hadn't stopped by from idle curiosity.

"The situation worried me, I'll admit," Bill said, "but Dawn knows you, trusts you. Gordon is, well, you know, he can't get enough of this place." He waved around the room.

"He's done for the year," Jerrod said matter-of-factly. "We won't be diving much longer and with the concussion he's not allowed, anyway."

"He'll be almost a year older when it comes up again," Bill said. "He liked diving up on the lake, so I knew I'd never hear the end of it if…"

"If his mother forbids it?"

Bill nodded at Dawn. "I suppose. But look, I'm done here, so I'll be on my way. I feel better having stopped in."

"Nice to meet you, Bill." Jerrod spoke up quickly before Bill left. "I'm not just saying this to be polite, but you and Dawn have raised a great kid."

Bill grinned and waved. Then he was gone.

"Well, that was an odd interruption," Dawn

said, "but not unpleasant. I guess I need to talk to Gordon."

"No, *we* need to talk to him." Jerrod was prepared for anything. Having your diving instructor as your stepdad might seem cool, or it could seem really awful. Only time would tell.

"Okay, it's a deal. We'll figure out when it would be best to do it."

"Now I want to talk business," he said with a laugh in his voice.

"You do? Now?"

"We have an end-of-season dinner to plan, Ms. PR Maven. Aren't you the one who suggested it?"

"That was me," Dawn said, giving him a lopsided smile. "Let's get to work."

Dawn insisted she needed her planner and went to her car to get it. In the few minutes he was alone, it occurred to Jerrod he had one more really important thing to do.

CHAPTER SIXTEEN

THE LAST FRIDAY NIGHT in September had rolled around and Dawn was now ready for the thank-you party to be over. She enjoyed the planning well enough, but she had other things on her mind since she and Jerrod were spending time at each other's houses and at the Bean Grinder and the Half Moon Café. They never tired of each other's company. The two kids, her work and Jerrod himself filled her days. Ever since that day in his office, when they'd settled things between them, it had been a whirlwind of activity.

The night had arrived unseasonably warm, meaning they could open the verandah doors of the yacht club and let the guests gather outside if they wanted. They could light a fire in the stone fireplace later if it turned cold. It was a casual party, jeans and sweaters, but Melody, with Carrie's help, had chosen the blue-tinted candle holders lined up on the top of the verandah wall. Tea candles had been dropped into them so they could be lit and protected from the wind. Carrie had wanted white fairy lights draped around the fireplace mantel. Dawn's future stepdaughter had very specific ideas about where she wanted them.

When Miles and Lark joined her, they stood on the verandah watching Brooke and Carrie playing tag on the grass at the side of the building. Evan and Gordon were keeping an eye on them. "How did we get so lucky to have such nice boys?" Lark asked.

"Luck had nothing to do with it," Miles said. "The two of you need to give yourselves some credit."

Lark shrugged. "You could be a little biased."

"Maybe so. But that doesn't make me wrong." Miles took stock of the guests coming into the room. "So many people I don't know. Can you fill me in, Dawn?"

"I can trace all the people Jerrod invited to something specific. They could be local customers, journalists and the librarians here in town. And Nelson and Zeke. Each one boosted—in some way—Jerrod's presence here in Two Moon Bay. Some of the

Two Moon Bay task force accepted the invitation, as well. It's a going away party of sorts for Wyatt and Rob. Melody is staying here for Carrie."

"What a summer," Miles said, his expression thoughtful. "I learned to dive and I got a taste of what it would be like to be caught in a wild storm in my own backyard. That alone taught me a lot about shipwreck diving."

"Miles." Lark gave Miles an exasperated look.

Dawn laughed. "Don't worry, Lark. We all learned something that day. And besides, Gordon is fine." In her case, maybe what she'd learned was about trust. Realizing, deep within her, that Jerrod, Rob and Wyatt had done everything they could to take care of the people they'd had out on the water when that terrible storm had hit. No one could prevent every possible mishap. "It reinforced the idea of preparing for something and not letting fear get in the way. My thirteen-year-old son taught me that."

"I'm hungry," Lark said. "Let's get some of that pizza. It smells so good."

The scent of sausage and tomatoes, onions and garlic, had drifted outside. She was ready to fill her plate, too. "Good ol' Lou's pizza," Dawn said. "A match for the casual atmosphere."

As Dawn filled her plate, she looked around the room but didn't see anyone she needed to catch up with. She had appointments scheduled with potential clients, and that was good enough for the moment. When she turned to find a drink, she almost bumped into Jerrod.

"I was wondering where you were," she said. "Lark and Miles and I were out on the verandah admiring everything from the lights to the food aromas floating in the air."

Taking her elbow, he guided her to an empty corner. "I'm going to make a quick speech, then later, when we're alone with the kids, there's something I want to say."

"Sure. I doubt Gordon will mind sticking around and keeping an eye on Carrie." She touched his arm and smiled up into his face. Sometimes she couldn't stop smiling—all day.

"Carrie's counting on that," Jerrod said, glancing outside where the kids were still on the lawn. "She thinks the best thing about the party is seeing Gordon."

He patted his blazer pocket. "I made notes so I wouldn't forget anything—or anyone."

"You're not nervous, are you?" she asked. "You, the seasoned speaker."

Jerrod's eyes softened when he answered. "It's going to be hard to say everything without sounding, oh, too sentimental. Or worse, lame. I want to cover everything, but not bore people and make them wish they could sneak out."

Dawn groaned. "Like that would ever happen."

"I hope you're right." He did a quick scan of the room. "Okay, people are still here. I'll greet the ones I haven't talked to yet and then go up front to wrap this baby up."

"You'll be great. And I'll be listening."

He raised his eyebrows and said softly, "I hope so."

Dawn finished off her food and got herself a glass of wine from the bar. She preferred to stake out a place in back and be alone when she listened to Jerrod. She couldn't explain why.

She took a few sips of her wine and looked outside at the nearly full orange moon reflected on the flat surface of the water. The second moon of Two Moon Bay. It was never more romantic than in the fall.

Earlier, when Jerrod asked her to hang around after the party was over, he'd looked at her with his wonderful tender expression, warm and inviting. Once their relationship found its foundation, and she could count on it, she'd let herself melt like a schoolgirl with every look, touch, and kiss.

When Jerrod tapped a fork against a glass, the room quieted. "Now that I have your attention," he quipped, nodding at Dawn.

He didn't have a mic, but didn't need one for this relatively small crowd. His voice was at his best, deep and able to project into the room.

"I decided to throw this party to thank all of you for what you've done for me, my crew, and my family."

Spontaneous applause rippled through the room. His eyes opened wide in surprise.

Dawn smiled to herself. He didn't get it yet. Of course they applauded him. The people around here had taken to him. She'd seen it as it happened. To Wilson and Morton, he represented the future of Two Moon Bay, especially because of his interest in the past.

Out of the corner of her eye, she saw Gordon and Evan come through the open verandah door with Carrie and Brooke in tow. They led the girls to a space across the room from her. She smiled at them, not knowing if they'd see her. It didn't matter.

Jerrod went down the list one by one, but kept the pace moving along, talking again about his strong feelings for what Great Lakes shipping represented in the history of the region. Jerrod singled out Nelson and Zeke. "You can't keep boats without docks and spare parts and all kinds of gear, so I especially appreciate the hospitality they showed to me and my crew."

Zeke raised his glass and smiled. Nelson looked self-conscious. Dawn was 100 percent sure he hadn't expected the special words.

Time to finish, Jerrod, she said under her breath. He was going on a little long, and risked losing the crowd.

"There's one person here who began this chain reaction. Kick-started doesn't begin to cover it." Jerrod lowered his head. When he looked up, he gestured to her.

The tingling started at Dawn's fingertips and traveled up her arms. The tender look was public and all eyes were on her, leaving her self-conscious, embarrassed. But she held his gaze.

"Of course, I'm talking about Dawn Larsen, who many of you know and have worked with. I realize how much you all respect—and love—her. Dawn was referred to me by a friend and agreed to take on my business. In a matter of weeks I'd launched my Great Lakes location of Adventure Dives & Water Tours."

More clapping. Dawn felt warm in her sweater and the tingling in her arms was intensifying and moving through her body. So many pairs of eyes were on her now. Like Nelson, she hadn't expected this attention.

"But more than that, Dawn made me and my little girl feel welcome, and we in turn were able to find a home here in Two Moon Bay. And she introduced me to all of you."

Her arms weak, even shaky, she put her wineglass on the table next to her and clutched her hands in front of her to keep them still.

Jerrod had recaptured the audience, so he took a few seconds to release a deep breath. "By now, you've likely seen some of the news stories about my life before I came to Two Moon Bay. Some of you have heard me speak

publicly about my earlier life. I lost some people close to me in an act of violence meant to
destroy. And it did. I thought I was destroyed
as well, alive only to raise my little girl."

Jerrod stopped talking and for a few seconds, the room was so quiet only the sound
of the gentle waves lapping the shore broke
through the silence.

"It was here in Two Moon Bay with all of
you, but especially because of Dawn's heart,
that I started believing in my future. With
great employees at the Key West location,
open all year round, I'm heading in a new
direction. I'll be working on a book about
shipping and shipwrecks in Lake Michigan,
and the way the shipping industry shaped the
culture of the region."

So, it wasn't their secret anymore, Dawn
thought. They'd talked about how he'd work
on the book during the winter, while also
planning periodic visits to his Florida offices.
The pieces of their life together were falling
into place one by one.

Jerrod paused, still held the attention of
the room. "I'm tempted to leave it at that, but
I've got one more thing to say. I've already
mentioned Dawn Larsen and her huge heart

and incredible energy. But now it's time for me to admit that she won *my* heart." With a huge smile, he said, "I've fallen madly in love with Dawn."

He turned to her and said, "I've listed a dozen reasons I'm staying, and they're all true. But being with Dawn is the best reason of all." He lifted his glass.

Somewhere, Dawn found the poise to reach for her glass and lift it to match Jerrod's gesture. She was giddy. And shocked. Mostly, though, she was in love.

That was the end of the speech, and with it, something had shifted in the room. It had turned into a celebration.

"People can't get enough good love stories," Lark said, approaching her as the crowd thinned out. "I didn't know Jerrod had it in him to be so public about...you know...you!"

"Me, neither," Dawn said, leaning toward Lark. "I'm just happy, though. Now we've told the kids, so it was time to be a little more public. Jerrod was so quiet when he first arrived, but look at him now."

Lark gave her a quick hug and headed toward the door, hollering something back about their Thursday coffee at the Bean Grinder. Dawn wouldn't miss it.

A few minutes later, everyone was gone, except for the four of them. After putting a plate of cookies on a table for Carrie and Gordon, Jerrod led her out to the verandah.

"Are you warm enough?" he asked.

If he only knew how good the cool air felt on her face after she'd flushed during his talk. "Absolutely warm enough, especially my heart. And your party was quite a success, huh? So many people were touched by how you feel about Two Moon Bay."

"Come here and sit on the brick wall with me," he said. "We can let the kids munch their snack while we watch the moon."

She pointed to the flat second moon on the surface. "We lucked out tonight with the weather and the moon."

"Lucky in lots of ways."

"Now everyone knows you'll be writing your book all winter," Dawn said.

Jerrod gazed at the water and smiled. "I'll promote Wyatt and Rob to be general managers. Meanwhile, I can develop this other side of myself."

She took one of his hands in both of hers. "Sounds so good to me."

"I'm thinking about our family," he said. "I mean, starting a family, and not waiting too long."

She glanced inside and saw the kids still at the table. "It won't always be easy with the two we have, you know." She rested her head on his shoulder. "I'm just being honest."

"If you're sure, I'm sure," Jerrod said.

She moved so she could see his whole face and look into his eyes. "Oh, I want our baby, but I've also been doing a lot of thinking over the summer about my direction. And I know now that if it doesn't happen for us, then I'll accept that. I'm so grateful for the two we have."

Jerrod pointed with his chin to the kids at the table. "Those two will get restless soon, so I better get down to it."

"To what?"

"You'll see."

Jerrod reached in his pocket and took out a box. "We talked about taking it slow, but we also want to be a family with our kids. And I realized I never formally asked you to marry me."

She glanced at the box. "Oh, Jerrod." It was another moment when she might have danced in circles and grabbed his hand and done the jitterbug. Instead, she kept a lid on her excitement and glanced into the room. "You're doing this right here, right now, with our two great kids munching cookies?"

"Right. Gordon is probably listening to one of Carrie's long tales." Jerrod laughed. "Here's my secret. I bribed Gordon with the cookies in order to get a few minutes alone with you."

"You mean Gordon was in on your scheme? A scheme that started with putting me in the spotlight during your speech." She gave him a playful look of warning. "I was beyond self-conscious. I got shaky inside."

"So, Dawn Larsen, will you marry me, sometime in the next, say, four or five months?"

He opened the box and revealed a ring, an opal set in a ring of diamonds.

She gasped when she saw it. "It's perfect, Jerrod." He took it out and Dawn extended her hand so he could slip it on. "And it fits."

"Well, I lucked out," he said.

"I never imagined an engagement ring,"

Dawn said, holding out her hand and having a look at it. "I really didn't." She pursed her lips. "Maybe because we're serious adults with children and all that."

Jerrod looked shocked. "You don't want it?"

"Oh, real funny. Of course I want it. I'll treasure it. I'm just bowled over, that's all." The air around her swirled with exciting, dizzying romantic energy. Love really was in the air.

Jerrod wrapped his arms around her. "I thought the other day about the need to go back and forth to Florida regularly this winter, and how we'll try to time the trips with school breaks so we can all go together."

"We'll work all that out, but not tonight." She put her hands on his chest. "Along with everything else. Remember the day Carrie asked me if I could be her mommy? We were all thrown by the question." She'd tried to deny the complicated feelings involved, too. "I told her anyone would be lucky to have her. That's how I feel."

She lifted her face and found his lips, firm and warm, and when she inhaled his scent she thought of red maple leaves, the full moon and the holidays, and the spring and summer and another fall after that and on into the future.

He smoothed his hands over her hair. "I've got one more thing on my mind and then we should go."

She drew her head back. "I'll bite. What is it?"

"I'm going to need you to trust me about something."

Dawn looked into gray eyes, soft now and full of love. She had a sense of what was coming. She'd said yes to everything else. She was about to trust him with the rest of her life. She could hear him out. "You want me to dive with you. Right?"

"Hear me out."

And she did.

"I don't want to see anyone walk away from adventure out of fear," he said. "That's all this is about. All I'm asking is for you to give me a chance to help you get past the fear. I'll take you on a dive, step by step, watching you every minute. I won't let anything happen to you."

Trust. That's what he was asking for. He trusted her to be with him and his child, start a family, take a chance. She could trust him to help her break through a barrier from her past.

"It's not only about love, is it?" She leaned against his chest and closed her eyes. "It's about trust, too. So, my answer is yes."

"Good. Thank you." He stood and pulled her to her feet.

She stepped back and did a little dance step before he caught her in his arms again. "Did I ever tell you how much I like to dance?"

"No, but I can't say I'm surprised. You'll have to teach me."

"Anytime."

They stood with arms around each other, gazing at the moon on the lake. They could have stayed that way all night, Dawn thought, but that plate of cookies wasn't going to last forever.

"Let's go," she said.

Hand in hand they went inside. Both kids looked up and smiled.

* * * * *

*Don't miss author Virginia McCullough's
debut title for Harlequin Heartwarming,
GIRL IN THE SPOTLIGHT.
Available now at www.Harlequin.com!*

Get 2 Free Books,
Plus 2 Free Gifts—
just for trying the Reader Service!

Get 2 Free Books,
Plus 2 Free Gifts—
just for trying the Reader Service!

LIS17R3

Get 2 Free Books,
Plus 2 Free Gifts -
just for trying the Reader Service!

Get 2 Free Books,
Plus 2 Free Gifts—
just for trying the
Reader Service!

HRLP17R3

Get 2 Free Books,

Plus 2 Free Gifts—

just for trying the Reader Service!

READERSERVICE.COM

Manage your account online!

- Review your order history
- Manage your payments
- Update your address

> ### We've designed the Reader Service website just for you.

Enjoy all the features!

- Discover new series available to you, and read excerpts from any series.
- Respond to mailings and special monthly offers.
- Browse the Bonus Bucks catalog and online-only exculsives.
- Share your feedback.

Visit us at:

ReaderService.com

RS16R